HATTIE
BRINGS
THE
HOUSE
DOWN

HATTIE BRINGS THE HOUSE DOWN

PATRICK GLEESON

NO EXIT PRESS

First published in the UK in 2024 by No Exit Press,
an imprint of Bedford Square Publishers Ltd, London, UK

bedfordsquarepublishers.co.uk
@noexitpress

ISBN
978-1-83501-003-7 (Paperback)
978-1-83501-004-4 (eBook)

2 4 6 8 10 9 7 5 3 1

Typeset 10.5 on 13.8pt Minion Pro
by Avocet Typeset, Bideford, Devon, EX39 2BP
Printed in Great Britain by CPI Group (UK) Ltd, Croydon CR0 4YY

For Maddie

Love's Labour's Lost
By William Shakespeare

CAST

Berowne	Adam Dilloway
Rosaline	Belinda Morley-Smith
King Ferdinand	Emile Velasquez
Jaquenetta	Atlanta Greenwell

[Reg, can you fill in the rest of the cast? Getting all the names lined up in columns is a right pain in the posterior, but apparently it's 'house style' for cast listings here – HH]

CREATIVE
Hashi Hassan – Director
Raven Hiscock – Set & Costume Design
Carrie Lewis – Lighting Design
Regine Kalinina – Assistant Director

[I hope you don't mind being at the bottom – it's just a political thing re Carrie – HH]

PRODUCTION
Keith Macaulay – **[Can you check whether he wants Producer or Artistic Director here? I'm not giving him both! – HH
P.S. Also, does Robin need/deserve a credit? If so, as *what*?]**

CREW
Steve Felton – Production Manager
Moira Macleod – Head of Wardrobe
Laura Harris – Head of Lighting
Miguel Mota – Sound Engineer
Hattie Cocker – Stage Manager
Kiki Bennett – Deputy Stage Manager
Davina Aggarwal – Assistant Stage Manager

[Finally, can you check with Steve – do we really need to list all of the above? On a minimalistic programme like this it sort of diminishes the emphasis if everyone and their dog gets a credit…]

Prologue

There's an old joke they tell backstage sometimes: the circus has come to town, and everyone lines the streets to watch the parade. It's colourful and glamorous and glorious, but once all the horses and elephants and clowns have gone past, bystanders see a solitary figure shuffle into view. He's dressed in rags, carries a bucket and shovel, and he slowly collects up the dung dropped by the animals. As he works he mutters a continual stream of complaints.

'Work all day, work all night, barely get food to fill my belly, just a pallet to sleep on, blisters on my palms from this splintered old shovel, hole in my bucket, and the smell, oh the smell...'

A well-meaning passer-by, hearing him rant, calls out to him, 'You know, they're hiring down at the mill. The work's easy and the pay's good. You'd never have to shovel dung again.'

The man looks up and replies, aghast: 'What? Quit showbiz?'

– From the introduction to The Art and Craft of Stage Management *by Donna Fletcher*

The Tavistock Theatre was not a grand building. It wasn't strictly speaking a building at all. Fundamentally it comprised one large, slightly damp room, connected to a couple of smaller, rather damper ones, all tucked behind and above the Tavistock pub. The pub staff and the theatre staff viewed one another with varying levels of disdain, but they were by and large mutually tolerant so long as neither was overly disruptive to the other.

So when Hattie Cocker came to visit Keith Macaulay, artistic director and technically sole employee of the Tavistock, at a little before eleven o'clock in the morning, she knew to walk round to the side entrance in the yard rather than go through the pub and bother the manager, who was doing whatever it is that publicans do on a Monday before their premises open.

Hattie was not a particularly large or heavy-set woman, but she wore an enormous thick coat that hung stiffly around her, rendering her external geometry almost entirely cylindrical. It was a good coat, which over the years had seen her through freezing cold overnight get-outs in Minsk, improbable outdoor performances in the Hebrides, and that one awful dress rehearsal in New York when the aircon was left on full blast in winter (as bizarre union rules meant they weren't allowed to switch it off themselves, and the in-house technician was on holiday). It was a bit tattered now, but Hattie liked it and trusted it, and besides, new clothes were so depressingly expensive these days.

The side door should, strictly speaking, have been locked, but as usual it had been left on the latch. Hattie slipped through, into the dingy low-ceilinged hallway just inside. There was one door dead ahead leading into the auditorium, and another on the right leading to the dressing rooms. A crumbling staircase on the left led up to the office. The familiar backstage smell of cheap stage paint and badly plumbed drains wafted up to greet her like a drunken uncle at a wedding as she turned and, refusing to acknowledge the twinges in her hip, made her way up the stairs.

Keith, always the fidgety sort, was practically vibrating when Hattie found him. He was doing little circuits through the mess of scripts and bills that littered the office, while his intern Robin – young, rather effete, and frowning nervously – perched on a table edge in the corner.

'Morning, then,' offered Hattie, uncertainly.

'Well, that ended quickly, didn't it?' exclaimed Keith abruptly, as he turned to look at her.

'What did?'

'The show. The season. The whole blessed theatre. Typical Hashi too, he had to blow the bloody lock off just to make a statement.'

Keith was a small man, with dark, bulging eyes, a crooked smile, and receding hair. He had a certain charisma to him that was perhaps attractive in its own way. 'Ugly-sexy', was how someone – Hattie forgot who – had once described him, and the epithet had always stuck in her mind. Of course, that charisma was rather lost when he was in the middle of a panic-driven meltdown.

'Er… Sorry, I don't follow,' Hattie confessed. 'Which lock?'

Keith waved expansively at the corner of the room. Hattie's eyes followed the direction of his gesture and alighted on the bright yellow safety cupboard standing, open, in the corner. The one that was compliant with Control Of Substances Hazardous to Health (COSHH) regulations, that was supposed to be used for storing stage pyrotechnics, but that Keith used like a safe and had insisted on keeping the… oh. Oh dear.

'Right. Just so I'm clear,' she ventured, 'are you telling me that something has happened to that… mask?'

'Happened? *Happened*? Yes, I think it's safe to say that something has happened to the mask. Hashi has taken the mask.'

He slumped down into his chair and groaned.

'A week. We got a *week* into rehearsals and the wheels fell off. I knew he was prickly but I swear on Derek Jacobi's codpiece I didn't know he'd try to take down the whole theatre.'

Hattie considered all this. In the world of theatre, feuds and dramatic gestures were commonplace, but actual, proper, calculated theft was not. The idea of it was repugnant. Theatre people did lots of things that they shouldn't, but they didn't *steal* from one another. Still, it was important not to jump to conclusions.

'Um,' she said eventually, 'now obviously I'm coming at this from the outside, so apologies if it's a stupid question, but are you sure that it was Hashi, and are you *sure* that it wasn't some sort of a misunderstanding?'

'Look!' shouted Keith, his voice cracking as he jumped up again and strode over to the cupboard. He scooped up something from the floor next to it and tossed it onto the sprawl of papers on the desk in the middle of the room. It looked like the mangled remains of a padlock that appeared to have been... melted? Dissolved? Perhaps it had been blown apart by an explosive. Whatever the case, it did indeed look like a deliberate act of destruction.

'And he left a note. A... a receipt. Look!'

Keith pointed at yet another pile of papers, atop which was a sheet of A4, on which was scrawled, in black Sharpie, the words 'Love's Labours Repaid'.

'Pretty clear now, isn't it? He even forgot the second apostrophe again. Moron.'

Keith resumed his frantic pacing.

'Well now, let's not jump to conclusions,' began Hattie soothingly. 'If it was someone upset about the pay issue, it could have been—'

'Who? The twitchy little sound assistant? *You*? Or, I don't know, how about the obviously unstable, temperamental prima donna director who's already explicitly threatened to nick it?'

'I think he was just making a jo—'

'Jesus H. Sondheim, I never should have let him anywhere near this place. As soon as he said he wanted to do *Love's Labour's Lost*

I should have seen he was completely off his rocker. No one in their right minds would pick a sodding Shakespearean comedy in a theatre like this, especially not given where he's coming from. And now he's going to destroy the whole theatre.'

'That's a bit of an exaggeration, surely?'

Keith glared at Hattie.

'Is it? Oh, great, I hadn't realised. What with being the only person in the world who understands how this house runs and what keeps it ticking, it's no wonder I misunderstood. Thanks for keeping me informed. For God's sake, Hattie, I wouldn't joke about this sort of thing. That mask is vital, *vital*, to the continued existence of this place.'

'How?' asked Hattie, genuinely confused.

'I don't... I don't have time to explain all of this to you. All you need to know is that if I don't have it in my hand on press night, two weeks from tomorrow, the theatre will fold before your show ends its run. Just remember that: it's your pay cheque on the line.'

Hattie looked over at Robin, who met her eye and gave an agonised sort of half-shrug. Poor thing, he must have been trapped in this room with a raving Keith all morning. This can't have been what he signed up for when he applied for work experience at the Tavistock. Hattie decided to stop winding Keith up with more questions, and instead tell him what he wanted to hear. The fact that he had called her instead of big Steve suggested that he was probably hoping for a diplomatic intervention of some sorts, even if he was too agitated at the moment to actually ask.

'This sounds like the sort of thing that could possibly be fixed with a few quiet words in the right place,' said Hattie cautiously. 'Shall I go and have a chat with Hashi and see what he has to say about the whole thing?'

'Sure, and if you wouldn't mind telling him to shove his face down a toilet, that would also be great, thanks,' replied Keith sourly.

'I think I'll reserve the right to include or omit that suggestion as I see fit,' said Hattie, eliciting a small smile from Robin.

Keith ignored her.

'I just don't know how we got from kisses and smiles to breaking and entering in the space of a week,' he said dejectedly.

'I'm sure we can sort it out,' Hattie replied encouragingly. She was still choosing to believe that, in the absence of definitive proof to the contrary, Hashi couldn't possibly have stooped so low as to have stolen the mask. *But if I'm wrong*, she thought to herself grimly, *I'll make him rue the bloody day...*

'You're a lifesaver, Hattie. My fixer *par excellence*.'

'It's all part of the job, Keith.'

Hattie went downstairs and decided to poke her head into the auditorium before she left. It looked much as she'd last seen it the previous week, the seating blocks laid out in a traditional proscenium arch format (which was just a fancy way of saying that all the audience chairs were at one end of the room, and the stage was at the other). Onstage were a few flimsy bits of scenery left behind from a young am-dram company's production, which had just finished its run. The theatre was looking no grubbier than normal, although a certain level of shabbiness was unavoidable in a place like that. The walls and floor had had so many coats of paint applied over the years that every surface was slightly warped in shape, and every so often an inch-thick chunk of various strata of coloured emulsion had crumbled away, only to be hastily painted over again, leaving pockmarks all over. It really was incredible, Hattie thought – not for the first time – how such an unprepossessing little room could, with the right lights, the right sounds, and the right bodies onstage, be so transportive, so *transformative*.

While she was here she decided it would be worth quickly re-familiarising herself with the layout backstage. She'd done at least one show here, long ago, but they all blended into one in the memory. Was this the one with the loo with the noisy flush that you couldn't use during a performance? No, that was that place in Stratford. Wasn't it?

She swung herself up onto the stage. *Ah yes, here we go.* No room for a prompt desk back here, so the deputy stage manager would have to cue the show from behind the audience, alongside the sound and lighting board operators. While there were wing spaces on both sides of the stage, they weren't connected, not unless you took a good metre off the size of the already poky performance space by hanging a big cloth curtain at the back to create a corridor.

There was a table for props in the stage right wing, that is, the left-hand side of the stage when viewed from the auditorium. The exit to the dressing rooms was stage left. Walking through that door, and noting how much it creaked when pushed – it would have to be propped open during the show, then – she found herself in the men's dressing room, which was a polite name for what was a slightly wider-than-normal corridor. At the far end of the room was another door. That must lead to the women's dressing room, which in turn presumably had a doorway through to the hallway by the side entrance.

Ah yes, this was the place that didn't have a backstage loo at all, which meant that if an actor was caught short during a show they'd have to hop out from the side, run round to the front of the building, and use the toilets in the pub. Which, depending on their costume, could be something of a hassle. Well, it was just one more thing to think about. Hattie made a mental note about the number of chairs that could fit in the men's dressing room, and then made her way through into the women's.

In this last room, the first thing she noticed was that the lights around one of the mirrors had been left on, illuminating on the desk in front of them a large, mostly empty bottle of brandy, accompanied by a mostly full glass. The second thing she noticed was another glass, this one cracked, in the outstretched hand of Atlanta Greenwell, who was lying on the floor, very unambiguously dead.

Act One

1

'The stage manager,' Hattie began uncomfortably, 'is the calm at the eye of the storm. We are the quiet voice of reason amid the squabbling and screaming. We are the solid foundations upon which every stage production is built.'

She paused a moment. Donna had left behind comprehensive notes, and Hattie had hoped she could get through her first session by reading the pre-prepared welcoming remarks more or less verbatim. But the words weren't her words, and they sounded ridiculous coming out of her mouth. So she put down her note cards, took a deep breath and tried again.

'Look, it's a tough job, and if I'm honest I don't really know *why* we do it. We don't get our names up in lights, we don't take a bow, and we never get the appreciation we deserve. But I'll tell you something: I've been in this industry for not far shy of forty years, and in that time I have never even considered doing anything else. If you're a theatre person you're a theatre person, it's that simple.'

Hattie was in the small performance studio at the Arrowsmith Conservatory of Dramatic Arts, addressing the new intake of the two-year stage management and technical theatre diploma course. Of the dozen-odd students clustered in the front seats of the auditorium, two were scribbling notes furiously. The rest were less engaged. One was doodling on her hand, a couple were playing with their phones, and one overweight, scruffy man, well, man-in-waiting – late teenager, perhaps? – was staring slack-jawed straight up at the ceiling. Hattie hoped he was inspecting the lighting rig, and not just catatonic.

One of the keener students had a copy of Donna Fletcher's *The Art and Craft of Stage Management* on his lap. Hattie eyed it suspiciously. She didn't believe for a moment that any of the important stuff about being an SM could be learned from a book, and she was secretly unconvinced that it could be taught in a classroom either, but Donna, Hattie's predecessor as stage management tutor at ACDA, had written the damn thing, and it was no wonder that some of these students would have read it. Hattie just prayed she'd get through the term without being interrupted by a sanctimonious youngster complaining: 'But the *book* says...'

Hattie had never been a teacher in any formal sense, but since she'd had to stop touring she was low on employment options, and when Donna had quit halfway through the summer term she'd managed to snag the gig as an interim replacement while they looked for a permanent successor. Now, at the start of the new academic year, she was tasked with turning these newbies into disciplined, capable entrants into the industry. After having had a look at them, this was feeling like a more and more daunting responsibility.

Today was mostly about introductions, though. These fresh-faced first years were still finding their feet, and the last thing they needed was an overload of information. So Hattie tried to keep it general. Make it seem fun, emphasise that it's hard work, start building up trust, that was what mattered.

'The thing you need to realise is that as much as anything, the job of a stage manager is to step in when things go wrong. And things do go wrong. Props get lost, scenery falls over, you name it. And that awful cliché about how "*the show must go on*"... well, it's only a cliché because it's true. Once the curtain has gone up, your job is to do everything in your power to keep the performance going. I had an actor collapse backstage, and once we'd called the ambulance we got the understudy into costume and half the audience never even noticed. I did a show once where there was a power cut, and we lit the whole of the second half with the crew's head torches, and it got a standing ovation.'

She was getting more attention from the students now, and beginning to feel she was getting into the swing of things. Stories, that's what they needed. Tell them facts about what it's like and they'll be bored, but spin them a yarn and you'll take them with you. Stories were what theatre was all about, after all.

But then a gawky-looking, very blond young man stuck his hand up, and, without waiting for any kind of acknowledgement, called out, 'Um, Miss, this morning the Principal was talking to us, and he said we were never allowed to say... you know. The thing we're not allowed to say. Is that true?'

'Um...' said Hattie, as much surprised at being addressed as 'Miss' as anything else. 'First of all, call me Hattie. Second of all... well, I mean, I don't know which thing you mean if you don't... say it.'

'He was talking about saying "no",' explained a woman in the front row, evidently amused by Hattie's confusion. 'He was saying we should try never to say no to a director. He said that when he used to direct shows he banned the crew from saying it. Which seemed a bit... I mean, really? It made it sound like we're basically their servants.'

Hattie, relieved, smiled.

'*I'll see what I can do*,' she replied. 'That's the trick. When the director asks you for something, if it's doable you say "yes", and if not you say, "I'll see what I can do".'

That got a couple of smiles.

'You want to help them whenever you can, but you've got

to be careful what you promise, you see,' Hattie continued. 'I once worked on a show where the director wanted a revolving swimming pool onstage...'

Having made it back to the land of anecdotes, she carried on storytelling for the rest of the session, delighting in the looks of surprise, fear and occasionally disgust she managed to elicit from the more attentive members of her audience. However, a few of the students, most notably the large, scruffy young man and the gawky blond, remained completely unengaged. *Ah well*, Hattie thought. She was never going to win them all over straight away.

Her allotted time drew to a close, and she started to finish up.

'Now, you won't see very much of me for the next few weeks. We've got a few classes together here and there, but I think your construction, lighting and sound classes will be keeping you busy for most of the next month. But from early October I'll be back full time, and we'll start stage management in earnest. I'll look forward to working more with you then!'

There was an awkward silence while the less engaged students slowly noticed that the class was over and this was their cue to leave, so Hattie decided to lead by example, packing up her notes and, with a last smile at her audience, making her way out into the halls of ACDA's teaching complex.

She was nearly at the main entrance when she heard a husky cough behind her.

'*Do you remember September when we were just fools in love...*' crooned a slightly wobbly baritone voice.

Hattie stopped and rolled her eyes, but she allowed herself a slight smile as she did so.

'Hello, Rod,' she called out.

'Harriet Mildred Cocker, you are a vision, an oasis for the soul in the desert of modern life.'

Back when she had been young and fit, while Hattie hadn't

really thought much about her looks, she'd generally been quietly confident that she scrubbed up pretty well. Or at least would scrub up well if she ever had the time to scrub up at all. Now, with her face a little weathered, her hair greying, and cruel time having done its general thing, she never wasted a moment worrying about what other people thought about her appearance, scrubbed or otherwise.

But no one is completely immune to flattery.

Shaking her head in good-natured exasperation, she turned to face the Senior Sound Tutor. Older than her, with a well-groomed grey beard to add edges to a ruddy face that would otherwise be lost in a mass of neck and jowl, Rod always gave the impression of someone making a half-hearted attempt to pretend he wasn't *actually* a wizard. He had a penchant for broad-brimmed hats, and a small silver earring in one ear. It was rumoured among the students that he had been living in his VW camper in the ACDA car park for the last thirty years, and while that wasn't, strictly speaking, true, it nevertheless captured quite well the overall impression that Rod gave off. Hattie, who had known him since the late eighties, reckoned that what he really was was a silly old bugger who got away with far more than he should. But she liked him anyway.

'Shouldn't you be settling down for your morning nap?' she asked, drily.

Rod drew himself up in mock shock.

'I will have you know that I never do so crass a thing as *sleep*,' he replied haughtily, then his voice softened. 'I do, however, have a fondness for a cup of tea and a Hobnob, if you would care to join me.'

'Sorry,' replied Hattie. 'I've got to hotfoot it to Pimlico for a first read-through.'

Rod frowned.

'You've got a gig?'

'Just a quick one, squeezed in before my timetable properly kicks off here. It's a Shakespeare, at the Tavistock.'

'Any good?'

'Don't know yet. We'll find out today. Oh, Miguel's on sound, and I've got Davina working for me.'

Rod looked blankly.

'You know… they graduated in the summer. Davina, the highly strung one, and Miguel, the… quiet one.'

Recognition dawned.

'Ah… yes. Well, do send Davina my regards. Miguel too, of course.'

'Of course. See you later.'

'Oh, I do hope so,' said Rod, waggling his eyebrows. 'Until next time, my queen.'

Hattie, with a smile, waved a dismissive hand at him, and turned to leave the building.

She had arranged to meet Davina at the rehearsal venue, so she was a little surprised to nearly stumble over her seated form as she turned out of ACDA's main entrance onto the pavement. Small and birdlike, Davina always had a slightly crumpled air about her, which belied her energetic and emotionally intense personality. The impression Hattie had formed when tutoring her in her final term as a stage management student back in the summer was that she worked phenomenally hard, but she risked being slightly too *intellectual* in her approach. It often happened with the ones who'd done an academic degree first, Hattie reflected. They got so caught up in ideas and opinions that sometimes they struggled to put their heads down and get things done.

But she meant well, and she normally got there in the end, and when she had confessed to Hattie that she was having trouble finding work since leaving ACDA, Hattie had sympathised, had a quiet word with Steve, the production manager on the new Tavistock show, and got her in as assistant stage manager. It would be fun to work with her on a real production, Hattie assured herself. Or at least, if it wasn't exactly *fun*, helping Davina navigate her first steps in the industry would be a Good Thing To Do, and Hattie could take pleasure in that.

'Hello,' said Davina, scrambling to her feet. 'I hope you don't mind, but I thought I'd try to catch you here because I was in the area anyway and, and…'

She broke off and gave a rather large, wet sniff, and, it seemed to Hattie, appeared to be fighting to hold back tears.

'Oh, now… it's OK, my love,' Hattie said uncertainly. 'Do you need a moment?'

'No,' said Davina miserably. 'I'm sorry, it's nothing, it's stupid, I just… I've just been dumped, that's all.'

'Oh my darling,' said Hattie sympathetically, although she noted, disappointed in herself, that she'd had to suppress a minor urge to sigh. *Of course* Davina was an emotional wreck, in the middle of a traumatic life experience. She had undergone many such crises even during the half of a term that Hattie had known her. None of it was ever her fault, of course, but… she did seem to get significantly more than her fair share of personal drama. In that respect she was rather more like an actor than a stage manager.

'Do you need to take some time out? It's not the end of the world if you miss the read-through.'

'No! No, I'd really like to be there. And I'd just be kicking round by myself otherwise,' Davina sniffed. 'I'm fine. I'll be fine, especially if I can have you with me. I just need to get it together.'

Hattie put an arm round her shoulders and gave her a squeeze, then steered her gently in the direction of the tube station. They walked in silence for a few moments, then Davina blurted out: 'It wouldn't be so bad, but he never even ended it with me, he just started seeing someone else while I was out of town, and then he acted almost surprised that I was upset when I found out. I mean talk about gaslighting! And I'd put in so much work to make it happen, and I even did the most disgusting... but now he's not even... I mean he's not even being discreet about it like he was with me.'

Alarm bells started sounding in Hattie's head.

'When you say you were discreet... do you mean there was a reason you weren't supposed t—'

'Oh God,' Davina gasped, horrified. 'I've already put my foot in it. I can't... Well, I can't say more, but... look, it wasn't exactly *appropriate* for him to be seeing... well, either me or my replacement.'

Oh dear. That explained why Davina had been at ACDA this morning. Hattie remembered noticing last term that she had been making eyes at Shane, the admittedly rather handsome construction tutor. He was much older than her, and married, but... well, it wouldn't be the first time a student and a staff member had had a dalliance at ACDA. It sounded like it wasn't the last time either. How disappointing. She'd hoped Shane would have known better.

'Well, it sounds to me like you're probably better off out of it then,' she suggested gently. 'Which isn't to say it's not going to hurt for now, but hopefully it'll make it easier to move on in the long run.'

'You're right,' said Davina, without much conviction.

'Anyway, if you're sure you're going to be all right for now...'

'Yeah, I'll be fine. Thank you.'

'Then we should talk about the show,' said Hattie, hoping that talking shop would help Davina buck up. 'You've read the script?'

'Yep,' Davina.

'And what did you take away from it?'

'Well,' said Davina eagerly, 'I think it's really all about the tensions between the emotional and the intellectual, as experienced in different social strata. You see very clear parallels between the narratives that occur on each social layer: King Ferdinand and the Princess represent symbolic love, Berowne and Rosaline have the passionate love, and so on. I know it's billed as a light comedy, but I think there's a lot of serious social commentary in there...'

Hattie sighed gently and cut in before Davina could get into full swing: 'Do you remember what we talked about last year? About different hats?'

'Oh,' said Davina, deflating. 'Yes. Sorry, I've got my arts graduate hat on, don't I?'

'Yes. And so what happens when you take that off, and put your stage management hat on?'

Davina frowned.

'Well… OK, so there's not much in the way of props mentioned in the script. There are a few bits of paper, but other than that it's going to be up to the director's vision. So we can't really start propping until we get some input from him.'

'True,' said Hattie. 'Anything else?'

'Well… oh! Quick-change. Act five scene two. To get the lords out of their Muscovite disguises. So we'll need to see what the costumes are like to work out how much help the actors will need backstage.'

'Good spot!' praised Hattie, and Davina beamed. 'The stage manager hat fits you very well, you know.'

They had now arrived at the tube station, and once through the barriers they made their way down to the platform to wait for a train. Hattie stole a sidelong glance at her protégé. She was looking perkier already. That was the thing about Davina: she seemed to change her mood with the wind. It made her a bit of a liability, but it was hard not to be fond of her, Hattie thought as the train arrived.

2

The four technical roles that are the most often confused by outsiders are the production manager (PM), stage manager (SM), deputy stage manager (DSM) and assistant stage manager (ASM). To keep things simple:

The PM is the boss.

The SM is a sort of shepherd/bureaucrat/therapist who answers to the PM.

The DSM is the SM's spy in the rehearsal room.

And the ASM is, in the nicest possible way, the SM's general dogsbody.

– From The Art and Craft of Stage Management *by Donna Fletcher, Chapter 1: Roles and Responsibilities*

St Eustace's Hall in Pimlico was a much sought after rehearsal space. Which is to say that it was cramped, cold, damp and smelly, and therefore, given its central location, refreshingly affordable. Most theatre companies in London operated on a shoe-string budget, and a well-situated, reasonably-priced rehearsal room that was large enough to accommodate a decent-sized cast was hard to come by. Hashi Hassan's season-opener at the Tavistock was no exception financially, and big Steve Felton, the bald, tattooed production manager, had scored an early victory in managing to secure St Eustace's for the entire rehearsal period.

Hattie and Davina got there a little early, but they weren't the first to arrive. Kiki, the deputy stage manager, had turned up before them, ostensibly to mark out the dimensions of the Tavistock stage in chalk on the floor. Hattie knew that her ulterior motive was to get in early to nab the most comfortable chair and least wobbly table and set them up in the nook next to the heater as her base for the weeks ahead.

Kiki and Hattie had worked together a few times in the past. Kiki was a short, taciturn woman with frizzy auburn hair and round, ruddy cheeks, whose innate shyness meant she came across as a little cold sometimes. But she knew her job well, and was a safe pair of hands who could be relied upon to keep her head.

Hattie made introductions, but Davina was looking a little bit emotional again, and Kiki didn't make much effort to be welcoming, so the conversation sputtered out pretty quickly. To avoid things getting awkward, Hattie gave Davina £20 from petty cash and directions to the nearest corner shop, to buy milk, sugar, teabags, instant coffee and enough biscuits to keep the company chirpy for the next few hours.

Then she and Kiki set about putting out a big circle of plastic stacking chairs.

'Seen Nick recently?' asked Kiki.

Hattie rolled her eyes.

'Hardly. He's been touring pretty much non-stop since March. Got a text on our anniversary.'

'Miss him?'

'Well... sometimes. It's funny, when I was travelling too I didn't mind that I hardly saw him. But now I'm not touring myself' – she patted her right hip absent-mindedly – 'I do sometimes miss him.

But then I remember how he snores and the feeling passes. How's Miranda?'

'Same old, same old,' replied Kiki noncommittally.

Davina returned, and they set up a refreshment table, raiding the kitchenette for mugs and a kettle. Hattie had Davina laying everything out neatly when a very beautiful young woman wandered in, wearing a headscarf, a lot of eye make-up, what appeared to be fleece pyjamas, and a blank expression.

'Er... yeah...' she said vaguely, to no one in particular, looking both disappointed and expectant.

Kiki and Hattie exchanged a look.

'Hello,' said Hattie, as warmly as she could. She was pretty sure she recognised the face from the list of cast headshots. 'Belinda, is it?'

The woman raised her eyebrows and nodded silently.

'Don't worry, you're in the right place, you're just the first to arrive. Make yourself comfortable, and—'

'Oh great!' said Belinda, her eyes lighting up as she saw the drinks table. She turned to Davina.

'Can I have a mint tea? Two sugars.'

'Oh, er...' stammered Davina.

'I'm afraid we only have bog-standard tea and instant coffee,' said Hattie firmly, 'but you're very welcome to *help yourself* to either. And do take a biscuit.'

Bloody actors. Always assuming everyone else was their own personal servant. You had to establish some boundaries early on or they'd walk all over you.

'Do these have gluten in them?' asked Belinda, again to no one in particular, pointing at the biscuits.

'Um... I think they... yes, they do, sorry,' said Davina, flushing. 'I'm so sorry, I didn't think of that. I can probably—'

'Oh no, no, it's fine,' replied Belinda airily. 'I'm not... I mean, it's fine. I'll just...'

She picked up a biscuit, and plonked herself down in a chair in the corner, nibbling at it while she played with her phone. Kiki and Hattie exchanged another look. Belinda was going to be one of *those* actors.

The second arrival came hot on the heels of the first.

'Darlings!' boomed a voice from the doorway, and Hattie turned to see another very beautiful woman, this one perhaps in her fifties, wrapped in a large fur stole and striking an exaggerated pose with one arm floating upwards, and the opposite hip thrust out to the side. Hattie, unsure exactly how to react to this unnecessarily showy entrance, realised she was staring rather awkwardly at the newcomer. Which, she pondered, was perhaps the intent behind the posture in the first place.

'Oh, hello,' said Belinda, looking up.

'Ah, yes!' cried the woman, holding up a finger to her temple. 'Now, don't tell me, don't tell me, I've memorised this... *Belinda*!'

She snapped her fingers and beamed. She had the sort of voice that belonged on 1950s BBC radio.

'Call me Bums,' replied Belinda cheerfully.

'Oh God, really?' asked the new arrival, making a face.

'Everybody does. It's my initials. Belinda Ursula Morley-Smith.'

'Bums it is then,' the woman replied, swiftly recovering her composure. 'Glorious. How do you do? Atlanta Greenwell.'

Belinda, or rather Bums, stood as Atlanta crossed to her, and they exchanged air kisses.

'I love your... thing,' said Bums, pointing at the stole. 'I wish I could afford something like that.'

'Oh darling, one should never *buy* fur. It's unbearably cruel and rather tacky. No, I'm of the opinion that furs should only be worn if they were given as a gift, or if they've been in the family for generations. Don't you agree?'

Without waiting for a reply, the older woman turned to the SM team.

'Now, you must be the lovely stage managers, is that right? Let's see, let's see, you must be Davina, and Kiki, and Hattie... Oh! Harriet! Goodness, when I saw your name on the sheet I didn't realise it was you! My love, my love, how are you?'

Hattie smiled and nodded, and said she was very well thanks. Truthfully, while she dimly recognised Atlanta, she couldn't just now recall when they'd worked together before. There were just so many of these actors and actresses...

Davina, clearly awestruck by this charismatic woman, breathlessly offered her drinks and snacks.

'That's quite all right, quite all right, I've brought my own!' replied Atlanta, pulling out a stainless-steel flask from her bag and brandishing it enthusiastically. 'Camomile tea. It's the *only* thing I can drink if I want to keep my voice... you know... tip-top. Well, that and brandy. But I don't think, for a first read-through, that would be quite *de rigeur*. If I could just trouble you for a cup...'

Over the next few minutes, more cast and crew members filtered in. Miguel, the young sound assistant, greeted Davina and Hattie warmly if a little awkwardly. He had been in Davina's class at ACDA, graduating the previous summer. He was a strange little man. Despite always being superficially friendly, his constant awkwardness prevented him from making many real friends. But he didn't seem too fussed about it. He was happiest when he could be tucked away in a corner fiddling with something. He was the sort of person whose ideal job would involve being handed a bucket of broken sound cables and asked to spend an afternoon fixing them one by one. Which was quite fortunate really, given the career path he was headed down. Hattie felt affectionate towards him in a sort of pastoral sense, but couldn't say that she liked him, exactly.

Then big Steve sauntered up, and greeted Hattie with his standard 'Ey-up?'. Hattie gave a friendly nod in return. They'd toured together several times in the past, and had a good sense of each other's working styles. He looked like a thug and had a

31

real temper when provoked, and it was generally understood that his first career had been as an enforcer for a north London criminal gang. It was rumoured that his nickname at one time was 'Kneecaps', and no one had ever dared ask him exactly why. But broadly speaking, if you treated him with respect he'd reciprocate, and when in doubt you could sweeten him up by buying him a Guinness and a packet of pork scratchings and asking how Arsenal were doing.

In too came the rest of the crew. Some familiar faces were first: Carrie and Laura – the lighting designer and head of lighting respectively – entered together, but were too busy bickering to acknowledge anyone.

'... "monthly in arrears" means you get paid *after* the end of each calendar month, not *at* the end,' said Carrie, sounding somewhat exasperated.

'Sure, but then why did he *say* we'd be paid on Friday?' responded Laura, sounding equally frustrated.

'Right, right, and like I say, it's not that I'm saying I don't believe you. Like, I believe that that's what *you* believe you heard.'

'You can argue about what you believe as much as you like, but if I don't get some money at the end of the week there'll be hell to pay, because I was very upfront about—'

'That's just... oh bloody hell.'

Carrie had stopped, mid-sentence, and was staring across the room. The object of her attention, who was quite oblivious to it, was Atlanta.

'Never mind,' finished Carrie quietly. 'Let's just get on with it.'

They made their way over to the drinks table and furnished themselves with instant coffees, Carrie shooting suspicious glances at Atlanta all the while.

Then came Moira, the dour, sour-faced head of wardrobe whose undisguised loathing of almost all actors and directors made her choice of career a surprising one. She had had some sort of accident or illness years ago, the details of which she never disclosed, but ever since walked very slowly, with an awkward hobbling limp. She used this as an excuse to stay in the quiet of her studio whenever possible. Hattie and she had crossed paths, but never really got to know one another.

The only person Hattie hadn't come across before was Raven, the scenery and costume designer. She was a small woman, dressed entirely in black, with spiky, peroxide blond hair and a silver hoop through her septum. She gave some small smiles when she first walked in, then quickly sat down and occupied herself with her phone.

It was a slightly bigger team than one would normally hire for a show at a low-budget venue like the Tavistock, but Hashi, the director, had been insistent, and Keith was only too happy to oblige. This was to be a big production, launching the first new season at the Tavistock after the death of its chairwoman and principal patron, Dame Joan Haygarth. Questions were already being raised as to whether the playhouse was a viable venue without her, as it had been seen by many as her personal passion project in the past, with resident artistic director Keith really just her pawn. So in response Keith had brought in Hashi Hassan, fresh from a critically acclaimed show that had transferred to the National, to prove that the Tavistock could still stage contemporary, relevant theatre without Dame Joan at the helm. Quite why they had chosen a light Shakespearean comedy as their tent-pole production was a mystery to Hattie, though.

The director himself arrived a few minutes late, in a flustered whirl.

'Sorry, sorry, everyone,' he called as he manoeuvred two large carryalls through the narrow doorway, his phone still clasped to his ear as he impatiently dismissed whoever was on the other end, and managed to drop his loose-leaf script with his other hand. Davina scrambled to pick it up for him, but was beaten to it by the tall, blond, energetic-looking girl who emerged from behind Hashi. That must be Regine, the assistant director. They seemed to get younger every year.

Oblivious to the clear-up operation behind him, Hashi did a round of greetings, offering elaborate air kisses to the designers, big friendly waves to the cast, and only slightly forced smiles to the crew. He was a petite, beautiful man, delicate of feature, elegant of dress and flamboyant of gesture.

'Terrible, isn't it? A director who turns up late to his own read-through. Fire that man! Regine, you can take it from here. No, no, not really, I'm joking, my love, no need to look so eager. I'm not quite that easy to supplant. OK, first things first, I'm going to need a proper coffee. There are some things I absolutely cannot live without, and real coffee is about five of them. Now, I do hate to be an entitled little whatsit, but there's a charming Portuguese cafe next to the tube station. Could someone lovely possibly nip out and fetch me a double macchiato?'

He pulled out a battered leather wallet and extracted a fiver, which he waved around the room hopefully. One of the actors hopped up from his seat.

'I can go!' he said brightly. Adam, that was his name. He was playing Berowne, the male lead.

Hattie shook her head. The thing about being a stage manager was that, while it wasn't your job to let actors walk all over you, it sort of *was* your job to let directors do it. There was a hierarchy after all. Actors and techies were adjacent but separate, but the creative team and producers were very definitely *above*. And catering to a director's fussy caffeine requirements was the sort of task best delegated to…

'Davina, can you handle that?' she asked.

Davina beamed, happy to be useful. She took the note from Hashi's hand and scampered away before the eager Adam could get close.

'Right,' said Hashi, brightly, and arranging himself in the last empty seat. 'So. *Love's Labour's Lost.* Now, you may or may not know about my work, but broadly speaking my *métier*, as it were, is, sort of, hyper-naturalistic slice-of-life character studies. So in some ways, the more stylised form of Shakespeare is a bit of a departure for me, which is I think why Keith challenged me to do it. Is Keith here, by the way? No? Oh. Anyway, I think this is going to be a great opportunity to experiment, and bring a more collaborative energy to the piece than I'd normally use. And with that in mind, I've deliberately tried not to come in here with a predetermined interpretation of the play. I want to discover the meaning as we go along. So for that reason we're doing it as a black box: no set, and pretty minimal costume, so Raven hasn't had much to do, have you, my love? Probably we'll need some fur coats and fake moustaches for that bit with the Muscovites, but not much more. Against that, I want to play with soundscapes to give us a lot of dynamic freedom in terms of the *mise en scène*, and that will help us create a really original audio-visual language with which to tell this story. Does that sound... does that sound good?'

There was a chorus of 'Yeah's and 'Wow's from the actors, and enthusiastic nods. But Hattie caught Steve's eye, and his cynical smirk told another story: the director had more or less just acknowledged that he had no idea how to approach staging a Shakespeare, and hadn't bothered to think about it in advance. That had left no time to design and build any scenery, and reliance on telling the story through abstract soundscapes and collaborative experimentation would be fine as a fallback if it wasn't *completely* at odds with the director's own self-professed directorial style. Not that it was remotely Hattie's or Steve's place to comment on such things, but this was not a promising start.

However, Hashi was putting a different gloss on it, and the cast didn't seem to be complaining. Best not to rock the boat.

Hashi handed over to Raven to talk about the production design, which, there being no scenery and minimal props and costumes, didn't amount to much. A few minutes later Davina reappeared, clutching a coffee in one hand, and a big cylinder of rolled-up paper in the other. Her eyes were red again: perhaps she'd taken advantage of her time alone to have another little cry. She scuttled over to Hashi and handed both to him.

'I bumped into Keith's intern just now; he gave me this to give to you,' she explained.

'Hold on,' said Hashi, downing most of his macchiato in a single enormous slurp. He closed his eyes, swallowed, sighed contentedly, re-opened his eyes, then turned his attention to the cylinder. Upon removal of the rubber band that secured it, it turned out to be an A3 poster for the show, with a Post-it note on it saying:

Just got these from the printers – Keith.

Hashi held up the poster, which was cooed over admiringly by the assembled company. Stark and simple, it had the words *Love's Labours Lost* in big white sans-serif capitals on a black background, and not much else.

'Good,' said Hashi. 'Solid. Impactful. Crisp. That'll do.'

'Yeah,' agreed Raven.

'Oh, that's interesting,' said Davina to Regine. 'Was that a stylistic thing? To only use one apostrophe?'

Regine's eyes widened and her mouth opened into a tight little 'o'. Hattie, overhearing, flicked her eyes over to Steve, who already had his phone out.

'Hm?' said Hashi.

'Uh… I think there's a… typo,' murmured Regine. 'Um… "Labour's" should have an apostrophe.'

Like a light switching off, Hashi's face darkened abruptly.

36

'Oh, for God's sake,' he snapped. 'That wretched little man. What kind of theatre doesn't proofread its own posters?'

'Hi, Keith, just wanted to give you a quick, heads-up,' Steve was saying softly into his phone. 'There's a small typo on the posters, just a missing apostrophe, give me a bell and we can talk about reprinting costs.'

'I mean, look at it!' Hashi continued, building up a head of steam. 'The poster is literally just three words, and one of them is spelled wrong. I have *never* worked somewhere that was this unprofessional. Not in London, not in New York, certainly not in Copenhagen, Jesus, they'd take your head off if you did something like this there. And this whole piece was his idea anyway! UUUGGGHH!'

He cast his face up to the ceiling, flung his arms down and outwards and shook them back and forth while exhaling noisily. There was an awkward silence, until he brought his gaze back upon the cast.

'Sorry,' he said, teeth gritted. 'We're five minutes in and already you're seeing me having a hissy fit. This is not going to do wonders for your morale or my reputation, is it? Tell you what, let's all have a rousing chorus of "fuck off, Hashi", shall we? Ready, one, two three…'

'Fuck off, Hashi,' murmured a couple of the actors, uncertainly.

'Oh, no no no,' Hashi tutted. 'You're going to need to do better than that. Come on, everyone, I want to hear this loud and clear, because these are going to be words you're going to be repeating at every rehearsal, I promise you. One, two, three…'

'FUCK OFF, HASHI!' came a more spirited response.

That helped reduce the tension, and everyone relaxed a little bit as they moved on to the main part of today's meeting: the read-through.

'Act one, scene one: Navarre, the King's park,' Kiki read. 'Enter the King, Berowne, Longaville and Dumain.'

'Right,' began the actor playing King Ferdinand, whose name, Hattie recalled, was Emile, clearing his throat. '*Let fame, that all hunt after in their lives...*'

And with that, they were away. First read-throughs could be tedious things. You didn't learn much from them that you couldn't get from a quick flick through the script in the quiet of your own home. But they were traditional, and there was nothing so traditional as the theatre.

The first act of the five gave way to the second, and Hattie allowed herself to tune in and out of the action. The slightly tiresome Belinda, inevitably, turned out to be brilliant as the leading lady Rosaline, imbuing the part with far more pathos and comedy than was apparent in the script. That was so often the way with actors: the better they were at their craft, the more precious and self-centred they were as people. It was something about the fact that acting required you to focus so intensely and precisely on yourself, Hattie supposed. You had to be a narcissist to be any good at it.

Atlanta was glorious and charismatic and oozed sophistication in a way that slightly jarred with her given role as Jaquenetta, a Shakespearean country bumpkin. Adam was a bit over-earnest, Emile didn't seem to be trying at all, and the rest... well, actors had a way of all blurring into one, didn't they?

She looked round at the crew. Laura, the head of lighting, was very obviously playing on her phone. Moira had leaned back and closed her eyes and could very well have been asleep. Davina was following the action, enraptured, drinking in every syllable. Carrie was still fixing Atlanta with a malevolent eye, and Atlanta still appeared not to be aware of it.

And odd little Miguel was gazing off into the middle distance, playing with... a padlock? He seemed to be slowly opening and closing it over and over again. There was something almost hypnotic about the slow, deliberate intensity of his hand movements. But looking closer, Hattie noted that he didn't seem to have a *key*. Just a couple of bent bits of metal. Ah yes, that was it: one of Miguel's many pet interests was, somewhat surprisingly, lock picking. Not, he assured everyone, that he had ever picked a lock that he didn't own. He seemed to think of his hobby as an activity in the same category as Rubik's cubes, or maybe knitting. Something you did to keep your fingers busy. Hattie supposed there was nothing wrong with it, but the periodic clicks were *slightly* annoying, now that she noticed them.

They took a quick break at the end of Act three. People jumped up, desperate for various combinations of coffees, cigarettes, and toilet breaks. Hattie made herself a cup of tea, then took a moment to check in with Davina.

'All right?'

'It's wonderful,' Davina breathed. 'There's just so much *energy*. I mean, I always think that at read-throughs, but you can already tell, can't you, that this is going to be a special production... Ooh,' she suddenly yelped, breaking away and grasping at the arm of a passing actor, 'I just wanted to say, I *love* what you're doing with Dull. I think it's so *interesting*, if you'll excuse the pun.'

The young man glowed.

'Well thank you,' he said. 'I'm so sorry, I didn't catch your name...'

Hattie left them to it, albeit disapprovingly. It wasn't that she didn't believe in fraternising with the talent, it's just that there was a right way and a wrong way of going about it. One didn't *gush*. It created the wrong dynamic.

Meanwhile Atlanta had – surely accidentally – managed to put herself at the centre of attention by nearly tripping over an inconveniently placed handbag on the floor.

'Whoopsadaisy!' she called, and staggered exaggeratedly, clutching on to Moira's arm for support. This caused Moira to drop her biscuit, which shattered into several pieces at her feet.

'Oh no!' cried Atlanta, beaming as she held her hands to her face. 'It's a digestive disaster!'

Within seconds, throngs of younger actors were prostrating themselves at her feet, gathering up errant crumbs of biscuit, while Atlanta took a restorative swig from her flask, and Moira, glaring furiously, muttered quietly something Hattie couldn't quite catch but part of which sounded almost like '... put poison in yer tea, ya wazzock...'

Hattie picked her way past the kerfuffle and went out to the foyer in search of Steve. On her way, she passed behind Hashi, who was having a muttered conversation with Raven.

'... my career narrative, you know?' he was saying, worriedly.

'It's not that bad,' replied Raven. 'Is it?'

'A quaint Shakespeare comedy at a pub theatre? After the *National*? Oh my lord. And the fact I couldn't even cast it myself. I mean, Atlanta playing Jaquenetta? Really?'

'I'm sure there are ways of solving that one,' offered Raven.

'What, like hoping she gets dementia so we can sub her out before opening night? I've got half a mind to... *Anyway...*'

Hashi, noticing Hattie, abruptly changed his tone. Hattie said nothing, kept her eyes down, and kept walking. Not her problem right now, not her place to say anything. But something to remember. Another variable to keep in mind for later.

She also had to skirt around Bums, who was standing in the middle of the main entrance doorway, on the phone.

'I tried to be nice, honestly. And the first thing she did was call me tacky. I know! Honestly, when people rub their money in your face it really gets to me, you know?'

Hattie found Steve having a quiet smoke outside, standing a little way apart from some vape-wielding actors.

'Any word from Keith about those posters?'

Steve grimaced.

'He's a bit het up, playing the blame game at the moment. It'll be fine in the end, we've got contingency budget. We've just got to wait out the hissy fits.'

'It's not often they start before the first read-through,' remarked Hattie.

'Reckon it won't be the last one with this lot.'

He finished his cigarette and dropped the butt into the ashtray mounted to the outside wall of St Eustace's.

'Ready for round two?'

3

' *The words of Mercury are harsh after the songs of Apollo. You that way; we this way. Exeunt.* Oh, sorry, in my script that's formatted like it's part of my line. Uh… yep. *We this way.*'

The read-through ended without calamity. The cast gave one another a rousing round of applause, as is traditional, and the crew joined in with rather more restraint, as is also traditional.

'Good,' said Hashi, emphatically, as everyone rose and stretched. 'Great, in fact. Well done, everyone. Well, that's the literal shape of the thing. Our task over the next two and a bit weeks is to find the emotional shape of it. And we'll start… tomorrow. For now, I believe there's a drink waiting for us at the Tavistock? Steve, is that right?'

Steve nodded. This news pleased the actors immensely, since, as a tribe, actors are generally the sort never to turn down free food and booze. As all parties were gathering up their things to go, Davina sidled up to Hattie.

'If it's all right, I think I'm just going to go home. I'm still feeling a bit… raw. And I think I'd rather just have a quiet evening.'

'Of course,' Hattie assured her. 'Are you sure you'll be all right?'

'Yeah,' she replied, nodding. 'Thanks. What's the plan for tomorrow?'

'Well, we don't have loads to go on, but meet me at ten o'clock at ACDA – we can base ourselves in the SM office – and we'll see if we can get ahead of things on paperwork. We'll also need to start researching fake Russian moustaches.'

Davina laughed.

'Sounds delightful! I'm looking forward to it. Enjoy your evening.'

'You too. Take care, my love.'

Hattie herded the company northwards towards the Tavistock. Some took public transport, some cycled, and Emile offered some a lift in his car. When those who had elected to take the tube were settled on the Victoria line, Atlanta started to tell a story about a raucous night she'd spent on a boat on the Thames with Sir Simon Russell Beale ('although, of course, this was thirty years before he got the knighthood, and at that time, trust me, no one would ever have dreamed that he'd be, well, an *establishment* figure'), and had the younger actors so enraptured that half of them were too slow to get off before the doors closed when they changed lines at Green Park, and Hattie was left shaking her head as the train whisked them away, with Atlanta calling through the doors, 'My fault, darling, all my fault. Don't wait for us, we'll meet you theeeere…'

It was with a much reduced group, comprising mostly techies, therefore, that Hattie arrived at the Tavistock. She shepherded them round to the side entrance where Keith was waiting.

'Hello my duckies!' he cackled, ushering them through to the auditorium. 'Welcome, welcome, welcome. Don't spill drinks on the seats, don't touch the scenery, fags out the back, and drinks by the lighting desk.'

Hattie's phone started to ring as the actors who'd taken other means of transport started to get in touch to ask for directions, and she spent the next twenty minutes rounding up lost strays. When she finally made it back inside, the errant tube party had arrived, and Keith and Atlanta were already in a full-throated, albeit very good-natured, argument about whether Strindberg's

A Dream Play could or could not be considered a realist work, where the objective appeared to be not so much who could win the argument as who could use a more expansively camp gesture to accompany their interruption of the other with the words, 'No, no, but, darling...'

Bums was talking to some of the other ladies of the cast, and the topic appeared to be 'Things that Bums feels aggrieved about'.

'I just don't know why there isn't a bit more of a culture of respect for the new generation of talent. I mean some of us are on the verge of having to take demeaning jobs as, I don't know, *waiters* or something, just to earn enough to be able to pursue our art, and then the ones who frankly should be long since retired, taking parts they don't deserve and swanning around shoving their fur coats in our faces...'

In various other corners, gaggles of actors were comparing notes about agents, cleanse regimes, sleep tracker apps and auditions. And at the back, Laura, Steve and Miguel were stolidly working their way through the supply of cans of Red Stripe. Hattie made a beeline for her people.

'Wotcher,' nodded Laura. 'Beer?'

'Wine if there's any,' said Hattie.

Kiki emerged from a dark corner, clutching a bottle of Hardy's red.

'Here you go.'

Carrie sauntered up as Hattie poured herself a glass.

'Here you all are: it's nice when all the ones worth talking to are together. Oh look, and Laura's here too,' she said with a smirk. Laura made a face, and stuck up a middle finger, but couldn't help a little smile as well.

'So you've worked with some of these actors before, have you?' Hattie asked Carrie, curious about the way she'd been glaring at Atlanta.

'Have I?' replied Carrie.

'Oh. Sorry. I just thought you looked like you recognised, um, someone,' Hattie said, embarrassed.

'Well, yes. You could say that.'

'Is it—' began Hattie, but stopped when she felt a sharp pain in her side. She looked down to see Laura's finger swiftly retracting, then looked back up in time to catch a meaningful glance from the finger's owner.

'Drop it,' Laura mouthed, urgently.

Meanwhile Carrie's eyes had drifted over to Atlanta, and the crowd surrounding her.

'Look at her. She's practically a bloody OAP and she still gets every man in the room following her around like a puppy, just because she talks dirty in a posh voice.'

Hattie, confused, looked round again at Laura, who leaned forward and whispered into her ear: 'Caz was dating a guy a couple of years ago, bit older than her, an actor, bit of a narcissist but no more than they usually are. It was properly serious, they booked a trip to Rome and he literally told her he was going to propose to her when they were out there. But then he does a show with that one, despite the fact she's even older than him, ends up snogging her backstage, and he turns rounds and dumps Caz. And then Atlanta turns him down anyway, the idiot.'

'Bitch,' muttered Carrie, to no one in particular.

There was an awkward pause.

'Remember Swinney?' said Steve, helpfully changing the subject. 'Broke his hand just behind where you're standing.'

'What'd he do? Punch a speaker?' snorted Laura.

'Nah, silly bugger fell off a ladder. Pretty much ended his career that day.'

'Why? What happened to his hand?' asked Miguel, aghast.

'Oh, his hand was fine in the end. No, the problem was, he decided to try to sue the production team when it was clear to all and sundry he'd been drinking.'

'That must have been a non-starter, eh?' said Laura.

'Well, not really,' mused Steve. 'We had no way of proving after the fact that he was sozzled at the time, and no amount of polite requests would make him drop the suit. I ended up having to go and pay him a visit…'

Steve left that hanging, and Hattie found herself thinking: Hang on, when *was* the last time anyone heard from Swinney? And what sort of visit would cause someone to not only drop a lawsuit but retire from the entire industry? She was debating with herself whether she really wanted to know the answer when she was interrupted from her thoughts by a commotion behind her.

Hattie turned round to see Keith holding up his phone triumphantly towards Hashi, who threw his arms up in the air, exclaiming, 'Well I'm bloody dyslexic, aren't I? I didn't realise your "full-suite design services" just meant doing a blind copy-paste job on a WhatsApp message I sent you.'

Oh no. The poster typo debacle.

As quickly as she could, Hattie put herself between the two of them.

'Can I suggest that if we want to talk shop we do it in the office upstairs?' she suggested firmly. 'Or, even better, we do it tomorrow?'

Keith held his arms up placatingly.

'All right, all right, I'm not trying to be antagonistic here. It's all easily fixed. Let's have a drink and not get upset.'

'I'm not upset, I just resent being blamed for… oh never mind,' muttered Hashi. 'Well, I'll take a G and T.'

'We've got beer, wine or Coke. If you want anything else you'll have to go through to the bar and buy it yourself,' replied Keith impassively.

'Of course. Of course. Certainly. More than happy to oblige,' responded Hashi, equally deadpan. 'Raven my darling, would you like a gin? Yup? OK great, we'll be at the bar.'

And with that, Hashi swept out, his designer following in his wake, leaving many significant looks and scandalous whispers from the cast behind him.

'Er...' said Adam, the good-looking young man playing Berowne, looking uncertain. 'Is everything going to be OK here?'

'Oh, pay that no mind,' said Keith, dismissively. 'Never shag an actor, never piss off a stage manager, and never mind a director's tantrums. I was taught that when I was starting out, and you'll find they're rules to live by.'

'Well,' huffed Emile theatrically, 'one must hope that not everyone lives by *all* those rules, otherwise life won't be much fun for us actors.'

'Oh darling,' responded Atlanta smoothly, 'one does not *shag* actors in the same way one does not *snack* on foie gras. I, for one, have never been shagged in my life. However, when it comes to cataclysmically tantric lovemaking... now, did I tell you about the weekend I spent in Prague with Kenneth Branagh?'

She put on a cartoonishly innocent face and drew a few chuckles. Hattie began to think it must be very tiring to be Atlanta. She was a very skilful actor, and extremely capable of working an audience... but she never seemed to stop. *Everything* was a performance. And, charismatic though she was, her persona seemed to net her as many enemies as friends. Still, she'd managed to already defuse the tension from the earlier altercation. Never say that actors didn't have their uses.

Hashi and Raven eventually reappeared as the party wore on. Despite his earlier tantrums, the cast were all so keen to impress Hashi that they flocked to him like puppies to a chew-toy, and asked him all sorts of flattering questions about his 'craft'. Soon he was holding court comfortably.

He did take pains to stay on the other side of the room to Keith, though. The older man, who normally liked to be centre stage in any gathering, was tonight spending a fair bit of time with his young intern Robin, who stuck to his side like a shadow. Hattie recognised the type: young, impressionable, enthralled by the glamour of theatre, desperate to be a part of it, but far too shy to be an actor, and with no idea how else to make their mark. He would probably spend a year or so chasing the lowliest office administrative work in theatres, and then, disillusioned by how (let's face it) boring that was, give up entirely. Hattie resolved to tempt him out of the office and into backstage work. That, she was certain, was where young men like that would end up happiest, if they only took the time to learn the trade.

Meanwhile Regine, the plucky assistant director, was making her own rounds. She went from person to person, making contact, flashing smiles, making sure to mention her own name so that everyone remembered it. She had ambition, Hattie could smell it a mile off. 'Assistant director' was often a euphemism for 'director's PA', and lots of hungry would-be directors tried to work their way up, only to find themselves perpetually fetching the coffee and photocopying scripts. It took a lot of energy to turn an AD role into a springboard for better things. Regine had that energy in abundance.

Eventually people started to filter away in search of food, and at seven o'clock the smaller number that remained were chased upstairs by the stage manager of the amateur production that had hired out the Tavistock before its official new season began, who needed to start setting up for the night's performance.

Up in the office the stories and jokes and chatter continued, until, in a lull, Steve called out to Keith, 'Show us the mask then!'

'How in the name of Cameron Mackintosh do you know about the mask?' retorted Keith, quizzically.

'Steve knows everything,' said Laura, merrily. 'He's a PM!'

Steve just smiled and shrugged.

'What mask?' asked Hashi.

'That's absolutely none of your business, ducky,' said Keith sharply. Then, relenting: 'But if it was your business I'd tell you that it formed the bulk of the bequest from Joan's estate.'

'Joan...?' echoed Adam the actor, nonplussed.

'Oh for God's sake,' groaned Keith.

'Dame Joan, darling,' said Atlanta, as if by way of explanation. 'Gods, she was marvellous. We *loathed* each other, but she was marvellous. If I were ever to have taken a woman for a lover it would have been her. She owed me a new cocktail dress, you know. I still haven't forgiven you for that, you know, *ma chérie.*'

Atlanta offered that last bit to the ceiling, seemingly addressing Joan's ascended spirit. Adam continued to look blank, along with several of the younger members of the cast.

Seeing their expressions Keith sighed and said: 'All right, gather round, kiddy-winks, and let uncle Keith tell you the story of the Tavistock theatre. There once was an English stage actress turned director called Joan Haygarth. Huge figure for a while in the eighties, but fell out with the wrong people and got slightly written out of London stage history. Anyway, she married well and divorced even better, and in the early two thousands decided to put her money to good use by revitalising a failing little fringe theatre behind a little pub called, wait for it... the Tavistock. She put in enough cash to get things going again, got some high-profile friends in to work on a season of shows, hired yours truly, and within a year had put the Tavistock back on the theatrical map. Got us on a par with the Finborough or the King's Head and made us into a going concern, and we've stayed that way ever since. Until, that is, her sad passing earlier this year—'

'May she rest in peace,' broke in Atlanta.

'Well yes indeed. Anyway, obviously she wanted us to be able to carry on, and so... Robin my love, would you do the honours?'

Keith fished a keyring out of his pocket and tossed it to his intern in the corner, who fumbled one of the keys into a padlock attached to the battered metal security cabinet next to him. With that removed, he opened the canary yellow doors and withdrew a small jewellery case, as the onlookers waited in hushed silence.

Robin passed the case gingerly to Keith, who took it, and with theatrical care presented it to the room.

'And so…' Keith repeated, 'she bequeathed us *this*!'

With a flourish he opened the case, revealing inside an ornate Venetian mask. It was finished in black velvet, with criss-crossing strands of gold thread forming a diamond pattern on top. At every intersection of the threads sat a small, sparkling stone.

'My God,' breathed Atlanta. 'It's to die for.'

Everyone automatically craned forward for a closer look, and Keith abruptly snapped the case shut and whisked it away.

'Stay back, you pilfering little varmints. The entire financial future of the playhouse rests on this thing. I can't risk grease-monkeys like you slobbering all over it.'

'You can't sell it, surely?' asked Atlanta, aghast.

'No, no, my love, no, not at all,' said Keith with a smile, deftly replacing the box in the cabinet. 'Don't get me wrong, I wouldn't bat an eyelid if I had to – just as I would cheerfully murder each and every one of you here if that's what it would take to keep the theatre going. But no, when it comes to the mask, I don't have to sell it. This mask serves a far more important function. But it can only come out on special occasions. The rest of the time it must stay under lock…' he said, snapping shut the padlock '…and key,' he finished, putting the keyring back into his pocket.

'Were those… you know… diamonds?' asked Adam.

His co-star Belinda elbowed him in the ribs. 'Of course they're diamonds. I mean… aren't they?'

'It's a fair question,' replied Keith. 'It's technically costume jewellery. In that she wore it as part of her costume in her starring role in *Antony and Cleopatra*. But that costume was paid for by her husband, actually before he was her husband, back when he was courting her. And I told you she married well, didn't I? So, yes, they're real enough.'

Hashi looked dubious.

'Far be it from me to tell you how to run your own operation, but that doesn't seem the highest security lock-box in the world,' he said, with an edge of scorn in his voice.

'Oh really?' replied Keith, eyeing him suspiciously. 'Well, if it goes missing I'll know who to interrogate first, won't I?'

'Oh don't worry,' grinned back Hashi. 'So long as you don't bugger me about I'm sure I won't be tempted to nick it. Whereas…'

'Ladies and gentlemen, the house is now open, the house is now open,' came a crackly voice over the speaker in the corner of the office.

'What's playing?' asked Atlanta. 'I didn't see any posters.'

'Marber,' replied Keith. '*Dealer's Choice*. Not an official part of the season. Amateur production, they're just renting the space.'

'Any good?'

'Well, you know Marber,' Keith replied with a shrug.

'I do, actually,' said Atlanta, brightly. 'Well, I met him at a party. Wonderful man. He has a very large… *presence*. Do you know, he said to me…'

As Atlanta launched into another one of her anecdotes, Hattie decided it was time to let herself go home. It was late, and her hip was hurting. So she said some quiet farewells to the crew and those actors who would make eye contact with her, and took herself down to the street and back in the direction of her tube.

Home, when she finally reached it, was too hot. Something was up with the thermostat. She hadn't had a chance to work out what, but she was already worrying about what it would do to the heating bill. It was a little flat in Chiswick: a bedroom, a kitchen, a sitting room, a bathroom and a glorified walk-in cupboard they'd squeezed a desk in and called the office. She and Nick had lived here for nearly thirty years. Back in the day it had been a great place to call home, particularly when rent was cheap and they were never there enough to get claustrophobic. There had been a time when they had had a chance to buy it, and Hattie regularly cursed herself for not doing so. In the absence of any savings, property in London might have been enough to set them up in retirement. They could have rented this place out for a decent sum, moved somewhere cheap up north, and lived off the difference. Whereas now she was having to scratch around for any work she could find, and it wasn't entirely clear how she could ever afford to stop...

Gods she was tired. First read-through days were always the hardest. After opening nights, of course. And fit-ups. And get-outs. And all those other hard days too. She looked wistfully up at the little carved wooden box sitting temptingly on the mantelpiece. Nope. Not on a school night. That was the rule. But one more glass of wine wouldn't go amiss.

Hattie helped herself to a Merlot from the box on the counter and curled up on the sofa under the ratty fleece blanket that smelled of once-spilt aftershave. On a whim she got her phone out and called Nick. It went through to voicemail. Of course. He'd be on the lighting desk at the moment, probably. She decided to leave him a message anyway.

'Hello, it's cockatoo. Started working with Kiki Bennett again today. You remember her? The DSM. Lesbian. You once walked in on her and Miranda Whatshername snogging in a Luckings van and I had to pull you away, you dirty old git. Anyway, she asked after you. Well, that's me. Take care, my love.'

She played on her phone for a little bit, and did a couple of cryptic crosswords from her puzzle book. Then, once the wine was finished, Hattie Cocker put herself to bed.

4

The key to a smooth rehearsal process is clear communication between all departments. The deputy stage manager is responsible for keeping every department informed of what decisions are being made in the rehearsal room. Furthermore, through weekly production meetings the production manager keeps all departments abreast of one another's movements. But there are still myriad opportunities for things to fall between the cracks, and so to prevent this, the stage manager should be in touch with absolutely everyone, at all times, about everything. Sound impossible? Well, maybe it is. But that's the ideal towards which we strive.

– From The Art and Craft of Stage Management
by Donna Fletcher, Chapter 2: Meetings

Looking back later at that first day, Hattie would conclude that there had been warning signs aplenty that some things were seriously amiss, and that the following Monday's discoveries of both the absence of the mask and the presence of Atlanta's dead body, while absolutely not predictable, were perhaps presaged by those signs. But at the time, none of it seemed more than the usual feuds and intrigues that were inevitable whenever a group of creative and passionate people were brought together on a performance project. This being so, the next morning Hattie had nothing particularly on her mind above and beyond the usual administrative concerns of a stage manager on the job.

She met Davina at ACDA at the agreed time, and they settled down in the SM office for the morning. Hattie had her assistant research false moustache options while she herself dived into the preparatory paperwork: provisional prop lists, call sheet templates, risk assessments and more.

At midday she checked in on Davina.

'How are you getting on with your moustaches, my love?'

'Hmm? Oh... sorry... Umm... I've not got very far,' Davina replied shyly.

'No? What's the problem?'

'I'm sorry, I just... I'm getting distracted. I'm in a situation that's putting me in close proximity to my... my personal life.'

Of course. Hattie cursed herself for being so stupid. Shane's workshop was just at the other end of the building. If they really had had a tryst, then asking Davina to come back to ACDA to work on the show must be excruciating for her.

'I'm so sorry, my love. How thoughtless of me. Look, let's just get you away from all of this...'

'No!' said Davina, her eyes widening. 'No, I'm a professional now, I need to act like it. I'm sorry, this is my fault entirely. You're trusting me to ASM for you, and all I've done so far is mope. I'm just frustrated because... well, I wanted to put it all behind me and forget about it, but I can't because he's right *there*, so I thought maybe it would help if I could just talk things through with him to get some, some *closure*, only he's ignoring my calls so now... But I'll pull my socks up, I promise. Right now. Honestly, a fresh start.'

'Bless you,' said Hattie. Then on a whim, not quite sure whether she was motivated by benevolence or selfishness, she added: 'Tell you what, why don't you take the afternoon off? There's precious little real work to do at the moment, and this'll be your last chance for some free time in a few weeks. Let's have a go at that fresh start tomorrow.'

Davina protested, of course, but once Hattie had assured her several times over that there really was nothing urgent she could be doing right now anyway, she eventually agreed to take her leave, and Hattie got a quiet afternoon to herself to ring round prop stores and enquire about fur coats.

On Wednesday, well before the start of the morning's rehearsal session, Hattie dropped into St Eustace's to see how things were going. She found the rehearsal room in a state of unexpected disarray. There were upside-down chairs strewn everywhere. Kiki's desk had been transplanted to the farthest corner of the room. The chalk outline of the stage on the floor had been hastily and incompletely scrubbed out, with other shapes chalked in instead. Several sheets had been torn out of the flip-chart that lived behind the tea table, and scattered along the floor, with words like 'fame' and 'love' scrawled on them.

Oh for goodness' sake, she thought. She'd hoped Kiki would be keeping the room in a better state than this. Still, maybe she had had a good excuse for not tidying up last night. Ever a team player, Hattie decided to help her deputy out, and began to clear away some of the mess.

She hadn't got far when a horrified yell rang out behind her.

'Nooo! No no no no no, that absolutely *mustn't* be touched!'

Hashi had materialised, and was staring at her, horrified.

'You can't just *move* things like this, they've been very carefully set up and put in places for a reason!'

'Not a problem,' replied Hattie cheerily. 'I'll just put this one back *here*, and that one... um...'

'I've taken photos,' sighed Kiki, coming through the door

behind Hashi. 'Don't worry, we can match things up to how they were. I know you were very particular about this... layout.'

Hattie looked again at the mess around her. It really didn't look intentional. Besides...

'You... do know that this staging won't fit on the Tavistock stage, right?' she asked gently.

'No no, you misunderstand what we're doing here. We're not defining the literal positions of the actors, we're working through the *emotional cadence* of the piece,' explained Hashi, exasperatedly. 'Look, we were going through it yesterday. There are four basic emotional axes here, from *fame* to *lust,* and from *love* to *excellence*. And for now we represent those physically to help us understand the journey of each character. See, so... OK, technically *two* axes, one axis from this corner, starting from fame and going across to lust... oh, was it that fame to excellence was one, and lust to love was the other? No, hang on, I'm sure we were opposing fame with lust. Wait, where's Regine? Regine!'

There was a little scuffling noise, and Regine, who had evidently been in conversation with one of the cast in the hallway, came sprinting in at the sound of her name, and the two of them started on an in-depth conversation about narrative structure as the cast filed in.

'Has it all been like this?' asked Hattie quietly to Kiki.

'Yep. From the get-go. No discipline, no structure: it's a madhouse. The plan was to be well into act two by now but they're still mostly doing looking at "power dynamics" in the opening scene. Still, at least they're all enjoying it. Except Atlanta. She's not impressed, and she's not doing a great job of hiding it.'

Meanwhile Miguel had now arrived, juggling a battered old laptop, an even more battered-looking pair of speakers, a couple of plug-in hard drives, and a spaghetti of cables. Hattie got up and helped him get everything placed down on a table to one side and plugged in. Hashi noticed them, and called out to Miguel.

'Ah, excellent, the soundscapes are here. Right, we're in a park. Now, like yesterday, we don't want literal park noises. We want the abstract feeling of openness. I'm wondering if we can do something with maybe wind, or waves, or something a bit *bigger* than just normal park noises, to contrast it to the closeness of the previous scene. What can you do for me?'

'Uh… let me see,' muttered Miguel, clicking around on his laptop. 'How about…?'

The room was suddenly filled with a tinny rendition of a tropical hurricane from Miguel's little speakers.

'Oh I love it!' exclaimed Hashi. 'It's far, far too much, in the best possible way! Good, let's get that ten per cent louder and make sure it's on loop. I want this atmosphere *all morning*.'

Over the course of that day, once she had returned to the office at ACDA, two requirements came through for Hattie from the rehearsal room. The first was that Hashi wanted to represent all paper documents – letters, laws, oaths and so on – with 'ethereal orbs' onstage, so Hattie set Davina off with an assignment to research as many different sorts of glowing spheres as she could think of, from Christmas ornaments to novelty juggling balls.

The second was that Hashi, warming to his new idea of using the physical positions of the actors in the rehearsal room to denote the characters' emotional state and relationships, now wanted to expand his system in the third dimension. He demanded to be furnished with a set of 'resizable, collapsible, stackable blocks' that could be arranged however he liked such that his cast could sit, lie or stand on them at different heights as a means of symbolising their shifting social status.

Hattie immediately replied to Hashi that she would, of course, see what she could do. She then followed up by asking, as innocently as possible, how much Hashi wanted to spend on this, and which department's budget it should come out of. Hashi responded that she should take it up with Steve and Keith, but that he expected she could use the contingency budget he knew they'd set aside.

The next 24 hours were characterised by increasingly fraught negotiations between, on the one side, Hashi, who thought that having a few simple wooden blocks in the rehearsal room was a perfectly reasonable and easy-to-accommodate request, and on other side, Steve and Keith who were adamant that reasonable or otherwise, *there was no bloody money available*, as the contingency cash had already been spent reprinting the posters.

On Thursday afternoon Hattie eventually engineered a grudging compromise from all parties: the Tavistock had some old oblong seating blocks that were used when they wanted to reconfigure the performance space 'in the round' (seats on all sides, stage in the middle). These blocks weren't resizable or collapsible, and would have to have some bolts and latches temporarily removed from them, which Keith grumbled about, but they would just about give Hashi his different levels to play with, without busting the budget.

However, in the course of negotiations, Keith and Hashi failed to conceal their increasing contempt for one another, and so by Friday lunchtime, when the crew and creative team reconvened in the rehearsal room for a production meeting, relations were already somewhat strained.

Hattie and Kiki managed between them to shoo the milling actors – packed lunches, iPhones, scripts and all – out of the room, before setting up tables and chairs for everyone to sit round. Other than the cast, the only person who'd been present at the read-through who was absent now was Moira, who had made excuses. Or rather, in true Moira fashion she'd simply told Hattie she wouldn't be coming, and left Hattie to make excuses for her.

Steve was chairing the meeting, and had a printed agenda to work through.

'Morning all,' he began, when everyone was assembled. 'Let's just crack on, eh? First thing, how are rehearsals going? It sounds like progress is a little slower than we were anticipating?'

Hashi folded his arms and leaned back.

'Well… look,' he said, truculently. 'It's *Love's Labour's Lost*. For whatever reason, it's the piece Keith wanted to stage, and I'm happy to do what I can with it, but let's be honest: it has more potential for sheer blandness than really any other work in the canon. Now, if you want me to just go through the motions in the rehearsal room and put on something bland, then fine. But really, my job should be to *challenge* that, and find a way of discovering the truth of the piece, and… look, that's a messy process. OK?'

'That's fine,' replied Steve patiently. 'So long as, when it comes to the tech rehearsal, the actors know where they're standing so we know where to point the lights.'

'I… sure,' said Hashi dismissively. 'If all you care about is where they're standing, I'm sure we can tell you where they'll be standing.'

'Perfect,' replied Steve, ignoring Hashi's sulky tone entirely. 'Now, next up, lighting…'

They worked their way through a list of minor niggles: Miguel wanted to hang some speakers from the same place that Carrie wanted to hang some lights, and he half-heartedly made his case before a stern glare from her made him back down. Hattie wanted to check how much of the cost of the Russian disguises in the second half could come out of the costume budget instead of the props budget, and in Moira's absence Steve ruled that the fake fur coat hire could, but the fake moustaches couldn't. Hattie made a mental note to ring Moira to smooth that one over personally before the minutes of the meeting were distributed. The wooden blocks were, perhaps sensibly, not mentioned.

'Lastly, thanks everyone for filling in your timesheets for this week,' finished up Steve.

'Actually, about that. It's the last Friday of the month. Can someone just clarify for me: are we getting paid today?' asked Laura.

'For God's sake,' said Carrie. 'For the last time, arrears doesn't mean at the end of—'

'The cast were all paid for their first week this morning,' put in Kiki. 'Although I suppose they're on different contracts.'

'Everyone's contract is worded the same,' murmured Steve.

'Well then: if the cast have been paid today then we should all be too,' said Laura. 'And I certainly haven't been.'

'Typical,' said Carrie, rolling her eyes. 'Actors get to jump the queue.'

'Tell you what,' said Steve. 'Sounds like there're a few crossed wires here. We're pretty much done, so how about I give Keith a bell now, double-check what's going on? All right?'

The team indicated its assent through a collection of nods and grunts, so Steve took out his phone and stalked off down the corridor. Everyone else remained seated, and there was an awkward silence for a few moments.

'So... did you really not want to do this play?' asked Davina of Hashi.

Hashi shrugged.

'I thought it was a joke. I honestly thought it was a joke at first. I mean... if you look at the arc that the Tavistock's on, and then you look at the trajectory of my career, I mean speaking purely objectively here, I can see why Keith was wooing me to open his new season. Right? And I thought, great, let's do some new writing, or something punchy... you know, a Ravenhill or a Kane or something. But then he comes at me with a bunch of weird casting requirements, and a pre-prepared list of show options to choose from. They're all ghastly, but to cap it off there it is on the list: *Love's Labour's Lost*. And I'm sorry, but that's the complete *opposite* of what I should be doing, or of what he should be putting on, frankly. So I literally mentioned that one, as a joke, like, *obviously* a joke, but then his eyes lit up, and next thing I know he's sending me a contract for *Love's Labour's Lost*. I mean can you imagine? And telling me I've got to cast some faded has-been in a role she's a terrible fit for. And look, I'm a professional, I'll do what I can, but, you know…?'

Davina was nodding along attentively, but Hattie could see behind her Laura miming shooting herself in the temple. As directorial visions went, 'I'm doing this play because I had no choice' was not ideal.

'Still,' Hattie forced herself to say brightly, to fill the awkward silence that followed, 'it sounds like you've found a fresh way of approaching it. And the actors are all full of enthusiasm.'

'Well… most of them,' replied Hashi, dismissively, and the room lapsed into silence again.

A few minutes later Steve returned, his face unexpectedly dark. He still clutched the phone in his outstretched hand.

'Right,' he said grimly, 'Keith, I've got you on speaker with the production team, so could you please explain to them what you just explained to me?'

'Look there's no need…' came a voice from Steve's phone, but it was drowned out by a few '*Hi Keith*'s from the room.

'Hello, everyone,' Keith said cheerfully. 'Look, all it is, is a slight misunderstanding about contract wording. You're all getting paid, but you're getting paid a month in arrears, that's all. So you'll be paid for this month at the end of next month. It's completely standard.'

'So then why were the cast paid today?' put in Laura.

'Because they're being paid on a slightly different basis, that's all,' said Keith. 'They're being paid *monthly in arrears*, meaning they get paid for a month's work at the end of that month. It's just a different arrangement.'

'But their contracts are the same as ours,' Hashi growled.

'No they're not. They're completely different. You really mustn't make the mistake of comparing contracts.'

'Keith, the payment clause is the word-for-word the same for all contracts,' insisted Steve.

'Yes, but the wording of the actual written contract lends itself to many different interpretations, and the arrangement I have with the actors is just different to the arrangement with everyone else.'

'You are kidding me,' muttered Hashi.

'Look, it's all well and good grumbling,' came Keith's voice defiantly from the speaker, 'but the fact of the matter is that theatre finances are ludicrously complex beasts, and my job is to keep on top of cash flow. I am able to pay some people early, but not everyone, due in part to disappointing box office pre-sales for this production. But you're still all getting paid, I promise you. You're being paid at the end of the next month, as per your contracts, and *please* stop assuming that every rule that applies to the cast also applies to the crew and vice versa, and if you'll excuse me, I have a lot to be getting on with. All right? Right.'

He disconnected, and there was a moment's silence in the room, before everyone started talking at once.

'The little *shi*—' began Hashi.

'Oh for God's sake,' put in Laura.

'Unbelievable,' snorted Raven.

'Is this normal?' asked Miguel quietly to Kiki.

'Guys, *guys!*' snapped Steve. 'Look, it is what it is. Timings aside, you will all get paid for this gig, I promise you. I'll wring his neck if he tries anything.'

'I just think it's ridiculous,' said Hashi. 'That little worm has got diamond jewellery literally spilling out of his cupboards up there, and he's trying to screw us out of our wages?'

'I'm not going to stand for this,' muttered Laura. 'I'm going to—'

She didn't get to tell the assembled company what she was going to do, because at that moment the door clattered open and Atlanta thrust her way into the room.

'Now, darlings, I... oh. Oh, how terribly gauche of me. A thousand apologies, everyone, I didn't realise you had a meeting.'

She gave a well-crafted little giggle, and backed out on elaborate tiptoes.

'Don't mind me! You just carry on!'

Hattie noticed that Hashi and Raven exchanged a sour look as Atlanta left. The interruption curtailed any further discussion about pay arrangements, but no one came out of the meeting looking particularly happy about the situation.

And the next time Hattie saw Atlanta was three days later, when she stumbled across her corpse backstage at the Tavistock.

Act Two

5

Hattie had heard herself described, in the past, as a 'tough cookie'. The term wasn't always used as a compliment, but regardless of intention, as a general characterisation Hattie felt it left a lot to be desired. True, a rough-and-tumble career in a bruising industry had inured her to a certain extent to most of the common ways in which people, objects, events and circumstances conspired to grind her down, but Hattie always felt that her acquired toughness was something she wore on her exterior, not an intrinsic quality of herself. This cookie may have been burnt to a crisp on the outside, but it still had a soft centre.

One might take as evidence of this fundamental softness the fact that when, early on Monday, Hattie found Atlanta's dead body in the women's dressing room of Keith's theatre, her very first urge was to burst into tears. However, one might equally consider that to be a completely normal and reasonable response to a particularly rare and upsetting situation. Most of us get through our entire lives without having to be the one to unexpectedly discover a corpse, so most of us probably aren't in a position to make an informed assessment.

Either way, that initial impulse was very quickly superseded by more practical considerations. Hattie double-checked that the body was pulseless, breathless and completely cold, but, not being at all certain when and how resuscitation was a possibility, she called 999 anyway. The operator connected her to someone calm but rather bored-sounding, who dispatched an ambulance, and then walked Hattie through making, essentially, the same checks she had done by herself. By the time she had finished, the man on the other end of the line didn't sound optimistic.

'I mean, she sounds pretty... dead... to me,' he said. 'And you say she's in... sorry, was it the toilets in the pub?'

'No, the dressing room in the theatre at the back of the pub,' corrected Hattie, through slightly gritted teeth.

'Oh I see. Um... that's a bit unusual, isn't it?' the man suggested. Hattie, hoping that was a rhetorical question, remained silent, and he continued. 'I'm going to dispatch a police officer to your location. That's just what we do when things are a bit unusual. If you could make sure you stay on the scene until they arrive, because I'm sure they'll want to talk to you. Um... hold on just a second.'

Hattie's patience with the man was wearing thin. She felt there was a frustrating lack of urgency in his responses, even though she had to admit that she wasn't sure what urgent action anyone could take at a time like this. More than anything else, what Hattie really wanted was to not be alone in a room with a dead body any longer than she had to.

Eventually, though, she heard a siren approaching in the distance. She stepped outside, flagged down the ambulance as it arrived and directed the paramedics backstage. They, while initially very enthusiastic, quickly cooled in eagerness when they realised that they were dealing with someone who was indeed, in the operator's words, 'pretty dead'. But at least they were a bit more formal and dignified about it.

Keith poked his head out of the office door as Hattie waited in the hallway.

'What on earth is going on?'

Hattie was suddenly painfully aware that she didn't know the proper way to announce news like this.

'I'm so sorry, Keith,' she tried. 'Atlanta has… died. Um. In the ladies' dressing room.'

Keith gave her a quizzical look.

'*Atlanta* Atlanta? In there?'

Hattie nodded.

'Well, what the bloody hell was she doing in there, then?' he demanded.

'It looks like she was having a drink.'

'On a Monday morning?'

'Well, she may have been there for a while.'

'And you say she's…?'

'Dead, yes, Keith.'

Keith let out a long slow breath.

'Bloody hell,' he said at last. 'I'd better come down then.'

The paramedics were taking turns going outside for a surreptitious cigarette, leaving the other one to watch over the body. Keith, still looking perplexed, took a look into the dressing room. He re-emerged a moment or so later, his expression now abruptly switched from confused to aghast.

'Well, that's new,' he said, shakily. 'We've had ambulances out before, but never this. That's going to bugger things up for me *completely.*'

Hattie wanted to chide him for focusing only on himself, rather than worrying about, say, Atlanta's loved ones and dependents. But she too had been thinking about the practical ramifications. She was a stage manager; that was her job.

'It'll be a shock to everyone,' she replied. 'We'll need to give the cast some time off to process. That'll give us time to re-cast, and maybe we can open a week late…'

Keith was already shaking his head.

'Can't do that. Got to be open in a fortnight, financially speaking. It's too late to shift opening night.'

'If rehearsals were going well, we might be able to get away with a shorter period, but they're not exactly ahead of schedule at the moment,' Hattie remarked.

'Frankly, this whole production already feels like a shit-show. If I didn't know Hashi's name would put some bums on seats I'd have never let it happen. Never be afraid to say no, Joan always said. We're not some cheap receiving-house, we've got a reputation to maintain. I'm not sure this show is going to do wonders for it.'

They were interrupted by a tall and rather heavily built woman who emerged through the doorway from the pub into the auditorium, guided by a member of bar staff.

'Hello,' she said solemnly. 'My name is Jordan Burakgazi, and I'm a detective inspector with the police. I believe there was an... accident?'

'Well, yes,' said Hattie. 'You could call it that. It's this way...'

The police officer spent some time in conversation with the paramedics, then came back to Hattie.

'You're the lady who rang 999, is that right? Would it be all right to have a word?'

'Fine,' Hattie said, and the woman led her to a corner of the otherwise empty auditorium. Hattie could feel herself tensing up. She'd learned from hard experience never to trust the police, no matter the situation. It had been a long time ago, and she'd been young and naïve and just trying to do the right thing in a tricky situation, but the rozzers had stitched her up like a kipper, and years later she was still dealing with... but now wasn't the time to dredge through all that.

'Now,' Burakgazi was saying, 'I just want to make clear that this is completely normal procedure. We're not making any assumptions about what's happened, but because we don't know,

72

I'm just here to ask some questions to establish what's going on. Is that OK?'

Hattie nodded, not sure entirely what it was she was supposed to be OK about. The woman sounded rather like she was reciting a script from memory.

'I'm sorry to inform you,' she continued in a sombre tone, as if breaking some unexpected news, 'that the lady in the dressing room is dead.'

'I... see,' said Hattie, hoping to sound equally serious.

'Now, do you know her name?'

'Atlanta Greenwell.'

The officer took out a notepad and started writing.

'And your name?'

Over the next ten minutes she conveyed to the woman the basics of the situation. No, she hadn't known that Atlanta had come to the theatre. No, she didn't know when she had come. No, she didn't know why she might have come. Frankly, she was beginning to feel like she wasn't being any use at all, and started to worry that she'd be accused of being obstructive or something. But after a few last questions the woman smiled at her, put her notebook away and said, apparently satisfied, 'Thank you. That's all very helpful. Now, we will need to notify the next of kin. I don't suppose you know who that might be?'

'I do, actually,' replied Hattie, her relief at having survived her interrogation translating itself into eagerness. 'I've got emergency contacts for all the cast. Let me just check...'

She pulled out her phone and started to dig out the relevant email.

'I'm sure you can look that up later,' said the woman, rather impatiently. 'What's going to happen now is that I'm going to notify a coroner, and some of my colleagues will come and take a look at the scene, and then we'll arrange for the paramedics to take the body to the mortuary. There will be an inquest, which I know is a scary term, but it really just means that, because it's not immediately clear how the lady died, we need to get a coroner to do a medical examination. All right? Now, when you have details of next of kin, if you could pass them on to me – here's my email address – and I'll get in contact with them at some point this afternoon.'

'This afternoon? Shouldn't we really let them know as quickly as possible?' queried Hattie.

'Well, obviously you're very welcome to call them now yourself,' said the officer, just a touch defensively.

'Oh,' replied Hattie 'Me? OK…'

'Great,' replied the officer, and Hattie grimaced, realising she'd walked right into that one.

The woman continued: 'I, or one of my colleagues, may be in touch with you again, if I have any more questions. In the meantime, I'd like to have a word with your boss, Mr… Macaulay, was it?'

Once Hattie had introduced Burakgazi to Keith, no one seemed to have any need for her any more, so after hanging around vaguely trying to look helpful for a few minutes, she let herself out. With a heavy heart, she realised what her first action needed to be. Hattie rooted around in the inbox on her phone, until she found the number she was looking for, and called it.

'Hello?' answered an upper class-sounding voice eventually.

'Hello, is this Francis Greenwell?'

'Speaking,' replied the voice, a touch impatiently.

'Hello, Mr Greenwell. I, er, I'm afraid I have some bad news. Some very, well, sad news. Um, it's about your sister, Atlanta.'

'Oh crumbs, is she OK?'

'I'm afraid not…'

She broke the news as gently as she could. He didn't say very much. He sounded shaken, and unsure. She outlined, without going into too much detail, when and where she'd found Atlanta, and explained that the police would be in touch in the afternoon with details about where the body would be taken, and next steps.

'Do you have any sort of a sense of, I mean not that I'd expect you to, but, uh, was it in any way obvious what had happened? To her I mean?' he asked at the end.

'I'm sorry, I really don't know,' said Hattie. Feeling this was somehow insufficient she added: 'I think perhaps it could have been a… heart attack? It looked sudden, at any rate. I don't think she suffered.'

'Well that's a blessing, that's a blessing. Thank you. Yes, thank you very much. Uh. Well, goodbye then.'

'Goodbye. Do let me know if…'

But he had already hung up.

The next call was to Steve. He listened sympathetically as she explained what had happened.

'Christ,' he said, when she'd finished. 'Are you all right?'

'I can't lie: I'm a bit shaken,' she replied. 'I very much hope I never have to go through that again.'

'Need to take some time off?'

'Maybe once we've got everything sorted. But there's a job to be done. I need to talk to Hashi, so he can break the news to the cast. We should offer them some sort of support, somehow. Is there a… I dunno, a bereavement hotline or something? Most of them only knew her a week, but you know what rehearsal rooms are like.'

'I'll see what I can find. You sure you're up to it?'

Hattie took a deep breath.

'I'll be fine. It's very… odd. Did you ever have a death on a show?'

'Yeah, once. Very different though. We were doing the get-out, and a girl was up on the fly floor, Judie Whitmore her name was. There was a lantern she was trying to reach, should have used a cherry picker, but she thought she could get to it from where she was. Well, she lost her footing, fell thirty feet, landed head first on the stage, twenty people saw her neck snap. That was a rough tour.'

They were silent for a moment, then Steve spoke again.

'Well, if you can tell Hashi, I'll try to get hold of him and Keith later in the day and work out what this means for timelines.'

'Keith doesn't want to delay things at all, by the way,' she warned him.

'They never do. Callous bastards, the lot of them. Worse than some of the sorts I used to work for in the old days. But they're the ones who sign the cheques, in the end.'

Hattie took the tube back to St Eustace's in Pimlico. The rehearsal was in mid-flow, so she patiently waited and watched as the cast jumped, squatted and crawled their way through Act three, climbing over and around imaginary blocks, accompanied all the while by a recording of the sound of soldiers performing the Trooping of the Colour on loop.

When they finally took a break for lunch, and Hashi had finished giving notes to Kiki and Miguel about his latest thoughts on the sonic and visual aspects of the scene, he made his way towards the exit via the hall, where Hattie intercepted him.

'Hello, Hashi. How's it going?' she asked, as cheerily as she could.

Hashi grimaced.

'We're getting… somewhere. Something is happening in that rehearsal room. I don't know if it's theatre yet, but it's something.'

It was meant as an exit line, and as he finished it he made to stride off, but Hattie gently positioned herself slightly further in his way. Realising the interaction wasn't finished yet, Hashi forced a smile, and added, 'And how are you?'

'I'm well, thank you, very well.'

Hattie considered for a moment. She didn't like breaking the news out of the blue like this. And meanwhile, there was one other thing she was supposed to talk to Hashi about. The whole missing mask thing seemed fairly unimportant, given the current situation. However, theft was a serious thing, so she had to at least ask. So she continued, trying for the least clunky segue she could manage: 'I had a very nice weekend. Um, and speaking of the weekend… Did you happen to be in the vicinity of the Tavistock yesterday at any point?'

'God no,' scoffed Hashi. 'You wouldn't catch me within a mile of that place on my day off. Why?'

'Oh, no reason,' replied Hattie, as nonchalantly as possible. 'I just thought I recognised you there.'

'Well it wasn't me. I was in Oxford all weekend, trying to clear my head.'

'Ah. OK. Um… just out of interest, how are you feeling about this whole pay issue?' asked Hattie, uncertain how else to probe him.

'Pay? Oh, the month in arrears debacle? Frankly, I don't really care,' replied Hashi breezily. 'I mean, I think it tells you a lot about Keith that he'd prioritise paying the actors over the director, and rest assured, if I'm not paid in full by the end of this thing I'll rip his sodding theatre down brick by brick… but I mean look, none of us is in this for the money exactly, are we? And a few weeks' difference here or there isn't the end of the world.'

He didn't entirely sound like a man who'd been so incensed by late payment that he'd burgled a theatre in revenge. Hattie decided she'd need to report back to Keith before taking this any further.

'Was that all?' Hashi asked.

'Er… no. Sorry. It's about Atlanta.'

He made her tell the cast. By that point she was sick of telling people. It wasn't getting any easier with practice. And the director was supposed to be the *leader* in a situation like this. But he insisted that they should know 'first hand', as though the details of where and when she'd died were important. So she put on a brave face, gathered the company round, re-introduced herself and briefly explained that Atlanta had died over the weekend, that her next of kin had been informed, that she was sure there would be a funeral or memorial service in due course, that she was available to talk if anyone wanted to, and would try to help anyone who needed to access some form of support.

The cast reacted the way you'd expect them to. A couple burst into tears, a few looked shell-shocked, one or two seemed enthralled and fascinated by the whole thing, and they all kept asking probing and inappropriate questions.

'Without wishing to pry... was it a fast death? A painless one?' asked Emile.

'Honestly, I'm not sure. I think so, but we don't know exactly what happened yet.'

'Does that mean it could have been, well, foul play?' suggested Bums, her tear-streaked eyes lighting up with gruesome glee.

'Of course not!' replied Hattie, shocked. 'It was almost certainly a heart attack, or, I dunno...'

'Old age,' suggested Bums, nodding understandingly.

'Well, no, I mean she was no older than me,' Hattie couldn't help pointing out.

'Yes, but ...'

Bums was stopped abruptly by a firm tap on the arm from the girl next to her. Struggling to keep her composure, Hattie continued.

'Obviously we haven't yet worked out what this means for the production. Keith, Hashi and Steve will need to sit down and make a plan, but for the time being it would probably best to take a little time to—'

'Yes, absolutely,' cut in Hashi. 'Let's all take twenty minutes to clear our heads. Then we'll keep rehearsing this afternoon as normal, and tonight I'll come up with a plan for how to keep the production on track. OK? Thanks, everyone, and well done. It takes a lot to absorb this kind of news. Don't be afraid to explore that energy in the rehearsal room when we pick it up again.'

Before she left Hattie took a few minutes to check in with Kiki and Miguel. Kiki was a little tearful, Miguel just gawped, and neither had a lot to say. But equally neither of them seemed in imminent danger of a meltdown, so after a while Hattie left them to it. She'd had a message from Keith summoning her back to the theatre: he was impatient for an update about the mask.

6

'What, so he just *says* he wasn't in town and you believe him?'

Hattie was back at the Tavistock, and Keith was only interested in talking about the mask.

'Well, it seems like it would be quite an easy lie to debunk,' replied Hattie. 'And if he did take the thing, he'd surely have guessed why I was asking, and telling me an easily detectable lie would land him in a lot of hot water very quickly.'

'Um...' mumbled Robin behind them.

'Not if he knew you'd just accept his side of the story and never bother to check it,' Keith retorted hotly.

'I'm not saying he's definitely in the clear, I'm simply suggesting we might at least entertain the possibility that it *wasn't* him,' Hattie persisted. 'Especially given how, you know, there's now a dead person involved.'

'Oh nonsense,' said Keith dismissively with a wave of his arm, while behind him Robin said 'Um' again, slightly more loudly.

'Yes, my love?' Hattie prompted Robin, as much to shut Keith up for a second as anything else.

'So... on his Insta he was definitely posting pictures from Oxford yesterday evening. Look, he was in Trevor's Bar. He took a picture of his gin and tonic. Um.'

'There we go,' said Keith, warmly. 'I knew there was a reason I kept you around. See? Evidence. Proof. Well done, my duck. At least someone's got the right idea.'

That was impressive, thought Hattie: taking proof that she was right and turning it against her, so that he didn't have to climb down. Petty, but impressive.

'Indeed,' she said through gritted teeth. 'Then if we're agreed Hashi didn't take the mask, should we think about what else might have happened?'

'So someone *else* from your team took it,' said Keith with a shrug. 'I don't even care who, so long as I get the damn thing back. So I need you to get on it.'

'Well, yes but… look, being blunt, how much is it worth?'

'It's priceless. It's a piece of theatre history. One of a kind.'

'OK, but if you were to take it to a jeweller, how much would they value it at?'

Keith sighed. 'If you're going to be crass… let's say the right buyer would pay several tens of thousands for it.'

Hattie felt her eyebrows rising fractionally.

'Oh. I didn't realise it was quite that… Is it insured?'

Keith snorted. 'Lord no! I only just got my hands on the thing. Joan's executor brought it in at the beginning of the summer.'

'That's still several months… look, never mind. The point is, you've had something rather expensive stolen on the very night that Atlanta *died* in your theatre. Don't you think the two might be related?'

'I don't see why,' replied Keith, condescendingly. 'Atlanta was a darling, but she was utterly batty. Let's be honest, drinking herself to death in the dressing room over the weekend is hardly out of character. It's completely unrelated. Besides, she clearly didn't take the mask, otherwise they'd have found the damn thing on her.'

'Maybe not,' countered Hattie, 'but what if she was here with someone? Someone who took the mask?'

'No,' said Keith, firmly and dismissively. 'The police can poke around Atlanta's death all they like, and of course, if they find anything suspicious I'm sure they'll tell me. But until they do, I'm not going to concern myself with Atlanta's death, just like I'm not going to concern the police with the mask. We handle these things ourselves.'

Hattie frowned. On the one hand, she had a deep suspicion of law enforcement, and her default position was to have nothing to do with the police if she could possibly help it. On the other hand, things got rather more serious when a corpse was involved. But, back on the first hand again, Keith was almost certainly right: tucked away in her dressing room, Atlanta's death didn't seem like it was part of some grand heist.

Her hip was starting to hurt. With a submissive gesture, she took a seat on one of the rickety chairs poking out among the mess of the office.

'Fine. So tell me more about what happened. When was the last time you actually saw the mask in the cupboard?'

'Friday night. I put some paperwork in the cabinet just before I locked up for the night, and the box was there.'

'And you're sure the mask was in the box then?'

'For God's sake,' sneered Keith. 'It's not like someone stole the mask first, then came back, blowtorched the lock and left a note a day later, is it?'

'All right, all right,' said Hattie. 'You know me, Keith. I'm not the quickest, but I am thorough, and I do get there in the end. So, Friday night the mask is there when you lock up. And then come Monday morning you open up and it's gone. And what was it like over the weekend?'

'It was a fairly normal day on Saturday. I was up here most of the day, and stayed late, and the lock was definitely still on the door on Saturday night when I locked up. So it must have happened on Sunday. It was quieter then. There was no show, but I was still popping in and out. I had a bunch of scripts to read, and we did some auditions in the evening.'

'When exactly were you around?'

'I first came in at about three o'clock on Sunday afternoon, unlocked everywhere, and did some work upstairs. Robin came along later in the afternoon.'

Hattie's eyes flicked across to Robin. He was sitting so still and so quietly she'd already forgotten he was there. A strange young man, and no mistake. He must be taking his internship seriously if he was giving up his weekends for it.

'You didn't open the cabinet at any point while you were there?' she asked Keith.

'No, but we'd have noticed if the lock was off. We stuck around until about half past six. Then we went and got some dinner.'

'And you locked up when you left?'

'Ye-es… well, the downstairs door. I don't lock this door except overnight,' he nodded at the one leading from the office to the stairs. 'When I came back, at about nine-ish this was, I went straight into some auditions in the auditorium. When I was done I downed a quick whisky in the pub, then I locked up a little before eleven and went home. This morning at nine I unlocked and saw the mangled padlock.'

'OK,' said Hattie, thoughtfully. 'So we think someone got in overnight last night?'

'No!' replied Keith, exasperatedly. 'Because I locked the office door last night, and unlocked it this morning, I've got the only key to this door. So the thief would have had no way of getting in overnight.'

'So when did they take the mask?'

'I've just *told* you. It must have been between half six and nine.'

'But you came back to the office after that,' pointed out Hattie.

'No, I came back to the *building* after that, but I didn't come in here,' said Keith, through gritted teeth. 'I told you, I was doing auditions in the auditorium. No one came in after that point or I'd have noticed – I had the door from the auditorium to the hallway open – so they must have taken it before then, and I didn't spot it because I didn't look into the office before locking up.'

'All right, all right,' said Hattie. 'I know you're getting frustrated, but I wasn't there yesterday, and I haven't spent all morning working this stuff out. Just bear with me. So you're both in here at six thirty, you're sure the padlock was in place then, you head out, *not* locking the office door but locking the downstairs one. So you think the thief came in then... how? If the downstairs door was locked?'

'Through the pub, into the auditorium and up.'

'All right, and they come up here, break the lock on the cabinet, take the mask, go back out via the pub, and when you come back you don't notice because you don't come upstairs.'

'Finally,' said Keith. 'Yes, that's the only possible explanation.'

Hattie wrinkled her nose. 'Really?'

'What do you mean?'

'Well, we're saying that someone who knew you had the mask up here, and knew that the theatre was empty, but the office door was unlocked, snuck through the door from the pub into the auditorium hoping no one would see them, bringing with them... sorry, did you say a blowtorch?'

'See for yourself.'

Keith pointed to the remnants of the padlock, still in the middle of his desk. It certainly looked like it had been subjected to some extreme conditions.

'OK, so they smuggled in a serious, professional blowtorch, used it to open the cabinet, then smuggled both the blowtorch and the mask back out through the pub, again, hoping none of the staff or customers would notice, before disappearing off into the night? It just feels a bit... messy, to me.'

'Well, maybe they didn't have your eye for efficiency, Hattie.

But the mask *is* gone, the padlock *was* melted… what more do you want?'

'And what about Atlanta, then? When did she come in?'

Keith shrugged.

'I don't know. The way the paramedics were talking, she could have snuffed it at any point over the weekend. The last time anyone else was in the dressing room was the end of the show on Saturday evening. They did their get-out straight away, it was all done and dusted by nine-ish. But look, let the coroner investigate that, you just worry about my mask.'

Hattie thought for a moment. Keith was determined to play down the connection with Atlanta. Still, she had no reason to doubt him. For now.

'So who knew about the mask being here, then?' she asked

Keith frowned.

'Me, Robin. Steve, apparently. He was doing a bit of work from this office last week, must have spotted it then. Then he blabbed about it to your whole company, which I still haven't forgiven him for. Completely unprofessional.'

Hattie didn't remember Keith being so opposed to showing the thing off at the time.

'Anyone else?' she pressed. 'The *Dealer's Choice* people?'

'God no,' replied Keith. 'Not unless one of your lot told them.'

'Which is possible, I suppose,' mused Hattie. 'We don't know who mentioned it to who.'

'But, um, the note…' murmured Robin.

'Right, right,' acknowledged Keith. 'Thanks to Steve misunderstanding the contract, it was your team who got all riled about what day they were getting paid on. And the note – "Love's Labours Repaid" – confirms it.'

'True… although, isn't it at least possible that the note was… I don't know, a deliberate misdirection maybe? Without wanting to be rude, I can't imagine that our crew are the only people in the industry who, at some point, have come to believe the Tavistock owes them money? Rightly or wrongly?' Hattie added hurriedly.

Keith couldn't help but show a sly smile.

'Well yes, there have been some misunderstandings in the past. Not all of which were resolved to all parties' satisfaction. That's the price of doing business. But it's all water under the bridge. And none of those people will have known about the mask.'

Hattie didn't like this set-up. Keith's insistence that the mask had been taken by one of her company rubbed her the wrong way. But, as he *was* insistent, she had no option but to go along with it. And besides, he might be right. If there was a thief in the company she was determined to root them out.

'All right. So let's say for the sake of argument that it was one of ours. It must have been someone who could get their hands on a blowtorch. And I guess from the note that it's probably not one of the actors, if they're the ones who actually got paid last week. Although it does seem a little extreme as a response to being paid a bit late.'

'Not late, just later than they expected,' Keith corrected her. 'But I've thought about that: maybe they didn't realise exactly how much it was worth. Maybe it was more to make a point than anything else. In which case they probably haven't really thought about selling it, and I can't imagine they'd damage it or anything like that. So if we can find them quickly there's a decent chance we can get it back. I just need you to work out who it was and talk to them, point out how very badly this will end for them if they don't cooperate.'

'I can chat with everyone, of course I can,' said Hattie, 'but whoever took it didn't do it on a whim. If it was Friday that stirred everything up, they had all of Saturday to cool off. But they still went ahead with it. Which means they've surely already thought through the consequences, and it's not going to do much good me pointing it out to them.'

'Well, then you'll have to convince them some other way,' said Keith. 'Persuasion, that's your whole... whole skill set, isn't it?'

Hattie thought for a second.

'You know what would really help me, then?'

'What?' asked Keith, suspiciously.

'Well, if they really did do it because they didn't get paid... perhaps it would make sense to pay everyone?'

'Oh now don't start—' Keith huffed, but Hattie cut him off.

'I'm just saying, it might, what's the word, *mollify* whoever it was. At which point, if I could suggest to them that they might be able to put an end to the whole matter by quietly giving it back, perhaps that would give them an easy way out.'

Keith sighed. 'Fine. Let me shift some things around. I'll do bank transfers tonight.'

'Thank you,' Hattie smiled, relieved. As much as anything else, she was reassured that Keith *could* actually pay the crew. His alarming statements about the theatre's future earlier that morning had made her begin to doubt it.

'But now, we need to narrow down who it could have been.'

'Well, if it's about the money then it could have been any of the creative team or crew, apart from Hashi who we've already ruled out. So Regine, Raven and Carrie are possibles. Then there's Steve, Kiki and me, Laura and Moira. Finally there're the assistants: Miguel and Davina.'

'Davina?' asked Keith, his eyebrows furrowing.

'Davina Aggarwal, my ASM,' explained Hattie. 'Oh yes, she wasn't here to meet you on Monday night, was she? So thinking about it, she might not even know about the mask.'

'Still,' said Keith. 'Worth checking her out. I've come across Davina. She helped out on a one-off cabaret night back in July. Nice girl. Seems... *unlikely* to have been her, but...'

'But none of them exactly seem the burglarising type, do they?

Although Steve's not the sort of person you want to cross, and Miguel... I mean, his hobbies... well, never mind. I'll ask them all.'

'Ask them what, though? I don't want it getting out that the mask is gone, that would be ruinous.'

'I'll simply ask them what they were up to last night. That way we'll hopefully rule out everyone who it wasn't, and we can see who's left,' replied Hattie. Secretly she was hoping that she'd be able to rule them *all* out, at which point she could pass the whole mess back to Keith.

'All right, Hattie,' replied Keith. 'But for heaven's sake, do it quickly. If you really care about you and your company getting paid, for this show or any others at the Tavistock, I need that mask back.'

'I'll do what I can,' said Hattie, standing up slowly. 'I won't stand for stealing in my company, *if* that's what happened.'

'That's the spirit,' smiled Keith. 'I'm sure you can sort this out if you put your mind to it. That's why I, unlike everyone else, keep hiring you.'

Hattie winced. She'd hoped Keith hadn't realised yet that he had her over a barrel. She needed work, and now that she was off the tour circuit, her phone was ringing less and less often. Most of her old contacts had retired and been replaced by younger people who thought anyone over forty was over the hill. She had been hoping to stay on Keith's good side, because while he'd dropped hints that he'd like to hire her for a few more Tavistock shows this season, she didn't have anything in writing. She could really use the money, especially once her ACDA gig ended. But having Keith *know* how much she needed to stay on his good side gave him an unfortunate amount of power over her.

Before she left, she cast a glance around the room. It really was a mess. It wouldn't be so surprising if the mask had simply been put down somewhere. She half expected to see the blooming thing poking out from under a pile of old lighting plans. But, she reminded herself, there was the note…

And Keith looked uncertain in a way Hattie had never seen him before. He was always cool-headed, confident. This whole thing had him rattled. She still didn't really understand why the mask was so important. Was he planning on selling it? He'd denied it to Atlanta, but then again, Keith lied like other people whistled, reflexively and unthinkingly.

Meanwhile, the taciturn Robin looked on, barely saying anything. It occurred to Hattie that here was someone who not only knew about the mask, but also had regular access to it, and was a completely unknown quantity. Was his internship a paid one? If not, did he resent that? But then again, Keith said he was actually out to dinner *with him* when the lock was melted.

It was all very odd, thought Hattie, as she closed the door and made her way down the stairs. Still, she resolved to find out what she could.

7

Before she left the Tavistock building, Hattie popped into the pub. It was now late afternoon on the Monday, and the place was quiet, but not deserted. Behind the bar was a short, shaven-headed girl who looked about twelve.

'Excuse me,' asked Hattie, 'Were you working here last night?'

The girl wrinkled her nose and grimaced apologetically.

'Er, no. Sorry. I was here Saturday, if that helps?'

'No, sorry, it's the Sunday I'm interested in. I wonder if you could help me, then: I'd really like to speak to whoever was here.'

'Um…' replied the girl, uncertainly. 'What for?'

'Oh it's nothing, it's just… I'm working in the theatre, and there were just some comings and goings yesterday. I'm trying to work out who was around. For… compliance,' Hattie offered, knowing that people would normally accept all manner of weird questions if you made them sound bureaucratic enough. 'Do you happen to know who was behind the bar? I just want to ask them if they saw anyone going through that door into the auditorium last night. Some point between about half six and nine.'

'Oh, goodness, OK,' said the girl, still looking confused. 'I can check with my manager when he's back… he'll know the rota. But

I'm not sure I can, you know, give you their details. I think that might be… um, a privacy thing…'

'Not to worry,' replied Hattie. 'I don't want to put you to any trouble. But maybe if you could find out who was in, and then ask them to call me? My name's Hattie, and I'm a stage manager for a show at the theatre.'

Hattie reached into her handbag and retrieved a pen and a Post-it note (a complete stationery set being the sort of thing that no self-respecting SM would leave home without, even when they weren't working), and wrote down her details. She handed them to the girl, who took them slightly gingerly.

'Thank you so much. What did you say your name was?'

'Er… Rosie…'

'Nice to meet you, Rosie. I'll be popping in and out quite a bit over the next few weeks, so I expect I'll see you again.'

Hattie said it cheerily, but the subtext she hoped to impart was, 'So if you "forget" to pass on the message then you will have to look me in the eye and tell me about it later.'

Then she gave a friendly wave and took her leave.

She was overdue a check-in with Davina anyway, so she rang her as she walked towards the tube.

'Hi, Hattie.'

'Hello, my love. How are you?'

'I'm… I'm fine,' said Davina, not particularly convincingly. 'Still tracking down "coloured orbs". Hashi didn't like any of the ones I found last week. Apparently they don't look ethereal enough. I tried to explain that the way they look in a photo of an online shop isn't what they'll look like under stage lights, but he's convinced we can find something a bit more "formless".'

'Oh dear. Well, I'm sure you'll find something.'

Hattie knew she really ought to tell Davina about Atlanta, but she knew that that was likely to send her into a total tailspin, and she needed to do a little bit of detective work first. How to go about this?

'So… how was your weekend?'

'It was fine. Um. Pretty quiet.'

'I thought I saw you on the tube yesterday evening.'

'R-Really? Where?'

Was there a note of alarm in her voice? Hattie took a punt.

'King's Cross. At about seven, eight-ish.'

'Oh, then no, it can't have been me.'

'Oh no? What were you up to?' Hattie desperately hoped the question didn't seem too contrived.

'I was at the theatre. It's Action To The Word's new thing, at the Menier. A sort of musical version of *Titus Andronicus*, although that makes it sound a bit camp, which it really wasn't. It was more like a play crossed with a heavy metal concert.'

'Oh yes? Good, was it?'

'Really good. I'm so glad they did a Sunday show, otherwise I wouldn't have got to see it. Vix and I are basically Action To The Word groupies, we go to see everything they do.'

'So you went with Vix, then?'

'Yup. Why?'

'Er… just making conversation,' said Hattie, awkwardly. Vix was another ACDA grad, whom Hattie had interacted with a little bit during the previous term. An eminently sensible young woman, Hattie remembered.

'So it wasn't you I saw at Kings Cross.'

'No, the show started at seven. I was out and about at other points in the weekend though? Just running errands.'

The Menier theatre was far too far south and east. Unless this was the shortest production of *Titus Andronicus* on record, there'd be no way Davina could have made it up to the Tavistock before or after the performance.

Good. Well, that was one name she could cross off her list immediately.

'Fair enough. Well, sorry I haven't been in the office today. Um, I'm afraid I've got some rather sad news…'

Davina, of course, was immediately in floods of tears, and Hattie found herself struggling to offer any real consolation over the phone. To her knowledge, Davina and Atlanta had met precisely once, at the read-through, and besides a conversation about camomile tea they had had no interactions whatever. Hattie reminded herself to be charitable, though: death is an upsetting topic for many people, and no matter how little contact they'd had, Davina and Atlanta had been on the same team, which mattered.

Eventually Davina seemed in a stable enough state that she could be trusted to take herself home, at which point Hattie hung up and did the same herself. She got back a little after six, by which point rehearsals would have just finished in St Eustace's, and Kiki would be tidying up the room. She gave her a call.

'I may kill him,' growled Kiki, in place of a more traditional greeting.

'Oh dear. What happened?'

'He's changed his mind about the concept. Thanks to the news about Atlanta he claims to have had a "conceptual breakthrough". Apparently all this stuff with levels representing social status is too literal, so he's ditching the blocks entirely, and now he wants to use colour of lighting to depict social status, how loud the background soundscape is to represent emotional intensity, and the actors' blocking onstage is all about geometrical shapes that they create with their bodies – he keeps calling it "biomechanical", by the way – so even though we haven't even looked at the second half yet, we're going back to the beginning and starting again, but he's still not prepared to consider the *actual* shape and size of the *actual* stage, because apparently that's just a "minor practicality"' – she paused to draw a deep breath then continued – 'which means I'm supposed to keep track of which colour each actor is supposed to be in each scene, and pass that on to Carrie, but she can't *use* that information because she doesn't know where the actors are, so she doesn't know where to point the lights, and it's… it's just not how it's supposed to be done!' she finished with a wail.

'Maybe this is just his way of dealing with the news?' suggested Hattie placatingly.

Kiki grunted noncommittally.

'Or maybe,' Hattie tried again, 'this is more of a case of common or garden director panic. He's tried to throw himself into a new style of directing, he's realised he's not sure how to do it, and that means he's second-guessing every decision he takes, and undoing it. He wouldn't be the first. It's just that normally directors get slightly further along before the panic sets in. But maybe that means he's getting it out of the way early?' she finished, hopefully.

'He just doesn't seem to understand how much he's buggering up our jobs by not committing to any of this stuff. Poor Miguel just sits in the room all day, being asked every five minutes for a different sound effect, and Hashi never makes a final decision about what he wants. At best he just says, "That'll do for now, we'll come back and figure it out later." But I don't know when this magical "later" is supposed to be. Every day I have to produce the most wildly unprofessional rehearsal notes I've ever seen, with really vague, nebulous requirements for props and costume, and most of them contradict what I said the day before. I just… I hate this!'

Kiki, normally so reliably stoical, sounded remarkably close to tears.

'It's OK, my love. It's OK,' soothed Hattie. 'Of course you hate it. You want to do a good job. You want things to be neat and tidy and disciplined. But you know what I'm going to say, don't you?'

Kiki sighed. 'Yes, but say it anyway, I need to hear it.'

'All right: our job isn't to produce neat and tidy notes, or make sure the plan never changes, or even ensure that it's a good piece of theatre that gets put on at the end. Our job is to support the director in bringing his vision to life, and ultimately that means doing what we're told. If he wants to do things in a ridiculous, unproductive way, then so long as you make clear, when necessary, the repercussions of his choices, then you're doing the right thing by going along with them. Everyone in the company has a good sense of what that rehearsal room's like, and no one's blaming you that the notes coming out of it are a little... chaotic. You're doing a great job. Honestly.'

'Thanks, Hattie,' said Kiki, warmly. 'All right. I won't kill him. Yet. And maybe... maybe this is me just getting overly emotional about it all because of... you know. The news.'

'That's completely understandable,' replied Hattie, and then, because she had a job to do, she continued: 'Now, changing the topic entirely, how was your weekend?'

'Not too bad. Just had a quiet one with Miranda. Walked the dog. Watched some telly. Tried to have a proper date night last night. We cooked a fancy meal and all. But I think I ruined it by venting about work all evening.'

Hattie made sympathetic noises, while mentally crossing Kiki off her list.

Over the rest of the evening and the following morning Hattie rang round the remainder of the team for a casual check-in, to let them know and/or see how they were feeling about the news about Atlanta. In each case, feeling slightly ashamed as she did so, she used that as pretext to make only slightly unsubtle enquiries about everyone's weekends. When she needed to press for specifics, she used her line about thinking she'd seen them on the tube on Sunday evening.

Everyone had a story, but not all of them were very convincing.

Laura, who had seemed most angry about the payment situation, had arguably the most solid alibi: she had been at a barbecue with a group of friends that included Carrie. Carrie herself confirmed this, but was far more keen to talk about Atlanta than anything else:

'I just... I feel awful. Because I didn't like her. I mean, more than that, there were times when I literally wished her dead. Isn't that terrible? Now she is dead, I just feel incredibly guilty. Like I wronged her, and now I have no way of putting it right. It's doing my head in.'

Hattie had little consolatory advice to offer, so told her that that was understandable and normal and that it would all be all right in the end, and hoped that would be enough.

Meanwhile, Raven had been at a small gallery opening by a curator friend of hers, so was equally above suspicion. On the other side of things, Moira claimed to have been sorting out her studio by herself, Miguel was unforthcoming, and would only say he had been 'working on some stuff', while Steve cheerfully told Hattie to piss off and mind her own business, and she couldn't get hold of Regine at all. So, for now, that left four theoretically viable suspects.

Hattie also made sure to let people know about Keith's decision to bring forward payment, and gauged their reactions to the news. Everyone was pleased, but only Laura and Steve acted as though a great wrong had been righted. None of the iffy four gave the impression that they might have been so incensed about the whole thing that they'd consider stepping outside the law to take matters into their own hands.

Hattie considered the four suspects. They were an odd bunch: Steve did have a real temper. Miguel was, well, a bit strange, and did know quite a lot about lock-picking after all. She didn't really *know* Moira, for all that her mobility issues made her an unlikely cat burglar. And Regine emanated ambition and determination, although whether and under what circumstances such determination could translate into larceny was anyone's guess.

Keith, when Hattie reported back to him on the phone, was sounding much more assured and back to his usual self than he had the day before. Presumably the shock of it all had started to wear off. The tone of his dressing-down of Hattie was more disappointment than distress.

'Well, ducky, you've not brought me very much, have you? You've barely ruled out half the crew, and have got nothing solid on anyone who's left. Proof, that's what we need. Like I said yesterday, it's evidence that we're after, otherwise we'll never narrow it down. I need you to dig deeper.'

'All right, Keith,' replied Hattie, then added cautiously, 'but you might recall that we agreed that the best way of de-escalating this whole situation would be for you pay everyone, and then I could make clear that there'd be a sort of amnesty if the mask was returned unharmed. And I can't help but notice that my bank account is still empty...'

'If I didn't know you better I'd say you were using this whole situation just to squeeze more cash out of me,' grumbled Keith.

'Now that's not fair, is it? I'm simply pointing out that if someone does have the mask in their clutches because they're so angry with you, holding out on them isn't going to help calm them down.'

'I'm working on it. I'm just having to move some money around. Don't worry, it'll be done very, very soon.'

'Well then. Once that's done, I'll see if I can drop a hint that returning the mask would put an end to the matter. OK?'

Keith grunted.

'Fine,' he said. 'But I'm disappointed you haven't been able to do more, to be honest. You're a professional problem solver. And if the house has to shut down, and your show gets cancelled, that's definitely your problem. So solve it. The clock is ticking.'

He hung up abruptly, and Hattie let out a little snort of frustration. Keith was a rude little man. Calling people 'darling' and 'ducky' didn't much make up for constantly calling their competence into question. She wished she didn't so desperately need him and his theatre.

8

The 'bible', or 'book', or 'prompt copy' is the definitive description, for technical purposes, of a show. It normally comprises one or more lever arch files, to which information is continually added over the course of the rehearsal period. It starts with the script, with all cuts, alterations etc written in. Over the course of rehearsals, the 'blocking' (that is, the specifics of where onstage anyone stands, or sits, or lies, at any given point in time) gets added in by the DSM.

Then, once the cast has moved from the rehearsal room to the theatre, the DSM starts adding in the technical cues: at what point each successive change in lighting or sound happens, when the scenery gets flown in, pyrotechnics, projections, whatever. By the time the show opens, it's being used as a reference by the DSM in performances to 'cue' the show – i.e. tell everyone else when to do what. It should be totally comprehensive. If one night the DSM gets hit by a bus, anyone else should be able to pick up the bible and use it to cue the whole thing.

– *From* The Art and Craft of Stage Management
by Donna Fletcher, Chapter 3: The Deputy Stage Manager

In the afternoon Hattie had to turn her attention away from the show, and the Tavistock, in order to run a tutoring session at ACDA for the first years.

'So, who here's put together a bible before?' she asked.

A couple of the students put their hands up. Others shook their heads. Still more just looked confused.

'Do you mean, like, book-binding?' asked the gawky young blond man at the front. Hattie had had a brief go at memorising their names. Was he an Alexander?

She smiled wearily.

'No, my love, sorry, I should have been more clear...'

She spent the next hour walking them through the various acronyms and symbols that form stage management shorthand as used in a show bible. Some people picked it up pretty quickly, others... less so. In particular, Alexander seemed to misunderstand everything she said, and asked woefully confused questions at every turn, which were all premised on such a muddled grasp of the topic that they were almost impossible to answer. He didn't seem embarrassed or frustrated at being repeatedly corrected, and after every re-explanation Hattie tried to give, he simply nodded, his brows furrowed, and then a few minutes later asked another question that suggested he'd taken absolutely none of it in.

'So if they're stage left and you want them stage right, how do you move them?' he asked.

'Um... move who?' countered Hattie.

'The actors.'

'We don't... I mean, we don't move them. The director tells them where to move in rehearsals. We just... write it down,' she said, confused.

'No, I mean not in rehearsals. On the night.'

'Well... when it comes to performances the actors should know where to stand while they're onstage. They should remember it. From rehearsals.'

Alexander frowned, then nodded.

'Oh, I see. Then when a performance is happening, how does the DSM know where the actors are standing?'

Hattie gawped for a second.

'Um, she... she can... see them? Um, listen, we're running a little bit short of time here. Maybe we should chat about this afterwards. But for now, I've prepared a little exercise to practise your notation abilities. Could you pass these out? Thanks. I'm giving you a bit of the script from a play that was on at the Lyric a couple of years back. We're going to watch a bit of it on the telly, and you're going to write down the blocking as best you can. Don't worry, this isn't a test, this is just to get you into the habit of notating this stuff.'

After a couple of false starts she got the decrepit TV in the corner working, and put on a DVD of a hand-held recording of the last scene of an old production of *A Woman of No Importance*. She handed out some photocopied script pages to everyone and they started going through the scene, pausing every time an actor changed position. Hattie, trying to make it easy for them, gave broad hints at every turn.

'Now, he's crossing from downstage left to downstage right. Can everyone remember the symbol we use when someone *crosses* the stage?'

'Just remember, we're looking at this scene from the auditorium, not the stage, so when someone looks like they're on the left to us, is that going to be stage left, or stage right?'

'Now, when she sat down we noted it with a down arrow, didn't we? So now that she's standing *up*...'

When they made it to the end of the scene, she did the rounds, inspecting each student's work. Most of them had more or less got it. Alexander's handiwork was a glorious mess, with longhand, incorrect symbols and in some cases honest-to-goodness cartoon drawings of the actors mixed together in confused heaps on the page. However, the most alarming sheet didn't belong to him, but rather to another young man, Felix, who was sitting at the back. Felix was enormous, with shaggy dark hair, tiny dark eyes, and an awkward mess of dark wispy facial hair scattered around his jowls. He was the one she had noticed just staring off at the ceiling on his first day. This afternoon he had been sitting silently, hunched over his paper, and had looked as though he was doing the exercise. But when Hattie came to inspect his work, she saw his sheet was entirely blank.

'Oh,' she said, uncertainly. 'Did you... did you not have a pen?'

'I just... didn't do it,' mumbled Felix, without meeting her eye.

'Did you get a bit confused by it? Don't worry, I—'

'No. I wasn't confused,' he said.

'OK,' faltered Hattie. 'Do you want to... talk about it?'

He shook his head, then asked, emotionlessly, 'Am I in trouble?'

'No, no, not at all. But, er, just... try to... Well, maybe see if you can have a go next time,' suggested Hattie, lamely. She was out of her depth here. She wasn't a *proper* teacher, and no one had taught her anything about how to deal with difficult students. She could pass on what she knew, but only on the assumption that her students were relatively bright, and relatively keen, and were there because they wanted to learn.

The class drew to an end, and she watched everyone pack up and leave. She watched Alexander carefully, still trying to get the measure of him. But she watched Felix more carefully still.

The evening was filled with more phone calls. This time it was to the cast, to check in on how they were dealing with the Atlanta news. No hidden agenda this time, just the pastoral responsibility of a stage manager in a time of stress. Most of the actors had spent a week in close company with Atlanta, and it was understandable that they would be shaken. Hattie wanted to make sure no one was hit too hard by it, and be ready to follow through on her offer of help finding counselling if so.

The calls were, on the whole, terrifically awkward. Hattie had never previously exchanged words with most of the cast, and ringing up, out of the blue, and trying to talk about something sensitive was met with mixed responses. Some of them made no secret of finding the call unexpected and unwelcome. Some were polite but unforthcoming, asserting that they were 'fine' and leaving it at that. A couple of them, seemingly deciding that Hattie was offering them a phone-based therapy session, immediately jumped into long monologues about their attitudes to death, grief and personal relationships, to which Hattie did her best to listen sympathetically.

Emile, now the oldest cast member, was reflective. He'd had former castmates die before, he said, although previously they had always become 'former' castmates by dint of the show ending *before* they had become former in the more final sense. He wanted to talk about the evanescent nature of live performance, and what that meant for an actor's professional legacy, and Hattie let him opine and ruminate for quarter of an hour before gently trying to wind up the conversation.

Bums, by contrast, seemed to find the whole thing terribly exciting, and spent her whole conversation pressing Hattie for details about the death.

'Do you think it could have been Keith?' she asked abruptly at one point.

'What do you mean?' asked Hattie.

'You know. Keith who… did the deed.'

'Belinda, I really don't think it's appropriate to start—'

'Please, call me Bums. Everybody does. It's my initials. Belinda Ursula Morley-Smith.'

'Yes, I know, I—'

'So who else was in the theatre on Monday morning?'

It took Hattie some time to steer *that* conversation to a close.

Young Adam, the romantic lead, seemed the most affected. He had apparently skipped the morning rehearsal session entirely.

'I just couldn't seem to find a way to get my head round it,' he explained. 'It didn't seem right that we'd all just... carry on. I know we always talk about the show being the most important thing, but... something like this? Surely something like this is more important. This is *real*. And I didn't even know her. I mean, none of us did. Apart from Emile, I think, but he didn't seem to bat an eye. I mean, did she have friends? Family? Is someone, you know, mourning her?'

'I spoke to her brother,' said Hattie gently. 'So I'm sure he's let her family and friends know. I think it's easy to feel like we have more of a responsibility, having been the people who were around her... closest to the end. But she had her own life, with people in it, and in some ways they're the ones who've got to mourn her. Not that we can't be deeply saddened, of course. But if you feel that the other people around you aren't feeling the weight of it, well, maybe that might be why.'

'But it just makes me so angry the way that people like Bums are just... I suppose I'd hoped there'd be a little more, I don't know, empathy or something,' said Adam.

'Everyone handles these things differently,' offered Hattie uncertainly.

Adam sighed. 'I suppose so. I'm sorry for not coming in today.'

'No, no,' said Hattie, hurriedly. 'I'm not telling you off. If that's what you needed to do then that's what you needed. And if you'd like to talk to someone...?'

'No... thank you, but no. I'll just... I'll just deal with it.'

Halfway through working her way down the cast list, Hattie received an incoming call from an unrecognised number. She answered, and was greeted by a quiet but warm female voice she half recognised.

'Hello, is this Harriet Cocker?'

'Yes, that's me.'

'Hi, there. My name's Jordan Burakgazi, and I'm with the police. We met on Monday. I was hoping to talk to you some more about Atlanta Greenwell, if you have a moment?'

'Oh, yes, certainly,' replied Hattie, feeling herself tensing reflexively.

'Now that an inquest has been opened, I've been assigned as what's called the Senior Investigating Officer. My job is to work with the coroner just to understand what happened.'

'Oh. If there's an inquest, then… is her death, um… suspicious?' asked Hattie, hoping she didn't sound as ghoulish as Bums had.

'I wouldn't say suspicious, exactly. It appears that she died of pulmonary asphyxiation, which frankly isn't surprising when people drink as much as she appears to have done. All I'm trying to do is understand a little bit more about who Atlanta was, and why she was where she was when she died. Did you know her well?'

'No, not really. We've just started rehearsals on a show. She was in the cast, I'm the stage manager. We didn't have much to do with each other yet.'

'And you'd not met her before rehearsals started?'

Hattie paused. She sort of recognised Atlanta, and Atlanta seemed to have recognised her. Had there been a show once?

'Um, I'm not sure. Possibly. It's a small world, our industry, and we've both been in it for years. I'd say our paths probably crossed before, but I can't say I remember.'

The admission made Hattie uncomfortable. To her own ears she sounded shady, giving such a vague answer.

'I understand. And you found her yesterday morning, in the dressing room, didn't you?'

'Yes.'

'And you were there as part of your stage management duties?'

'Yes, sort of. I was at the theatre for a meeting, and afterwards I looked round backstage to re-familiarise myself with the layout,' Hattie replied, carefully leaving out any mention of the mask debacle that had brought her to the Tavistock that morning.

'I see. And would you have been the first person to go into that room that morning?'

'I think so. Keith said he reckoned no one had been in there since Saturday evening. Keith who runs the theatre, that is.'

'And you found her lying, face down on the floor, is that right?'

I told you all of this on Monday, Hattie thought to herself, irritably, but all she said was, 'Yes.'

'Did you move her?'

'Only enough to check her pulse and breathing. But she wasn't… I mean, it was pretty clear she was dead.'

'Yes indeed. We don't have full details from the post-mortem examination, but we believe she died between thirty and forty hours earlier. And you said you have no idea what she would have been doing in the dressing room on Saturday evening?'

'No, sorry.'

'All right. I don't want to dwell on the details any more. I would just like to ask, if I wanted to get in touch with Atlanta's friends, who would I talk to? Who were the people who knew her well?'

'Honestly, Atlanta seemed to know everyone in the industry. I think she had a million friends. She seemed to have a story about every actor in London. Um… I suppose you could start with her brother?'

'I tried. He said he didn't actually see her very often, and gave me a couple of names to call. But when I spoke to them, they all said they didn't know her very well either. She was a familiar face at parties and bars, but I've yet to find anyone who'd ever been inside her home, for example.'

'Sorry, then,' said Hattie. 'I don't know any particular friends of hers.'

'Fair enough. Finally... I've done some preliminary research on everyone who's in some way in proximity to Atlanta's death, and I've learned a little bit more about your... personal history.'

Hattie's blood ran cold.

'Oh yes?' she replied, as calmly as she could.

'I must say, I am surprised to see you've secured a position in an educational setting... ACDA, was it?'

'That's right.'

There was tense silence.

'Well, I won't keep you,' said Burakgazi. 'I'll be in touch if I have any more questions. Goodbye for now.'

She hung up.

Bloody hell.

Everyone did stupid things from time to time, Hattie told herself. And just because some things turned out to be monumentally more stupid than others, and leave one sadder, poorer, and deeply distrustful of law enforcement, shouldn't mean that one should have to carry one's past mistakes around forever (despite whatever the Home Office's Disclosure and Barring Service said to the contrary). There were very few people in the world who knew what 20-year-old Hattie had done. Apparently DI Burakgazi was now one of them. Why on earth was she bringing *that* up? Did it make Hattie look more like a suspect in this case?

But then again, what case? She'd said the cause of death was pulmonary asphyxiation... that meant suffocating or choking or something, didn't it? But if this woman was asking questions about Atlanta's social life, that suggested there was more to this than Atlanta getting a Werther's Original lodged in her windpipe. The question of what on earth Atlanta had been doing backstage on Saturday became ever more pertinent. The only comfort to Hattie was that Atlanta had died a full day before the mask had been stolen, which slightly assuaged her guilt at not telling Burakgazi anything about the theft. Keith had told her not to, of course, and she naturally inclined away from telling the police anything more than the bare minimum. But even so, she suspected that the police woman would not look too kindly on having been left in the dark about it.

9

Davina came in late the next morning. It was the first time Hattie had seen her all week, as the previous day she'd charged her with tracking down parasols and monocles in prop stores across London. Now her eyes were puffy, her hair was a mess, and she was constantly sniffing and wiping her nose with a tissue. She ignored Hattie's greeting and, wordlessly plonking herself down at a desk, busied herself logging in to ACDA's creaky computers and pulling up last night's rehearsal notes email from Kiki. As Hattie watched, she spent a few minutes staring blankly at her screen, then let out a loud wail, picked up the keyboard and hurled it hard at the wall, then buried her head under her arms on the desk.

Hattie, alarmed by this explosive outburst, approached her gingerly, and put a tentative hand on her shoulder.

'Oh dear,' she said, as kindly as she could. 'I'm guessing you didn't get very much sleep last night?'

Davina muttered something inaudible.

'What was that?'

'I didn't get any,' repeated Davina, this time lifting her head enough to allow her to be heard. 'The whole Atlanta thing... I just wanted someone to confide in, and he... he won't *talk* to me. It's like I never existed. It's all so messed up. All I want is a conversation. That's all. God I'm a mess, I'm just… I'm so sorry. I can't do this at the moment. I'm sorry.'

'It's OK, it's OK, my love,' soothed Hattie. 'Don't you worry at all. Just go home, try to get some sleep.'

'But there's so much to do!' wailed Davina.

'Don't you worry about that. I've got a quiet day, I'm sure I can cover it. I'd much rather you take the time to sort yourself out than be here feeling miserable.'

'All right. I'm sorry. I just… all right,' Davina mumbled.

She picked herself up and shuffled out of the office.

'Take care of yourself,' Hattie called after her. 'And take as long as you need!'

Oh bother. Hattie was beginning to regret getting Davina involved. Not only was she now without an ASM, but she'd also have to explain this absence to Steve. And given that she was the one who'd vouched for Davina in the first place, it wouldn't do her standing in his eyes any good.

But broken hearts took time to mend. What else could she do?

Actually, there was one thing she could do. Hattie logged off her computer, walked out of the office and took herself off down ACDA's long central corridor to the far end of the building, where the construction workshop was situated.

It was a large space, with a variety of lethal tools arranged on benches around the outside, stacks of lumber in the corners, and the comforting smell of fresh pine sawdust pervading everything. The ventilation fans were roaring away, and a number of the second-year students were busy at work at the benches, building the sets for the first trio of productions of the year. A bandsaw whined, a table saw zoomed, a pneumatic brad gun made a series of soft pops, and above the din of it all Hattie could just hear a radio blasting soft rock. The workshop was not a place for quiet reflection.

In one corner was what looked like a haphazard lean-to shed. This was Shane's 'office'. Hattie knocked, then, seeing him wave at her through the grubby Perspex window, let herself in. She closed the door behind her, and the sounds of tools faded fractionally, so that the din went from almost unbearable to simply unpleasantly loud.

'Good morning!' said Shane. He was working on some technical drawings on his computer, while slurping tea from a dirty, chipped mug.

No two ways about it, Shane was a good-looking man, in a sort of craggy way. His dark hair was beginning to pick up a few strands of grey, and his face was weather-beaten but kindly. He had the physique of a skinny man who's spent a lifetime lifting and carrying heavy things: he was lean and wiry, but very obviously strong. He spoke in a quiet voice with a gentle New Zealand lilt, and veered in the direction of hippie-ish. One would have a hard time believing he didn't meditate each morning, and while he wasn't the type to wear healing crystal jewellery, his wife absolutely did, meaning he was very well versed in all things alternative and New Age-y.

'Hello, Shane,' Hattie greeted him. Shane wasn't his real name. He was actually Michael MacShane, but as there were several Michaels in the faculty, Shane was just easier.

'What brings you down to the workshop?' he asked.

'Oh, just passing by, thought I'd drop in.'

'I thought you were off doing a show?'

'I am. It's at the Tavistock, but as they've no decent office space I'm working from the SM office here.'

Hattie paused. Shane had visibly winced when she mentioned the name of the theatre.

'Do you know the Tavistock?' she ventured.

'Er… yeah. I did some work for them once.'

There was another stark pause, which Hattie eventually filled by saying: 'I've actually got Davina Aggarwal working with me. You remember her?'

Shane smiled.

'Oh yeah. I liked Davina.'

I bet you did, thought Hattie to herself. Out loud she said, as innocently as possible, 'Did you keep in touch after she graduated?'

Shane's smile faltered.

'Uh... a little bit. But you know how it is, it's always a bit awkward moving from a student-teacher relationship to a... to a more personal one. So I'll admit I slightly let things slide.'

'I see,' said Hattie. 'And do you think that maybe... maybe Davina thought there was a bit more to your relationship than there actually was?'

Shane looked relieved.

'Yes, exactly. Exactly. And I didn't want to hurt her feelings, so... you know. Why? Has she said something?'

Hattie hesitated. This was delicate stuff.

'Not exactly... I just wonder if her feelings ended up getting hurt anyway. And I wonder whether, if she's been trying to get in touch with you recently... it might be worth you calling her back?'

'Well, if you're sure it wouldn't make things complicated...' said Shane uneasily.

Hattie nodded again.

'I think it would mean a lot to her. You know how she is, she's quite... sensitive.'

'All right,' said Shane with a deep breath. 'Leave it with me. Er, was that what you came here to talk to me about?'

'Oh you know,' replied Hattie awkwardly. 'Just thought it was worth mentioning. So I'll see you later then.'

'All right. Well, good luck with your show. And... be careful at the Tavistock, yeah? I don't like to speak ill of anyone, but... yeah.'

With that last remark hanging in the air he gave a little wave and turned back to his grubby computer. Hattie let herself out of Shane's little lean-to, and picked her way back through the mess of power tools out into quieter parts of the building. Her first thought was to head back to her office, but, upon checking her watch and realising it was nearly lunchtime, she decided to make a detour, and some social calls.

ACDA was a Franken-building. Originally a town house, it had been converted into a small dance conservatory a hundred years past, and then remodelled again in the sixties when it was repurposed as a drama school. As it expanded, several cheap and cheerful extensions had been bolted on in a hotchpotch manner, until the last-but-one chairman had led a massive fundraising drive to knock down most of the ad-hoc bits and replace them with a state-of-the-art facility with a large main auditorium, a secondary performance studio, rehearsal spaces, dance studios, music rooms, TV production rooms, technical workshops and a costume store. And while almost all the backstage departments had now moved into their new homes, one remained steadfastly in its original place in the oldest part of the building: Rod's sound department.

It was a poky little basement suite, almost every wall of which was covered in racks upon racks of CDs, cassettes and minidiscs of music and sound effects, all painstakingly indexed on typewritten cards, along with wall-mounted plastic colour-coded pots containing connectors, adapters, fuses, plugs and patch cables. Longer cables were coiled in neat figure-of-eights or wound around drums underneath the workbenches, and the cupboards were stuffed with amps, speakers and mixing desks, each neatly slotted into a space no bigger than what was needed to accommodate it. Rod had been teaching here longer than almost anyone, had set up everything just as he liked it, and had so far shown no interest in migrating to the fancy new sound-proofed room that awaited him on the other side of the building, with its colour-changing LED lighting and built-in air-con.

Hattie walked into the sound basement to see several first-year students fretting with what looked like props from an early *Doctor Who* episode, and getting increasingly tangled up in long strips of narrow brown tape.

'Oh for God's sake, *why*?' howled one young woman, Yoo-Kyung, as she struggled to slice through a piece of tape that appeared to be tethering her arm to the machine on the desk in front of her.

Hattie smiled. 'Going back to basics, are we?'

'Going back to the Stone Age, more like.'

'It's not the Stone Age,' said one humourless-looking, acne-bedevilled man with thick glasses and unexpectedly bushy nasal hair. 'It's a Revox B-77...'

'Mark Two Reel-To-Reel Tape Recorder,' chorused the rest of the class.

'I just don't see why we have to bother with learning about obsolete technology. We'll *never* use this out in the industry,' said Yoo-Kyung.

'Well, I don't know much about sound,' said Hattie awkwardly, 'So I can't really comment. Er, is Rod in?'

One of the older students, perhaps thirty-something, giggled, and nodded towards Rod's corner cubicle. Hattie poked her head round for a look. Rod was leaning back in his chair, his arms folded across his stomach, his chin resting on his chest, his eyes closed. Hattie nodded.

'Been there long, has he?'

'Ever since he set us going on this task. Does he often do that?'

'Do what?' asked Hattie sweetly.

'Er... fall asleep in class.'

'I am not asleep,' boomed Rod suddenly. 'I am sitting here listening. Listening and waiting. Listening and waiting and thinking. Listening to the sound of lots of very intelligent people having all sorts of trouble operating some relatively straightforward bits of kit. Waiting for some of these very intelligent people to ask me for help. Thinking that perhaps if these very intelligent people spent less time complaining about their tasks and a little bit more time thinking constructively about how to achieve them, then they might find this course a little bit more instructive.'

His students looked suitably chastened as Rod emerged from his cubicle.

'I am *also* thinking that it's high time for a lunch break. So why don't you take your good little selves off for an hour, and I'll see you back here at... ooh, I'll be generous, let's say ten to two, at which time I'll be more than happy to answer any questions you might have about these marvellous little devices.'

When the students, abashed, had left, Rod escorted Hattie to the staff lounge, where they took it in turns to microwave their lunches: a baked potato for Hattie and a mysterious stew-like concoction for Rod.

'And how is the Old Bill treating you?' he enquired as they waited.

'Hey?'

'Old Bill. Old William. William Shakespeare. You said you were working on one.'

'Oh right. Yes. I think it's going to be a rocky ride. I'm not sure the director really knows what he's doing.'

'Oh dear,' said Rod. 'How's Miguel getting on?'

'They've got him in the rehearsal room, messing round with soundscapes. I think he's enjoying it.'

'Good for him. I'm glad he's working. He'll be all right. Reliable sort, is that Miguel. And speaking of reliable... Davina?'

'She's going through some relationship heartache that's slightly distracting her from the task at hand...'

Rod made a face. The microwave pinged, and he retrieved his food.

'I'm not sure that she's quite cut out for this life, is she?'

'Well… we'll see. I'm giving her the benefit of the doubt,' said Hattie, uncomfortably.

They continued to chat as they ate their lunch. Rod had been around in the industry when Hattie was first starting out, and they'd always got on. They worked on several big shows together, and over time he probably got to know more secrets about her than anyone else in her life, even Nick. Then he'd been in a motorbike accident and duffed up his arm. Unable to rig kit or operate a mixing desk, he'd taken a gig as assistant sound tutor at ACDA, and got comfortable, so that even after his hand healed he'd ended up staying. Fast forward twenty-odd years and he'd helped put in a good word for Hattie when they needed a stand-in SM tutor, even though their paths hadn't crossed for years. Now they were the two old crumblies of the technical department, and they naturally gravitated towards one another when they got a chance.

Meals finished, Hattie cleared her Tupperware away. She hadn't told Rod about Atlanta. He had almost certainly worked with her, and she'd spent too much time recently breaking the news to people who knew Atlanta to relish doing it again.

'Now if you'll excuse me,' she said, 'I should drop in on Mark. I've not seen him since term started.'

'Hmm. Yes, cultivating good relations with Mark is important. I rather think… well, give him my love, of course.'

Rod shuffled off, leaving Hattie to make her way deep into the heart of the new facility, where everything still smelled of carpet shops and plastic. In the distance she could hear someone making their way through 'Luck Be a Lady' in a rather laboured baritone, while from another direction a frustrated dance tutor was calling out, 'Shoulders above your hips, shoulders above your hips! Come on, you can do better than this! I'd expect that sort of crap at RADA!'

Mark Britten, director of technical training, was in his office, snarfing down a packet sandwich while he fired off an email. He was a formidable character: vivacious, decisive, intelligent. Perhaps in the end slightly too intelligent, Hattie pondered, to commit to the life of a stage manager. Mark needed a bigger challenge, which is probably why he'd ended up here, as part tutor, part administrator, part brand ambassador, and part sly politician, navigating his way through the treacherous waters of ACDA's governance structures. Easy to like but hard to get close to, he was very much the sort of person you wanted to remain on the good side of.

'Good afternoon, Mark,' called out Hattie, keen not to interrupt him if he was in the middle of something.

Mark's head snapped up, and he smiled.

'Hattie! Do come in, do come in. Excuse the sandwich. Sit, please.'

Hattie sat, and Mark pinpointed her with his clear blue eyes.

'So,' he enquired warmly, 'how are you?'

'I'm doing very well. I just saw the new intake downstairs. I'm looking forward to getting to know them properly when my show's finished.'

'Ah yes. Tell me about that. Who's in it?'

'It's got two of ours from last year, actually. Miguel Mota is on sound, and Davina Aggarwal is my ASM.'

'Oh good, good, I'm glad she's got a proper gig,' beamed Mark.

'We're working out of the SM office for the moment, so you should pop by and say hi when you get a moment.'

The smile faded ever so slightly, and the brows creased just a tad.

'Oh… the theatre doesn't have its own office? Where did you say it was on?'

'Tavistock.'

The smile went entirely.

'I do wish the grads would listen to me and start off by doing touring or West End work,' Mark sighed. 'It's so much easier to get to know people, and you get taken much more seriously.'

'That's true,' replied Hattie, feeling a little defensive, 'but not many places are hiring right now, and the Tavistock is better than a lot of them.'

'I know, I know… But I just worry that if Davina keeps going back to the Tavistock she'll find it very hard to get hired anywhere else. And Miguel… well I mean he'll be fine in the end, but he's not good enough at marketing himself. He just needs to find someone to take him in hand. Who's the chief sound engineer on the show?'

'There isn't one, actually. He's by himself.'

'See, that's what I mean: on a big show there'd be a senior engineer. Miguel would work for them, Miguel would impress them, on the next show he did they'd remember Miguel and have a decent chance of hiring him. Tiny fringe gigs don't help them make connections. They're dead ends.'

Hattie winced. This particular dead end was the only gig she'd managed to land all year. Oh, she'd tried to dig up work, she'd really tried. She was terrified that that adage about theatre was coming true for her: you never really retired, you just realised one day that the phone hadn't rung in three years…

Mark sighed and shook his head.

'Sorry, I shouldn't complain. They're working, and that's the main thing. And at least we haven't lost them to the sodding cruise ship circuit!'

And just like that the smile was back.

'Now was there anything in particular…?'

'No, no, just popping in to say hello,' said Hattie. And trying to make sure I stay on the right side of you, so I can stretch out this ACDA gig as long as possible, she thought.

'OK great,' replied Mark, the finality of his tone clearly signalling that the meeting was at a close.

Hattie stood up.

'Rod sends his regards,' she said, remembering as she reached the door.

'Oh… yes… actually I did want to talk to you about that.'

Hattie stopped and looked back. Mark looked uncharacteristically ill at ease.

'Um… So look,' he began. 'I'm not sure that Rod has entirely embraced the new spirit of ACDA following the rebuild.'

'Not really one for change, our Rod,' agreed Hattie.

'Quite. And he's always had his quirks, but for the most part they've been something I can contain and manage. But his recent unwillingness to use the new facility has, shall we say, placed him under a slightly brighter spotlight within the administration.'

'Are you saying that the administration has only just noticed that he's a cantankerous old sod?'

'Well yes, to the extent that the administration has really only now noticed that he *exists*. Unfortunately, things have reached a bit of an impasse. Now, this is going to be very delicate, and I don't want to put you in an impossible position, but you're an old pal of his, and you're very charming and persuasive, so…'

Hattie sighed, and smiled. 'I'll have a quiet word. It might take a term or so to talk him into it, but we can probably get him out of his basement into the new sound studio.'

Mark grimaced. 'Ah. No. Sorry, that's not quite what I'm saying. I'm saying it would be helpful if you could broach with Rod the matter of his retirement.'

For a moment Hattie was stunned, and couldn't think of a rejoinder. Rod couldn't possibly retire. After all, he was only… sixty…? Well, sixty-something…

'Isn't that a bit drastic?'

'It isn't just the room thing. Come on, Hattie, he's supposed to teach technology, but he stopped keeping up with sound tech with the advent of the CD. Every year we all trot out these absurd justifications as to why it makes sense for our students to spend weeks messing with reel-to-reel tape recorders when the real reason is that *Rod doesn't know how to use anything else*. And that whole debacle last summer over extended DBS checks. I don't know what he's hiding in his past, but he more or less incited a staff mutiny to make the administration back off – and of course, it was me who had to negotiate that on his behalf.'

Hattie felt a twinge of guilt. She knew exactly why Rod had fought so hard against staff being subjected to detailed criminal background checks. But now was not the time to get into that.

'Look,' Mark continued, offering a conciliatory smile, 'I like him. You know I do. But the room debacle means that if he's going to stay I'm going to have to fight for him, and that means expending a lot of political capital at a time when I don't have much going spare. So, given that he's coming up to that age anyway, if he were to *choose* to retire, that would solve a lot of problems all at once. It's an HR minefield for me even to try to talk to him about it, and I doubt he'd listen to me anyway. So I'm just saying that if you could help me by planting the seed of the idea in his head, you would have my gratitude.'

Hattie considered for a second.

'I can certainly raise the topic with him,' she said, cautiously.

Mark gave her a measured look in response.

'Well, that's a start. Let's chat more about this next time you're in. We're still working out how to staff the SM department in the long term. There are lots of criteria of course, but a big one is finding someone who's a team player. I'm sure you understand…?'

Hattie nodded uncomfortably. Getting the permanent stage management tutor could give her a much-needed stable foothold in an otherwise precarious financial state. But she wasn't sure she was comfortable with the support for that foothold being a knife embedded in Rod's back.

Act Three

10

Hattie had hoped that, following her prompt, Shane would speak to Davina that night. But either he didn't talk to her, or the conversation didn't go as planned, because the next morning Davina messaged Hattie to say just that she wouldn't be coming in. Hattie replied, recommending that she take the rest of the week off, quietly cursing as she did so. Atlanta's death hadn't slowed down the pace of rehearsals. If anything, it had spurred them on to an ever more manic cadence, meaning Davina's absence would be all the more sorely missed. For once, Hashi and Keith were in complete agreement on something: both wanted to side-step the time-consuming re-casting process. So when the energetic and ambitious Regine helpfully volunteered to step into the role, they both jumped at the offer. The fact that Regine was about thirty years younger than Atlanta and a completely different shape, size and temperament wasn't a problem, apparently. To be fair, Atlanta had, to Hattie's mind, been horribly miscast in the role in the first place. Jaquenetta was a fairly bland comedy wench, whose main purpose was as a plot device to give both the clown Costard and the foreign nobleman Don Armado someone to fall in love with. Atlanta, while eminently fall-in-love-with-able, was older than both the male actors *combined*, which, at best, played as a slightly uncomfortable joke where her age was the punchline.

Despite her very different looks and unproven acting ability, having Regine in the role was, purely considering the quality of the overall production, probably not a fundamentally bad thing.

With Atlanta's part thus re-cast, Hashi and Keith were keen to press on as if nothing had happened, and rehearsals continued much as they had before.

Hattie dropped into St Eustace's on Thursday before the start of the morning's session to catch up with Kiki, and the first thing she noticed was a gaggle of actors sitting in a clump on the floor, chatting away, furiously excited.

'… jealous lover? I mean, she didn't exactly… you know…'

'But I mean, come on, wasn't she a bit past all that? I know she had stories, but they were all from years ago.'

'It just seems a bit… unbelievable to me.'

'Well, yes, I know what you mean, but *affairs of the heart* are the most common motive, aren't they?' said Bums excitedly.

'I thought it was family disputes…'

'… pretty sure it's money.'

'Guys, do we have to?' pleaded Adam.

'What?' asked Bums, innocently.

'I mean, come on. There's people here,' Adam responded.

Bums followed his gaze, saw Hattie, frowned, and then snorted. 'Well I don't think *she* cares,' she said dismissively.

'Cares about what, my love?' asked Hattie, sweetly but with a *soupçon* of edge.

'Atlanta,' Bums replied. 'The police are involved, they've been calling us all, there's an inquest and everything. So… you know.'

'Ye-es…?'

'It's murder. Right? I mean, they think it's a murder,' said Emile, uncertainly.

'I really don't think so,' said Hattie. 'They told me she died of pulmonary asphyxiation. That just means she choked. I think they're just going through the motions while they wait for the post-mortem results. I really don't think it's that exciting.'

She said the words with more conviction that she felt, being very strongly of the opinion that even if there was a sinister aspect to this whole affair, it shouldn't be allowed to interfere with the rehearsal process. If that made it her job to downplay the thing, then so be it. She was there to get the job done.

'But they won't say *how* she was asphyxiated. She could have been strangled, for all we know,' insisted Bums. 'And they found her *in the theatre*. There's no reason she should have been there in the first place. You've got to admit, it's pretty suspicious that she sneaked backstage and then wound up dead. They kept on asking me if I had any idea who she might have been meeting with there.'

'They asked me the same thing!' added another of the cast ladies, delightedly. 'So it must be important.'

'I don't think it's *that* surprising that they asked you all the same questions,' countered Hattie, but the conversation was already flowing away from her.

'Maybe she was shagging Keith!' announced Bums, eliciting a few gasps and groans from her peers.

'Seriously?'

'Well, they did have a sort of chemistry, didn't they?'

'Not to put too fine a point on it but… I mean he's very, very gay,' said Emile.

'Is he?'

'Oh God yes. Trust me, he plays on our team.'

'Maybe that was it then. Unrequited love. Classic.'

'Wait… she had unrequited love for him? So… who killed her?'

'I don't know. Maybe Keith's boyfriend got jealous.'

'Does Keith have a boyfriend?'

'He seems like the kind of man to have several.'

The door slammed suddenly, and Hattie realised Adam was no longer with the group. Perhaps he had walked out in protest at the crude and increasingly ghoulish turn the conversation was taking. Hattie couldn't blame him. She opened her mouth to encourage the cast towards a little more respect for the dead, but was interrupted by Hashi, who at that moment emerged performatively from the kitchen, prompting all the actors to jump to their feet.

'My warrior-poets! Time for another day's battle...'

Hashi was back in full creative flow, and as a result his requests for props were getting increasingly frequent and outlandish, and really required the attention of a full-time ASM. So, in Davina's absence, for the rest of the morning Hattie buried herself in propping, trying to source, among other things, a bag of golf clubs, a large metal bin – large enough for Dull to hide in, with a lid and strong enough handles to allow two cast members to carry it while it was occupied – and three large two-handed water pistols, all on a budget of slightly under a hundred pounds. It was all doable, but it required pulling in a lot of favours, sweet-talking some strangers, and a little bit of creative research, which, put together, meant for a busy morning.

She was made for a busy morning. It was only at lunchtime that she checked her phone and saw a message from Keith:

Everyone paid. Get cracking. Start with Steve and Moira. Remember what's at stake. Tick tock. xx

Typical Keith, she thought. Rude and demanding, with a couple of kisses thrown in at the end as if that cancelled it out. What a distasteful little man. But still, he'd given her a job to do. She reached for her handbag.

She found Steve working in a small glass-and-steel corner office, at the end of a glass-and-steel corridor, on the fifth floor of a glass-

and-steel building, tucked out of the way in Holborn. It was quiet, bright, and soulless. Safe to say this was *not* the natural habitat of a theatre technician.

'So this is where you've been hiding.'

'Fancy seeing you here,' said Steve coolly. Then his face cracked into a small but warm smile.

'Well, this is swish,' remarked Hattie. 'What on earth are you doing in a place like this?'

'I know a guy who owed me a favour,' Steve replied cryptically. 'Needed somewhere to work from.'

Hattie realised she hadn't seen a single other person on this floor of the building. Steve's office was almost entirely empty, apart from his chair and desk, which had on it a battered old laptop and a small pile of paperwork, including a set of technical drawings of the Tavistock auditorium.

'I thought you were going to be based in the office up at the Tavistock.'

'Tried it. Not my scene,' Steve responded, with a slight wrinkle of the nose.

'Didn't like the mess?'

'That too.'

'Hmm. Speaking of, have you checked your bank account? Keith's finally delivered the goods.'

Steve just grunted.

Hattie considered her next words carefully. Steve gave little away at the best of times. There wasn't an easy way of saying what she'd come here to say.

'Pissed you off, didn't it? The whole pay thing,' she tried as an opener.

'It's just unprofessional. If you're producing a show your number one responsibility is to pay people on time. And then the bastard asked me to smooth it out with the crew, rather than take responsibility himself. I don't like weasels.'

'Especially given that we know he's not short of money,' Hattie suggested. 'I mean, that mask…'

She left the suggestion dangling, and watched Steve's reaction carefully. But his face remained characteristically inscrutable.

'I hope that thing is worth as much as he makes out,' he replied. 'Because I don't think he's got much else. Tavistock was always a money pit. Keith would have driven it into the ground years ago if Joan and her pals hadn't kept bailing it out.'

'How did you know about the mask, anyway? I thought it was a secret.'

Steve snorted.

'Some secret. Every time I was over at the theatre in pre-production Keith was on the phone to someone or other, always banging on about the mask. He seems to think it's the holy grail.'

'Well,' replied Hattie carefully, 'let's hope he can hold on to it then. I'm sure it would be better for everyone if the Tavistock's future wasn't jeopardised right before we're supposed to open a show there. I think the outcomes wouldn't be great, for any of us, if Keith was put in a position where he felt he had to cancel the production.'

Steve scratched the side of his nose.

'Nah. If anything were to happen to it I don't think you'd have to look far to find the person to blame. Not far at all.'

'What do you mean?'

'I mean I know a crook when I see one, and Keith's a crook. He's up to no good in that office. I don't know what precisely, but I can't abide it.'

The vehemence in Steve's tone caught Hattie by surprise, and gave her pause for thought. On the one hand, his dislike of Keith marked him out as a more likely suspect. On the other, would someone who'd just committed premeditated burglary be capable of such genuine-sounding disdain for 'crooks'? Steve always did have a strong sense of right and wrong, despite the rumours about his past.

'Anyway, enough of that,' he said. 'You want a cuppa?'

'Can't stop, I'm afraid. I'm on my way across town, just thought I'd drop in and see your fancy digs. Doesn't it get a bit lonely here, when it's this quiet?'

Steve only smiled.

Hattie had known that Moira's studio was out of the way, but, turning down yet another back alley, her hip pain flaring up, she was forced to admit that she had underestimated quite *how* out of the way it was. She was walking amidst a jumble of Victorian warehouses and factories, 1940s council estates and anonymous, windowless, metal-clad buildings with no discernible exits or entrances. Hattie didn't like east London.

Eventually she came across a railway line, running above a series of brick arches, each of which had been walled up with a small door in the middle. Going through the fourth of these doors, she found herself in a dingy space under the archway, with rusty industrial light fittings and a concrete floor. On either side of the bare, central space were rows of little closed-off cubicle studios. A radio was playing BBC Radio 6 Music in one of them, loud enough for it to reverberate round the entire space. Hattie dimly remembered Rod explaining something about the unusual acoustic properties of barrel ceilings. Each cubicle had a wooden door, all in different states of repair, some dirty, some painted, some rotted. Each was emblazoned with a number. In some cases it was done using neat metal numerals screwed into the woodwork, while in others the number was scrawled in pencil.

Studio 36 had its number written in felt-tip pen on a scrap of paper that had been stuck to its plain wooden door with yellowing sticky tape. Underneath the number was written '(MOIRA

MCLEOD)' in careless lettering. Hattie knocked, and Moira's voice from inside called her in.

Moira's studio was a mess. Glorious, chaotic, overwhelming. Every wall was lined with shelves, every shelf held countless assorted plastic tubs, and every tub was overflowing with fabrics, beads, buttons, hats, feathers, tights, shoes, fluff, foam, paint, pins, and smaller boxes of undisclosed contents. There seemed to be no consistency in what items went in which container, and in the vast majority of cases the contents overflowed their containers entirely, lying sprawled across two or three tubs in big amorphous mounds.

In what space was left in the middle of the studio sat a chair, a desk with a sewing machine on it, as well as, of course, yet more piles of stuff, a couple of battered tailor's dummies, and Moira, looking her usual grouchy, sleepy self.

'Hello, Hattie,' she said in her gentle Scottish brogue, peering disinterestedly through jam-jar glasses. 'Tea?'

'Don't mind if I do,' replied Hattie, suddenly aware that she was gasping for a cup following her long journey.

Moira frowned.

'Right… I don't suppose you brought a cup with you?'

'No, sorry.'

'OK, OK. Well, let me see if I can borrow one. Come wi' me.'

Hattie followed Moira out of her cubicle to a tiny kitchen area at the back of the arch, where a very elderly kettle with a frayed electrical cord perched precariously on the drainer of a small, stainless-steel sink. In the basin were sitting several assorted grubby mugs. Moira picked out one that had printed on it: 'I'll deal with your bullsh!t when I've finished this coffee'. After a pause she picked up another one, white, chipped, with the logo of a sheet metal supply company on it.

'I think Barry's away today,' she muttered, sticking the kettle on. From under the sink she produced a couple of teabags of dubious provenance, and a carton of UHT milk.

'So how are you, my love?' asked Hattie, while they waited for the water to boil.

'Oh, I'm all right. Tough news about Atlanta, eh?'

'Did you know her at all?'

'Not really. We did a couple of shows together, had a natter backstage a few times. But actors come and go, don't they? Very sad life she had, though.'

'Really? From what I heard she made it sound like she spent her entire time drinking with celebrities.'

'Aye,' said Moira, with a serious look. 'And did you ask her what it was drove her to spend her entire time drinking in the first place?'

Hattie hesitated. 'No... no I didn't think of it like that.'

'Not a happy lady. Not sure why. Lost someone very close to her very young, I believe. Never really recovered. Shame that she grew up in a world where mental health wasn't talked about. Instead I think they taught her to put a brave face on it, you know? Just guessing that bit, from her personality, mind. I always worried she'd decide to go before her time.'

'You mean... commit suicide?'

Moira tutted. 'Don't call it that. Only crimes are *committed*. Leaving early is a choice.'

'But the police said... I mean, do you think that's what it was, then?'

'I'd have thought so,' shrugged Moira. 'By herself, in a theatre. That's how I'd do it, y'know? Here you go.'

Hattie accepted the cup and took a sip. The long-life milk made it taste pretty vile, but beggars can't be choosers.

'Anyway, what can I do for you? Is this about the fur coats? Cuz I told Steve, I can get them for way cheaper if you just leave it with me.'

'Oh really? Sorry. He didn't pass that on.'

'Oh... well maybe I didn't tell Steve. Either way, I don't mind it coming out of my budget, but if it is, at least let me save some money on it.'

'Of course. Sorry, I did mean to call you about it earlier, but… this week has been a bit mad.'

'No bother,' said Moira, starting to limp back towards her studio.

'Actually the real reason I'm here is I wanted to check whether you'd been paid now.'

Moira stopped and gave her a suspicious look.

'You came all the way out here to ask me about that? You could have just rung.'

'I know, I know, it's just… well, on Friday a lot of people got riled up about the whole thing.'

'Did they? I suppose if people had been banking on having the cash sooner… but you'd have thought they'd have double-checked before making assumptions.'

'I think it was more that some people thought it was unfair that the cast got treated differently from the crew even though the contract was the same.'

Moira rolled her eyes.

'For God's… They *are* different. I swear, I don't know if it's everyone getting *woke* or something, but the whole industry's getting more and more pissy about treating everyone identically. It's mad.'

'So you're not fussed about the payment thing?'

'God no. Rag-tag production like this, I'm just glad to be getting paid at all. Now that Joan's not about, I need to take the Tavistock off my list, it's just not worth the bother. Keith's fine, and I wish him well, but…'

Moira made a face, and then resumed her slow walk back to her studio. Hattie looked at her hobbling form. No way, she thought. There's no way this woman broke into a theatre and nicked an expensive piece of jewellery. This had been a wasted trip.

*

Having spent most of her afternoon hopping around London, and with her hip complaining at her, Hattie took herself back to ACDA, and decided to do the rest of her check-ins by phone. She rang Miguel, on the pretext of double-checking that he had now received his first week's pay. She used a similar line to the one she'd tried on Moira and Steve, emphasising that now that the money had been sorted it would be better for everyone if things could go back to the way they were. He seemed as much bewildered as anything else, and she came away from the call with no clearer sense of whether he had anything to do with the mask disappearing.

She also finally managed to get hold of Regine, who claimed to have spent Sunday night at a meet-up for aspiring female theatre directors. Apparently it was as much an emotional support network as a networking event. Hattie could well believe it: the world of directing was famously cut-throat, and the industry was still one where men had all the top jobs, so being a woman *automatically* put you at a disadvantage, and left a certain sort of (normally male) producer feeling that, as a result, he was entitled to take advantage of any woman who dared try to get a foothold. In such a climate one did well to find allies. More pressingly, here was an easily verifiable alibi, and furthermore, Regine scoffed as soon as she mentioned pay.

'The money is the least of my worries. Being blunt, it became clear pretty quickly that Hashi's coat-tails aren't ones to attach yourself to. No one has a good word to say about him, and frankly, being his AD was starting to look like a black mark on my CV. I'm much happier to be doing this project as an actor, to be honest. Not that I'm happy about… you know… the *circumstances*, of course.'

After that, Hattie was about to settle down to some actual show work when Kiki called.

'We've, um, we've had a bit of an upset here,' she said without preamble.

'What happened?'

'Bums found a note.'

'As in… a suicide note?' asked Hattie hesitantly, thinking back to her conversation with Moira.

'I wish. I mean, I don't wish *that*, but honestly… this was like something out of a slasher movie. There was a piece of paper left in her handbag. It's got a couple of quotes from the play on it, all about death, and also: *Atlanta didn't make the cut. I wonder who else will have corpsed by opening night…*'

'Bloody hell,' said Hattie, after a pause. 'How did the cast react?'

'Dramatically, as you'd expect. Some of them wanted to call the police right away. Bums has gone full-on *Famous Five*, and is launching her own investigation. She's started drawing up suspect lists and all. I think I've managed to convince them all to let us handle it. But I wanted to check in with you before anything else.'

'Thank you. Crumbs.'

'So… should we call the police?'

Hattie thought about it.

'Well, it's weird, I'll give you that. But it's not exactly a threat, is it? Or a confession?'

'So… what? Do you think it was some sort of prank?' asked Kiki.

'Is there any chance Bums could have written the note herself?'

Kiki thought about it.

'I mean, it's *possible*, I suppose. She's a bit self-involved, but that seems extreme even for her.'

'I just don't know,' said Hattie, screwing up her face. 'OK, tell you what: you tell the cast that we'll handle it. Then let's chat about it in tomorrow's production meeting. I don't want to go overreacting here.'

'Fair enough. Unless… you don't think anyone's in any imminent danger, do you?'

'I may live to regret this, but… no. I don't think so.'

'OK,' said Kiki, still somewhat hesitant. 'OK, we'll figure it out in the meeting tomorrow.'

'Last thing on that, though: was the note handwritten in Sharpie on an A4 piece of paper?'

'Handwritten on A4, yes, but no, this was written in biro, not Sharpie. Why?'

'Oh… no reason,' said Hattie. Was there a connection to the note left in Keith's office? There was no real way of knowing, was there?

Her call with Kiki complete, Hattie decided to ignore the work piling up in her inbox and allowed herself to go home. She cooked some pasta, spooned in a splodge of pesto, and ate at the little kitchen table as she worked her way through a crossword. From time to time she'd look up in thought, and invariably her gaze would land on the mantelpiece through the doorway in the sitting room, and the little box that sat on it. On days like these it was particularly hard to resist, but she held firm. Merlot and pesto were to be her only vices tonight. Well, and one of those posh yoghurts from M&S, the ones that are as much cream and sugar as they are yoghurt. A girl needed *some* comforts, after all.

11

On Friday, late in the morning, Keith called her back to the Tavistock. She resisted, pleading a heavy workload, but he wouldn't be swayed.

'Some things should always be talked about in person,' he insisted.

There was no way Hattie could put him off without saying an outright 'No' of the sort that a lifetime's training had taught her reflexively to avoid. So she trotted to the Underground and took a train up to see him.

When she arrived, she found Robin in the office, but Keith nowhere to be seen. Hattie felt she had yet to get the measure of Robin. There was something unnerving about him. Whether it was his slightly clammy complexion and sagging posture, or whether it was the way he tended to hover in silence in the background, he just made Hattie feel ill at ease. She decided to try to understand him a bit more.

'Oh hello,' she offered as an opening gambit.

Robin smiled shyly.

'I think he's just gone to the loo,' he replied. 'I'm sure he'll be back in a second.'

'That's fine,' smiled Hattie. 'OK if I make a cuppa?'

'Of course! Um, would you like me to…'

'No, no, don't mind me, I'm always happier if I can make my own,' said Hattie, crossing the room to root around in the PG Tips boxes behind the kettle, looking for one that wasn't empty. 'So how are you enjoying working at the Tavistock?'

'It's great!' replied Robin. 'I mean, I'm learning so much, and meeting so many people. It's really… great.'

'Good, good. I'd imagine it's mostly just you and Keith in the daytimes, is it?'

'Er, well people are always dropping in. But yes, basically I'm shadowing Keith all the time. I'm sure he's sick of me by now.'

'I'm sure he isn't. And what, er, what do you want to end up doing? In the theatre, I mean.'

'Oh, goodness,' said Robin, his eyes widening. 'Well, I mean I suppose the dream would be to one day have my own theatre to run, like this. But I don't know whether that means doing a bunch of producing, or starting off as a director, or whether I could start off in the office of a bigger theatre doing, I don't know, marketing or something. I don't really know, I just want to be a part of it all.'

Hattie nodded, knowingly. Another moth to the flame. She felt she was beginning to get the measure of him now.

'When you've got the theatre bug there's no point resisting. But have you ever considered working backst—'

'There she is!' announced Keith, shaking the last droplets of water off his hands as he entered the office. 'Bloody hell, making your own tea? Sort it out, Rob my boy. Whatever am I paying you for?'

'You're not,' replied Robin with a hint of cheekiness in his voice, and they smirked at each other. Hattie suspected this was a running gag between them. She was glad that Robin seemed comfortable around Keith. Personally, the idea of being locked in this cramped room with him day after day made her skin crawl ever so slightly. But if anything, this epicene young man seemed rather *too* comfortable. Hattie forced herself not to wonder what exactly went on between the two of them, tucked away together in this office

'I don't suppose the mask has reappeared overnight, has it?' she asked. 'I spoke to everyone yesterday.'

Keith made an expansive gesture, showing his empty hands.

'I'm as maskless today as I was last night.'

'Ah well.'

'And you spoke to our four suspects again?'

'I've ruled out Regine, and the other three… well, none of them gave any sign of having taken it, and if I'm honest I really don't think—'

'I know you don't, my love, because you're an optimist, and you want to see the best of people. But at the moment I'm afraid I don't need compassion. I need my bloody mask back, or the theatre will be bankrupt before your show can even finish its run.'

'I thought you said you weren't planning on selling it.'

Keith gave a condescending eye-roll.

'I'm not, my love. But you don't have to sell things to get value from them. I really don't have time to explain the fundamentals of finance to you.'

Hattie didn't care for Keith's tone, but if he was determined not to tell her why the mask was so important, there wasn't much she could do.

'Did you hear about the new note?' she asked, changing the subject.

'What note?' replied Keith suspiciously.

'They found it in the rehearsal room. It said something ominous like "*Atlanta didn't make the cut.*"'

Keith's face fell.

'Oh, so nothing to do with the mask, then?'

'Well, not explicitly, but I thought because it was another note—'

'Yes, yes, yes, two pieces of paper with words on them, very obviously connected, great sleuthing and everything… Come *on*,

Hattie. I thought we'd agreed: Atlanta's accident, tragic though it was, had nothing to do with the mask.'

Hattie was slightly unnerved by the knee-jerk certainty with which Keith rejected any connection between the death on the Saturday and the theft on the Sunday. She had to admit that at the moment the evidence for such a connection was fairly wobbly, but it didn't seem rational to dismiss it out of hand.

'You just worry about the mask,' continued Keith. 'And let the coroner deal with Atlanta.'

'All right then,' said Hattie. 'But I don't really see what else I can do.'

'Well, leaving aside Moira, Steve and Miguel for the moment, you can check some of these stories you've been given about Sunday night by the others. Take, for example… Davina,' he said, with sudden intensity. 'Can you actually prove it wasn't her?'

'Davina? Well, I don't think she knew about the mask, she didn't seem all that fussed about the pay issue, and she was watching a play at the Menier on Sunday. But, I mean, other than that…'

'Forget what you think she thought and knew. Can she prove she was at the Menier?'

'Maybe, but there's no way I could find out about it without asking some pretty direct questions, and she'd of course want to know why I was asking.'

'Hmm,' replied Keith. 'Then we might need a change in strategy.'

His eyes suddenly flicked up.

'Tell you what: there's a production meeting coming up, right?'

'Yes, and as a matter of fact I should probably get moving if I—'

'I'll come too,' said Keith. 'Do you know which of the cast is in this morning's rehearsal?'

'It's a full company call, I think.'

'Even better. Come on, Robin, we're off to Pimlico!'

*

144

The trip over was ever so slightly awkward, as Robin and Keith spent the whole journey in conversation with Robin insisting on staying on Keith's far side and speaking so quietly that Hattie could barely make out a word of what he was saying. So she sat in silence while they murmured to each other. However, the tube got them south quickly enough, and soon they were making their way into the foyer at St Eustace's. Hattie immediately heard a nasal, high-pitched whine. It sounded like a dentist's drill, and it seemed to be emanating from the rehearsal room. The door was closed, but through its little round window Hattie could see a cluster of actors doing... something. It didn't exactly look like a rehearsal. Hattie looked at Keith and gestured questioningly. He nodded, so she gently opened the door and the three of them slipped into the room to watch.

Inside, the whining sound was even louder, emanating, it transpired, from the speakers next to Miguel's laptop. Hattie looked over, and sure enough on his screen she saw that the name of the file playing was 'Dentist Drill 03 – Loop.wav'. Meanwhile in the middle of the room six actors were standing, all facing in different directions, all moving seemingly at random, bobbing up and down, stepping left and right, and occasionally spinning.

'THOU ART EASIER SWALLOWED THAN A FLAP-DRAGON,' boomed one of them, suddenly.

'PEACE! THE PEAL BEGINS,' responded another in hollow tones. They all spoke like bored priests reading a particularly dull communion text.

'What the hell...?' Keith breathed, and Robin let out an involuntary snort, which Keith then firmly shushed. In combination they made enough noise for Kiki to look round in annoyance. She made eye contact with Hattie, who gently raised her eyebrows. Kiki gave a small eye-roll in response, and nodded subtly at Hashi, who was crouching on the floor in front of the actors, apparently enraptured by their bizarre performance. The rest of the cast sat up against the walls, seemingly equally entertained by the scene. Or at least, the younger ones were. Some of the older actors were notably less engaged. Emile, in particular, was having a nap.

Meanwhile, Bums appeared to be hard at work arranging some sort of collage on the walls, oblivious to what was going on around her. Hattie looked closer, and realised that at the centre of it was a head-shot of Atlanta, around which were scattered yellow Post-it notes with the names of some of the rest of the cast and crew. Slightly higher up a piece of paper was tacked to the wall. On it was written, in blue biro:

'Let fame grace us in the disgrace of death'
Atlanta didn't make the cut. I wonder who else will have corpsed by opening night…
– 'The sudden hand of death'

Then there was a red Post-it slightly higher up on which she'd written:

Second victim: ??

So that was the note. Sinister though the message was, Hattie still found herself struggling to take it completely seriously. It just seemed so… theatrical.

The performers droned on, continuing their odd bobbing and shuffling, their delivery monotonous, making no eye contact with one another, until, abruptly, they all lay down and spoke no more. The other actors started clapping.

'Good!' announced Hashi. 'We've got the structure then. In which case we'll crack on with act five scene two after lunch. Great work everyone.'

'Er, Hashi my darling?' called out Keith, and as Hashi looked round Keith gestured for him to come closer. Hashi took a couple of steps towards him, but stopped well short of halfway, leaving Keith, with a shrug, to close the distance himself.

'What, um, what did I just watch?' Keith asked, with an air of obviously contrived nonchalance.

'Hmm? Oh, have you not been keeping up with the rehearsal notes?' responded Hashi, icily pleasantly.

'Yes, but I don't recall anything about turning the play into a pagan ritual. As I recall, it's nominally supposed to be a *comedy*.'

'Well yes, on a superficial and rather naïve level I suppose it is, but I rather thought you'd be interested in digging a bit *deeper* than that,' parried Hashi, condescendingly. 'Don't worry, you'll get your gags. But at the moment we're exploring something else. It's the process, Keith. Trust the process. I'm surprised that you're surprised by this, to be honest. But I suppose it's been a while since you've directed anything yourself.'

'And I'm surprised that you've spent two of your three weeks of rehearsals trying to work out what the play is actually about,' replied Keith, equally sweetly. 'Most directors would have that bit done before the first day, so that they can spend the rehearsal period, you know, *rehearsing*. But then again, it's your name on this thing, not mine. Now, if you'll excuse me, I just need to have a word with everyone, while they're all here.'

Keith turned away from Hashi before he had a chance to respond, and, raising his voice, addressed the room as a whole:

'Listen, while I have you all, I've got a little announcement to make. Over the weekend something went missing from the Tavistock. I won't go into the details, and I'm not here to make any accusations, but I will say that all the evidence points to it being taken by someone in this company.'

Eyes widened, as the actors took in this new information and, one by one, connected it in their heads to the *other* significant event that had happened in the Tavistock over the weekend, and the note from the previous day. Bums looked like she might explode from excitement, and was intently mouthing 'Oh my God!' at everyone she could make eye contact with.

'Now I don't want to put anyone's back up,' Keith continued (although Hattie thought that his preceding sentence had probably put paid to that intention), 'so all I'm going to say is this: so far, I have not got the police involved, and I would prefer not to. So if the item is returned over the weekend, no more will be said about it. But, if it isn't, the police will be called, and I can guarantee that it will end *very* badly for whoever broke in. Understood? Now, Kiki, could you follow this up with an email to the whole company repeating what I've said for anyone who's—'

He was interrupted by a clattering sound behind him. All eyes in the room turned to the source of the sound, which came from next to where Miguel was sitting. He immediately turned a bright shade of crimson. In his hands were his lock-picking tools, and on the floor was one of his practice padlocks, which he had just fumbled and dropped.

12

If it's a physical thing that appears onstage, and it's not alive, it's either costume, scenery, or a prop. And if they don't wear it, stand on it, sit on it or lie on it, it's a prop. A prop could be as small as a keyring, or as large as a car. It could be as cheap and simple as a piece of paper, or as expensive and rare as a vellum-bound first edition manuscript. And the assistant stage manager's job is to buy, make, rent or borrow whatever props the director deems necessary to tell their story.

– From The Art and Craft of Stage Management *by Donna Fletcher, Chapter 5: Propping*

Keith didn't stay for the production meeting, which was just as well, as tensions were already running high. Steve, who was being uncharacteristically brusque, ruffled Hashi's feathers by again noting that, in technical terms, they were well behind where they had expected to be in terms of finalising blocking, sound and lighting requirements and so on. Hashi responded defensively again and, perhaps as an act of defiance, suggested that even the props he had requested so far were only temporary, and they wouldn't know what actual props they needed until the following week. This prompted an unconcealed 'Oh for God's sake' from Kiki, but before anyone could respond to that, Hattie cleared her throat noisily and diplomatically pointed out that, while they would of course do their best to lay their hands on any props requested the following week, they were now working under significant time and budget constraints.

'Don't you have someone working on props full-time?' demanded Hashi. 'The brown one? *Yes I'm allowed to say that, stop being ridiculous.* Where is she, anyway?'

'Davina is unwell today. She should be back in action next week. Nevertheless—'

'All right, all right, I understand. Don't worry, my expectations have been managed,' Hashi huffed. 'God almighty, spare me from the unbridled pessimism of stage managers!'

'Moving on, then, Kiki, what's this note you wanted to talk about?' asked Steve.

Kiki, looking uncomfortable, pointed out the note on the wall, and explained to everyone how it had come to be found.

'… So the question we had was, really, how seriously do we take it, and what do we do about it?'

'We give it to the police,' said Laura, immediately. 'I mean, that's a no-brainer, right?'

'Is it though?' asked Carrie.

'I mean, it's a death threat. It's a possible clue to Atlanta's death. Why would you ever not?'

'Because,' said Carrie, 'as soon as you take it to the police, that's the show cancelled. Or at the very least delayed. They'll press pause on everything, they'll want to take over the entire rehearsal room, interview the cast endlessly, you name it. Which would be fine and sensible if we honestly thought this was a real threat, but…'

'What do you mean *if* it was a real threat?' asked Laura. 'Of course it's real, it's right there on the wall!'

'Carrie's not wrong,' said Steve. 'And I'm going to be honest, I've seen death threats before. Real ones. And they don't have flowery quotations all over them. I'm not sure this is legit.'

'Well look, it'd take more than a death threat to stop me from rehearsing my play,' put in Hashi.

'I'm just not sure that I feel safe,' said Kiki, and Miguel nodded his agreement.

'Bloody hell,' said Laura. 'I can't believe we're even debating this. Hattie, come on, you're the sensible one in the room. We tell the police, right?'

Hattie took a breath. The problem was, no one else around the table knew about quite how much financial trouble the Tavistock was in. From everything Keith had said, there was already at least a possibility that their next invoices would never be paid. If the show got delayed by a full police investigation of the note, that possibility became a dead certainty. If she thought the police could be trusted to assess the seriousness of the note, and act accordingly, that would be one thing. But given that she didn't trust them at all – particularly not that Burakgazi woman – the way forward was not obvious to her.

'I don't think we should take it at face value,' she said eventually. 'In the nicest possible way, actors are a pretty weird bunch, and I can easily imagine that this was written by one of them, and not meant to be taken entirely seriously. They're probably just ashamed to own up to it now they've seen how much of a kerfuffle it's created.'

'Fine,' said Steve, giving Hattie a curious look. 'Then it's decided. We keep an eye out for anything strange, but we don't get the police involved. Now, is there any other business?'

Hattie felt torn. Should she tell them about the precarious state of the Tavistock? Did they have a right to know?

No, she decided. Seeing how the pay issue had exploded the previous week, revealing this would likely cause a walk-out, torpedoing the show, and the Tavistock's future, for good. For all that these were murky waters, and despite Hashi's assertions to the contrary, Hattie was at heart an optimist. She chose to believe that there was indeed a path to getting the show to open and close its run as planned. In which case, the best thing she could do, rather than sabotage any chance of success now, was not to unsettle her colleagues, but rather to do everything she could to get that mask back.

The meeting drew to a close, and Hattie sidled up to Miguel. After Miguel had drawn all the attention to himself just before the meeting, Keith had made some pointed head-nods in Miguel's direction while locking eyes with Hattie. The meaning was clear: Miguel the lock-picker was high on his list of suspects.

'Miguel, my love, could I have a word?'

He gave her a nervous look.

'Um… OK?'

'Perhaps we could chat outside, where it's quieter?'

He nodded balefully, and followed her outside. She led him a little way away from the entrance, where various members of the company were milling around and eating their lunches.

'Now, the reason I wanted to chat was—'

'I didn't steal anything,' he blurted. 'I promise, I wouldn't do something like that.'

'I'm sure you wouldn't, my love,' Hattie reassured him. 'Don't worry, I'm not trying to accuse you of anything. I more wondered if you could tell me a little bit about what you know about locks.'

He looked relieved for a second, and then shrugged.

'I mean, I'm not an expert or anything. I just like learning how to pick them. I bought my practice kit online, followed some YouTube tutorials. Anyone could do it, with a little bit of practice, if it's a straightforward lock.'

He frowned, then his eyes suddenly widened.

'Was it… the cabinet in the office at the Tavistock? Was it the mask that they took?'

Hattie grimaced. 'It's not really my place to say. Sorry.'

'Oh,' said Miguel. 'It's just… I had a look at the padlock that was on there, and it's pretty flimsy. It was made by Alumantium. They make knock-off copies of premium brand locks, with fewer pins and cheaper materials. Half of their products can be raked open.'

He must have seen the questioning look on Hattie's face, because he went on:

'Sorry. That more or less means… well, there's no skill involved. You just need a turning tool and something to wiggle the pins with.'

'I see,' said Hattie. 'But suppose the lock wasn't actually picked. What sort of equipment would you need in order to be able to, say, melt the lock?'

Miguel looked surprised.

'Melt it? Like in a furnace?'

'Or with a blowtorch?'

'Oh, I see. Um, I mean, the body of the lock will have been made from aluminium, and I guess that melts pretty easily? I don't know what sort of temperatures, though, or what kit you'd need to do it. Someone like Shane would know this stuff. You could ask him?'

'Good idea,' said Hattie. 'I'll do just that.'

'I just… that feels like a difficult way to open an easy lock. I'd have thought it would be hard to melt the lock without also melting the cabinet it was attached to, or at least setting off the fire alarm.'

'That's true…' conceded Hattie. 'There was no sign of damage to anything except the lock. No singeing or anything that I could see. The lock was just, sort of, crumbled.'

Miguel frowned again for a moment, then all of a sudden his eyes widened again, and he squeaked, 'I know…'

Then he stopped himself abruptly.

'I mean… I don't know. I thought I had an idea, but I don't. Sorry. Um, good luck. I should really get some… lunch… before the next session starts…'

He was already backing away, almost stumbling in his haste to escape, as Hattie looked on confusedly. *Something* was going on there. What had Miguel worked out? And why on earth was he being secretive about it?

Annoyingly, she didn't really have time to chase after him, because she was due back at ACDA for an afternoon teaching session. She wasn't looking forward to it. ACDA worked its students hard, their weeks packed with classes, and come Friday afternoon they had normally spent all their reserves of mental energy. So they'd either be brain dead and morose or, worse, fidgety and hyper. Still, it was what paid the bills, so she took herself back to ACDA, idly wondering whether she'd have any luck trying to expense any of her travel costs to either the school or the Tavistock. Both possibilities seemed pretty remote in the current climate.

It was as bad as she'd feared. The topic of the session was prop-related paperwork, ranging from budget analyses to prop lists to borrow forms to purchase receipts. No one had ever pretended this stuff was *fun* exactly, but Hattie had hoped to communicate to her students the quiet satisfaction to be had from accurately completing and filing a neat set of documents. They didn't get it. They stared at her as though she was trying to deliver a seminar on self-assessment tax returns. Just you wait, she thought to herself, because in your final term we actually will deliver a seminar on self-assessment, and if you want to get by as a freelancer you'll damn well need to listen. Several of them played on their phones while she was talking, one looked on the verge of nodding off, and Yoo-Kyung actually *did* nod off, which meant that two more amused themselves trying to balance more and more stationery on her sleeping form, until she woke with a start, clattering pens, scale rulers and Post-it notes to the floor.

To give him credit, Alexander at least tried to pay attention. He failed utterly, but he did try. Within ten minutes he had started doodling on his hands with a Sharpie, then up his arms, then absent-mindedly on his nose, and then, inevitably, he stuck the damn thing in his eye, and had to be escorted to the bathroom by one of his fellow students to try to wash the ink out and alleviate the stinging pain that he felt the need to tell them all about in great detail.

Then there was the big lad, Felix. He didn't play with his phone, didn't fall asleep, didn't cause any fuss. He just didn't do… anything. When Hattie handed out some sample borrow forms for them to fill in, providing them with an imagined scenario where a local furniture dealer had agreed to lend them a period lamp in exchange for a free advert in the show programme, he took his paper and spent a few minutes hunched over it. But when she came to inspect his work, once again it was blank. He offered no excuse or explanation.

She let them go early. No one was getting anything from the class, and they'd all learn this stuff better when they came to work on real productions the following term, when they'd be filling out this paperwork in earnest.

Before Felix could shuffle out, she motioned him aside. She didn't particularly want to, but she needed to get to the bottom of this.

'Can I have a quick word?' she asked gently.

'Uh… can't,' he replied.

'Maybe on Monday morning, then? Before your classes start?'

'Sorry…' he said, not deigning to elaborate further.

Hattie gritted her teeth and smiled.

'Well, it's settled then,' she said forcefully. 'We'll chat Monday at the end of the day. Six o'clock, at the SM office. OK?'

'Uh...'

'Perfect, I'll see you then.'

She wanted to go home, but there was work to be done. There had been so many meetings in her day that the backlog of stage management admin had piled up. She really ought to spend the next couple of hours catching up on the props backlog, so that Davina's workload wasn't completely unmanageable if and when she returned to duty next week.

And yet...

This mask thing. Up until now she had never truly believed that it was anything to do with the *Love's Labour's Lost* company. But Miguel's strange reaction when he learned about what had happened to the locks niggled at her. Yes, he was acting, very credibly, like someone who hadn't known at all about the theft until she told him about it. But he also very clearly knew *something*. He'd joined some dots, and that meant maybe he knew someone who was involved. Besides Hattie herself, the only other person in the crew that Miguel actually knew was Davina, although he hadn't seen much of her lately. What was she missing about either of them? It would be helpful if she could somehow prove where they were when the mask went missing, without having to ask them. She remembered how Robin had checked up on Hashi's 'Insta', and shown definitively that he was in Oxford that night. Hattie wasn't at all clued up on social networks and things, otherwise she might be able to try the same thing.

She made her way back to the SM office, trying to work out how she could dig any further into this, but found her path blocked by a very nervous-looking Yoo-Kyung, who was skulking outside the office door.

'Hello,' said Hattie.

'Hi,' replied Yoo-Kyung in a small voice. 'I just wanted to say… I just wanted to say sorry. For falling asleep earlier. It was really rude of me.'

Hattie smiled. 'Oh, not to worry. Everyone's knackered on a Friday, and I don't blame you for nodding off.'

'Still, I feel bad. It wasn't that what you were talking about was boring, I promise! I don't want you to get a bad impression of me. I'm taking the course really seriously. Honestly. It's just that we were practising lighting rigging all morning and I was climbing up and down ladders and—'

'It's fine, my love. You're not the first, and you won't be the last. Forget about it. Go and enjoy your weekend.'

Hattie thought for a second.

'Although,' she added, 'if you wanted to make it up to me… are you any good with all that social media stuff?'

It took a little bit of bending the truth to get the brief across, but Yoo-Kyung was so eager for a chance to get back into Hattie's good books that she didn't ask too many questions. Armed with nothing more than a couple of names, she was soon curled up on a chair in the SM office, glued to her phone as she dived through various social media platforms hunting for evidence. Hattie looked on in awe. This whole world was a closed book to her.

'OK, here we are,' Yoo-Kyung piped up, turning her phone to Hattie. 'Look, Davina checked in at the Menier theatre bar at ten to seven that evening. See, there's her and a friend.'

Hattie peered at the screen. On it was a selfie of Davina and her friend Vix, tickets in hand. There were also a bunch of hashtags that Hattie could make neither head nor tail of, but the photo seemed to pretty unambiguously prove that Davina really was at the theatre on the other side of town with Vix while the theft was taking place.

'Wonderful, thank you. Anything on Miguel Mota or Steve Felton?'

'I can't find any accounts for Steve. But I found Miguel on Facebook, and just over a week ago he liked an event organised by a group called "The Treacherous Thieves". It's a private group, so I don't know anything about them, but the event started at seven o'clock on the Sunday, and they said to meet in the bar of the Black Boar in Camden at six. Then he actually checked in to the Black Boar on Facebook at ten to six on Sunday, so I'm guessing that's where he was for the evening. Is that helpful?'

'Hugely,' smiled Hattie. 'I've no idea what any of it means, but it gives me something to chase up. Thank you so much, and please, don't let me keep you. I'm sure you've got things to be doing.'

Yoo-Kyung, evidently delighted to have redeemed herself, let herself out, leaving Hattie to ponder more about mysterious Miguel. Was he really part of a group of organised criminals? A group who organised their meet-ups on Facebook? How bizarre. It had been a long week, and Hattie's brain wasn't cooperating any more, so she decided to give up and go home. She was about to log off her computer when she saw a new email in her inbox. Speak of the devil…

Hi Hattie,

Sorry for rushing off earlier, I suddenly realised I was going to be late for rehearsals. I just wanted to make sure I didn't give you the wrong impression earlier. While you were talking I had wondered if maybe the padlock you mentioned had been frozen somehow, to make it more brittle. I wondered if maybe you could dip it in liquid nitrogen and then snap it into pieces. I saw something like that in a film. Anyway, I've checked, and it turns out that unlike some metals, aluminium doesn't actually get brittle with cold, so that wouldn't work. So my idea was a dead end.

Anyway, sorry I couldn't be of more use. Good luck finding the mask!

Best,
Miguel.

Bless him. He was bright enough to realise that he'd been acting suspiciously, but, with the best will in the world, his 'people skills' weren't quite up to the task of assuaging that suspicion. Maybe he really had had a thought about freezing the lock, but there was definitely more to it than that. He hadn't run off because he thought he'd be late, he ran off because he panicked. Hattie resolved to find out why. Maybe it was tiredness kicking in at the end of a gruelling week that caused her also to think: *and if it turns out he had anything to do with the theft then God have mercy on him, because I won't.*

13

She unlocked her door, let herself in, hung her jacket and bag on the peg... and nearly jumped out of her skin when a figure appeared suddenly at the other end of the hallway.

'Oh bloody hell!' she exclaimed, clutching at her chest.

'Sorry, cockatoo,' replied Nick, chuckling.

'We need to get a bell and put it around your neck so I hear you coming,' she chastised her husband.

'OK, but not one of those girly little kitten bells. A big manly Swiss cowbell, that'll do me.'

He set down the half-empty pint glass he had been holding, then came forward and gave her a small kiss and a big hug. He smelled like a man who hadn't had access to a washing machine in a while, and who had dried himself off from his last shower with a damp, mildewy towel. As usual. It was good to have him back.

'What on earth are you doing here?' asked Hattie, leaning back from the hug to look him in the eye. 'I thought you were in... Norwich? Yarmouth?'

'That was last weekend. I've got this one off. Thought I'd come back to see you for your birthday.'

She thumped him gently on the shoulder. 'You know perfectly well it's not my birthday.'

Nick frowned. 'Oh? Then whose birthday is it? I'm sure it's someone's.'

'Oh you old sod… Happy birthday. I was going to call. This evening,' she said it confidently, trying to mask her dismayed realisation that her life partner's birthday had completely slipped her mind.

'Yeah, yeah… Anyway, I've ordered a jalfrezi. You can pop a candle in it when it comes.'

She finally disengaged from his embrace, and he sauntered back to collect his drink, giving Hattie an opportunity to take him in fully. He was looking maybe a little paunchier, a little greyer, a little more crinkly around the eyes, but otherwise, she was pleased to note, much like his normal self. That was good. These tours were a mixed bag. Mostly he was good at not letting it get to him when the going got tough, and riding it out with gentle good humour, but the long, chaotic days could take their toll. Sometimes when he limped back home at the end of them he immediately put himself to bed and stayed there for days recuperating.

'Show going well, then?' she asked.

'Can't complain,' he shrugged. 'Couple of the dancers have a quick-change right by the lighting desk. Boobies galore.'

'Oh you little pervert!'

'It's not my fault!' pleaded Nick. 'I didn't decide where they got changed. They could do it in the voms, they just said they preferred to see the action.'

'As do you.'

'Well, you can't blame me for enjoying the view.'

'I bloody well can,' she shot back.

There was a moment's tense silence, then she relented. 'Still, I suppose I can't really talk. Not after the *Full Monty* tour.'

'Or *Equus*,' put in Nick. 'Or *Hair*. Or—'

'All right, all right.'

The doorbell rang, and a motorcycle rider dropped off the takeaway Nick had ordered. Lamb jalfrezi for him, chicken dopiaza for her, with pilau rice, peshawari naan, and a tarka dhal on the side. They'd been getting the same order, from the same restaurant, a few times a year for well over a decade now. The quality varied, as new chefs and owners came and went. And originally part of the ritual had been walking over to collect it, an increasingly burdensome practice now rendered blessedly obsolete by the rise of cycle couriers. But the core meal remained the same, a pleasing piece of stability in their often unstable lives.

They ate their meal largely in silence. Nick seemed engrossed by his food and Hattie... Hattie was just happy to be in his presence for a bit. He wasn't the brightest, wasn't the handsomest, wasn't the kindest or most thoughtful, wasn't the most ambitious, wasn't the funniest... well, there were lots of things he wasn't. And quite possibly, if they ever spent more than a few days at a time in each other's company, she would start to find that his many, many flaws began to grate on her. He was a silly old fool, *but* it was nice to have him around sometimes. A bit like one of those big, smelly, hairy, daft dogs that some people kept as pets, thought Hattie to herself. Only slightly less self-reliant.

'What are you chuckling about?' enquired Nick, looking up from his plate.

'Nothing, nothing, my love,' replied Hattie quickly. 'So how long are you staying?'

'Got to be in Birmingham Sunday night for fit-up. I need to buy some new shoes, thought we could go to Westfield tomorrow.'

'I might have plans tomorrow,' replied Hattie disdainfully.

'Do you?'

'No, but I might have done.'

'Then I am glad you haven't. Hey, we could stop off at the cheese shop as well.'

'The cheese shop closed down years ago,' Hattie reminded him.

'Did it?' he asked, aghast. 'No one told me.'

'I told you,' replied Hattie exasperatedly. 'Last time you were here. In fact... wait, you told *me* last time you were here, because you tried to pick up a Camembert to bake but couldn't. You got very aerated.'

'Oh...' he murmured thoughtfully. 'Maybe I did...'

They finished their meal, and after he had tidied away the dirty plates and empty containers she was about to settle down on the sofa, when he tapped her on the shoulder with a mischievous grin.

'Hey... fancy some dessert?' he said, waggling his eyebrows.

'God yes,' she replied with a sudden rush of pleasure. 'I thought you'd never ask.'

They opened the big sash window that overlooked the downstairs flat's overgrown back garden and drew up two kitchen chairs next to it. While Nick fetched blankets from the cupboard to counter the autumn breeze, Hattie retrieved the little box from the mantelpiece and fussed with the contents, eventually producing a respectably sized, neatly rolled spliff. They arranged themselves on the chairs under the blankets, and lit up, passing the joint back and forth, and being careful to direct all smoke out of the window.

The first inhalation was, as always, delightful. These days, Hattie got as much from the ritual, and the nostalgia, as she did from the actual weed. It was like the first sip of a glass of local plonk when you'd just set up your tent on a camping holiday in France. Or sitting down in a scalding hot bath after getting drenched in a winter rainstorm. Or stepping off the air-conditioned coach on the first leg of a European tour and feeling for the first time the hot Mediterranean sunshine wrap itself across your face. Each experience reminded you of all its predecessors, letting you enjoy all the memories of the good old days while also quietly reassuring you, 'One day, this will be one of the good old days too.'

'Ooh my sainted bollocks,' Nick coughed noisily. 'What's in this? Rat poison?'

'I got it from Gaz,' Hattie replied. 'Seems the same as usual to me.'

'I must be getting old,' said Nick, clearing his throat repeatedly. 'Maybe we can make some more of the brownies next time.'

'Would you like me to mush them all up and spoon-feed them to you as well? That way you can take your dentures out and still get merry,' mocked Hattie.

'Aww, would you? That would be delightful,' responded Nick sweetly.

Hattie smiled and closed her eyes. Filthy habit, she thought to herself. But a little bit of filth was good for the soul.

They sat in silence for a while, passing the spliff back and forth, until Hattie was jolted from her reverie by a ringing noise. Her phone. Slightly muzzily, she picked it up and answered it. It was some mobile number she didn't have in her contacts.

'Hello, cockatoo… I mean, Hattie Cocker speaking.'

'Hi there. Rosie said you wanted to speak to me?'

It was a man's voice, and not one that Hattie recognised. There was a slight accent. French perhaps? Polish?

'Rosie?' asked Hattie. She screwed up her face. 'Sorry, I'm having a little bit of trouble…'

'At the Tavistock. She said you wanted to speak to someone who was working last Sunday night.'

'Oh yes, of course!' Hattie replied, blinking and shaking her head to try to make the fug recede. 'Thank you so much for getting back to me.'

'Rosie said it was something about the theatre?'

'That's right, that's right. I was wondering whether you might have seen anyone go through the door between the pub and the auditorium while you were working. Between about half past six and nine?'

'Is this about the lady who died? Because a woman did go through on the Saturday, after the final performance of that poker show. Older lady, smart clothes, definitely an actor, you know? I remember her, because I saw her as she went up to the door, and she gave me a wink and said not to worry, she was there on theatre business. She didn't look like she'd be making trouble, so I let her through. Was that her?'

'That sounds like Atlanta. I mean, yes, the woman who died.'

'Oh, well then. Yes, about ten o'clock. I didn't see her come back out again, of course.'

'Thank you, that's very... But did anyone happen to go through the door the *following* evening?'

'Hmm,' said the man. 'Not that I remember. I mean, Keith came through at some point, he always does, but that was right at the end of the night.'

'OK. Do you think someone could have gone through without you noticing at any point?'

'Mmm... It's possible, but it's hard to do it, you know... subtly. We keep the curtains in front of the door when the theatre isn't open, and the, you know, the fire door bit at the top, it's pretty noisy. So you'd have to open the curtains, make a noise going through the door, and then I don't think you could close the curtains until after the door was closed, and then you'd be on the wrong side. So it seems pretty unlikely.'

'I see. Thank you so much, that's really helpful. Sorry, I didn't get your name.'

'Pavel.'

'Thanks, Pavel. And, so I understand, what times were you at the bar?'

'My shift started at six both nights, and I was there until we closed. Rosie was with me on the Saturday shift, on Sunday it was just me. Are you trying to learn how the lady died?'

'No, actually, it's… it's sort of unrelated. There's a mask… er, sorry, I mean a marking… marketing thing.'

So much for being discreet. Hattie suddenly found herself struggling to contain a fit of the giggles.

'I mean, I wanted to know whether someone from the marketing team popped by. But it sounds like they didn't. So… thank you. Have a good evening!'

'OK, no problem,' said the voice, uncertainly.

'Great, speak to you soon, bye!'

She hung up, and let herself have a little chuckle. She wasn't exactly sure what was so funny, but that didn't seem to matter.

Nick looked at her quizzically. 'What on earth was that about?'

'I'll tell you in a bit,' said Hattie between laughs. 'Right now I'm too… Oh no. I said "speak to you soon", didn't I?'

Nick looked at her solemnly, and nodded sadly. Hattie pressed her palm into her face, and let out another little guffaw.

'At least…' began Nick, and then even he couldn't help but emit a little chortle. 'At least you didn't tell him you loved him.'

Hattie snorted, and then they were both off, giggling like idiots. It took them several minutes to calm down.

'So what *was* that about?' asked Nick, when he was no longer in danger of relapsing into laughter.

'God, where to start?' replied Hattie. 'This is all to do with the Tavistock. It's really not funny at all. An actress went backstage on Saturday night while the house was dark, and died back there. Very sad. And on the next evening they got burgled. Apparently. But Keith won't tell the police who are looking into the death about the burglary. He's convinced it was someone from my company, so he's had me sneaking about like the Spanish Inquisition interrogating everyone. As far as we can work out, whoever it was must have done it on Sunday evening while Keith was out to dinner, and I thought they'd snuck in through the bar, same way the actress had. But apparently not. And it's all for the sake of this ridiculous little mask, which, given how expensive it was, really should have been kept somewhere safer than a little COSHH cabinet in the office. Anyway, it's gone, and with the exception of one of the soundies acting a bit weird, and big Steve being big Steve, I've no way of knowing what happened. But apparently it's my problem now. I'll have to teach that to my first years, because it's new to me: it's the job of the stage manager to fight crime, alongside their other duties. Cape and mask not provided.

'Meanwhile the police officer has found out all about that business thirty years ago and is threatening to tell ACDA all about it. I don't know what she wants from me, it's not like I know anything about Atlanta. But I've still got this Burakgazi woman breathing down my neck. And they'll fire me if they find out, you know. Trust my luck. You spend a lifetime smoking grass and getting away with it, but you try to do one good thing in the world and they put a permanent black mark on your record. "Inexpungible". Bloody hell.'

She realised she was rambling, so she stopped. She looked across at Nick. He was staring thoughtfully at his shoes.

'Five years,' he said eventually. 'Six maybe. I think I bought them before *Miss Saigon*. Not bad. Suppose I've mostly been wearing my steelies since then, but still. Got some good wear out of them. Comfy. I'll miss them.'

'You silly old sod,' grunted Hattie. 'Shall we go to bed?'

They spent the weekend together, mooching around, chatting and semi-amicably bickering. On Saturday morning Hattie put it to Nick that, really, on balance and all things considered, it might be worth him having a rather more thorough shower than the sort he'd clearly become accustomed to, and that perhaps there were benefits to applying soap all over, rather than just mashing a bit on his tummy and immediately rinsing it off. Nick's counter-suggestion, that he damn well knew how to wash himself, and anyway, if she thought he smelt bad she should just come out and say it, was considered on its merits but ultimately rejected. Eventually, Nick took a nice relaxing, and pointedly very drawn-out bath, and while he did so Hattie quietly picked through his duffel bag and washed as much of the contents as she could.

After an improvised lunch at home they wandered over to the shopping centre so that Nick could buy some more trainers, and she had to wait around while he tried out micro drones in Man/Cave, the glitzy gadget store that sold overpriced toys to overgrown kids. Then he had the temerity to get huffy when she spent just a few minutes looking at a few tops on sale, and was quite rude about her figure when she wanted to try something on. They made up over overpriced lattes and a shared slice of chocolate tiffin cake, went home, cooked a couple of steaks, watched some *Who Do You Think You Are?* and went to bed.

On the Sunday Hattie did some housework while Nick slept in. When he got up he immediately started getting under her feet, trying to fry some eggs in the kitchen while she was cleaning the stove, spreading his stuff all over the living-room floor right when she wanted to hoover, and grumbling about the statement from the gas company as if he'd been the one at home using the gas in the first place. Eventually she tasked him with fixing the thermostat just to get him out of the way. That worked at first, but what he'd been certain was just a case of changing the settings soon turned out to be something rather more complicated, and his shouting and swearing at the boiler turned out to be even more annoying than his earlier interference with the housework.

So when it came time for him to head off, Hattie was sad but not distraught. She loved him dearly, but she'd also got used to being in control of her own time, and having him around messed with her routine. Also, he was in some ways the sort of person who's easier to miss from afar than appreciate up close. She did find herself thinking again about what on earth life would be like when they both retired. There would have to be a period of adjustment, that was for sure. But, she reassured herself, there was a decent chance they'd never be able to afford to retire, so the issue might never come up. This thought reminded her guiltily of Rod, as she realised she had been avoiding talking to him about the prospect of *his* retirement. Next week, she promised herself.

Nick gave her a kiss and said 'Goodbye, cockatoo', and she gave him a hug and said 'Goodbye, Cocker One', and she packed him off in his trusty, dusty Vauxhall Astra, and took herself back up to her flat. She put the kettle on, made a cup of tea, settled down on the sofa, and realised she was already starting to miss him. Ridiculous. An hour ago she'd been desperate to turf him out. What a silly thing it was to love someone.

She pootled about on her phone, until she found herself on the website of *The Stage*, looking for the latest industry news. None of the headlines jumped out at her particularly... until she spotted a familiar name in one of them, and, clicking through to the article, started to read the most recent obituary to be added to the site:

Atlanta Greenwell was a rising star in her native Sheffield before she came to London in the mid-1980s. She received early critical acclaim for her Rosalind in Matthew Cooke's As You Like It, *and regularly appeared in productions at the Crucible.*

At a party in her first week in London, she met fellow northerner Linda Sheppard, who was at the time keen to leave her current role, portraying Sally Bowles in the hit production of Cabaret *that was running at the Palace Theatre at the time. Sheppard made introductions to the producers, who arranged an audition, and Greenwell was offered the role soon after, launching her West End career.*

PATRICK GLEESON

A spell of illness cut short her time in the role; however, on recovery she soon caught the eye of director Sean Clifford, who gave her her National Theatre debut in his revival of Follies, *in which her performance was 'masterly and exhilarating' (*The Stage*).*

In the years that followed she became a familiar face in the London theatre scene, both onstage and socially, with noted theatre critic Susan Rush describing her as 'a legend in the making'. However, a series of bouts of poor health interfered with her career, and required several long sojourns away from the stage.

In later years she explored nuanced roles in independent and at times experimental productions across several of London's more niche venues, drawing particular praise for her performance in Wally Ngoyo's devised piece Iron and Skin *at the New Rose. She had recently begun work on the forthcoming production of* Love's Labour's Lost *at the Tavistock. The producers have announced they are dedicating the production to her memory.*

Atlanta Greenwell died on September 30, aged 63.

Sixty-three eh? thought Hattie. She had worn it very well. It was a good obituary, but… it hinted of sadness. Atlanta had dedicated herself to theatre fully and wholly, and had come close to stardom, but was continually thwarted by what was perhaps euphemistically referred to as 'poor health'. Was it depression? Anxiety? Panic attacks? Who knew. Either way, she ended her days doing 'experimental' work across 'more niche' venues, which was by far the most polite way of putting it.

Perhaps that was too negative a view, though. Lord knew there were precious few parts available onstage for women over the age of thirty – blame generations of male writers for that – and arguably the fact Atlanta had managed to find work at all in the latter part of her career was a triumph, even if Jaquenetta at the Tavistock was a far cry from Rosalind at the Crucible. Would she have been happy with her life as a whole? Hattie hoped so.

She was interrupted from her thoughts by a ping from her phone. A message from an unknown number:

Hi! It's Yoo-Kyung. I hope you don't mind me contacting you out of hours. I thought I should let you know that Miguel just checked in to the Black Boar on Facebook again, in case it's useful. x

Hattie looked at her watch. It was quarter to six. So much for her quiet evening in. She reached for her coat.

14

In her rush to get out of the flat, Hattie hadn't thought to grab an umbrella, and therefore, inevitably, it started raining as soon as she got off the tube in Camden. Not a heavy rain, just one of those persistent drizzles that gently envelops an outdoor setting and, no matter what's going on, makes it fractionally worse. For Hattie, whose hip tended to flare up in wet weather anyway, it exacerbated an already stressful situation, and it meant she lost her bearings and wasted five minutes walking down Greenland Road when she needed to be on Greenland Street. By the time she reached the Black Boar it was very nearly seven o' clock, and she was worried that she might have missed Miguel altogether.

She sidled cautiously through the door, keeping her eyes peeled. If Miguel was here she wasn't entirely sure that she wanted him to see her. Not until she knew what this thieves' club was all about. She couldn't spot him immediately, but the Boar was one of those sprawling pubs with several rooms, and it was fairly crowded. Keeping as low a profile as she could manage – the clientele here was a slightly 'alternative' crowd of youngish goths and rockers, and a middle-aged lady in a big tatty coat looked a little bit out of place – she picked her way between tables, on the lookout for a face she recognised.

Not in the first room… Not in the second… Was that him in

that nook at the back?… No, it was some other skinny curly haired man… She couldn't get a decent look at the fellow in the hoodie propping up the bar… Hang on.

She looked carefully at that last figure. He was facing directly away from her, and the edges of his raised hood covered his entire face. But the hoodie: she recognised that hoodie. It was black, and it had printed on the back in blocky white Arial font: *I just need a screw!* A second line of text was obscured by the bar stool, but Hattie knew its content from memory: *ACDA Construction Crew '22, Twelfth Night.* A few of the students who graduated over the summer had worn them sometimes. Apparently they'd got them made in their first year at ACDA when a bunch of them worked together building the scenery for the summer musical. It was a fairly standard techie bonding ritual: take a semi-funny thing someone once said while stressed and tired – preferably a not-very-subtle innuendo – print it out on an item of clothing, wear said clothing until it falls apart. It was harmless fun, although it did perpetuate the perception of backstage teams as a tribe apart from everyone else in the theatre. You never caught actors doing this stuff.

Either way, she'd found Miguel. He was in conversation with a tall, skinny man next to him, who had long, straight brown hair tied back in a ponytail, a beard, and a black leather trench coat. Well, sort of in conversation. Neither of them seemed to be saying very much, as both had their phones out. Hattie considered getting closer, but decided against it: if they weren't talking she'd gain little from being closer, but she would increase the risk of being spotted. So she slunk into a corner, pulled out her own phone and pretended to be deeply engrossed in it, glancing up every few seconds to check on Miguel.

For a few minutes nothing of note happened: Miguel and his friend stayed up at the bar, mostly playing on their phones, drinking their pints. Then, at seven o'clock precisely, Miguel looked up, and looked around. So did the long-haired man. And so too did about a dozen other people dispersed around the pub, almost all of them men. Lots of eye contact was made, but people kept looking around until their eyes all eventually converged on a figure standing in the corner. He was squat, bald, and wearing what appeared to be a wizard's robe. Rod would feel right at home here, thought Hattie. His hand was raised lazily, and he had a small, calm smile on his face. Slowly, everyone who had sought him out, Miguel included, finished their drinks, stood up, and made their way towards him. Once a handful of people had reached him, he turned silently and strode off down a corridor, with his followers forming a straggly line behind him. There was something deeply unsettling about the way all of this was conducted in silence. Hattie noted that none among those who remained in the bar seemed to comment on this bizarre exodus. Was this – whatever 'this' was – a weekly ritual?

Once the last of them had disappeared down the corridor, Hattie started to follow. She thought about keeping her distance, but no one seemed to be looking behind them, so in the end it was easier to join the back of the line.

They were led down a passage at the back of the pub, then up some narrow stairs, past the loos, and through a doorway with a paper sign next to it that had printed on it: 'Reserved from 6.30pm – The Treacherous Thieves.'

The group filed in, and Hattie, the last of them, dawdled in the doorway, trying to peer through to see what was on the other side before committing to follow. The room within looked like a fairly typical pub function room: small, cramped, and filled with the cheap and duffed-up furnishings they didn't want on the main floor any more. She could see four assorted tables surrounded by miscellaneous chairs, towards which people were slowly making their way after consulting a flip-chart in the middle. The chart depicted some sort of seating plan, underneath a drawing of what appeared to be a dagger and a key crossed one atop the other. On the tables were laid out sheets of paper, and on each table, in front of one of the chairs, was set up a small screen, behind which was a small pile of shiny hardback books. In the middle of each table was a pile of dice.

'Are you here for DnD?' asked a voice, and Hattie realised with a jolt that the bald man had materialised next to her. He was smiling at her encouragingly.

Hattie's mind blanked, and she just let out a strangled, 'Er…'

'*Dungeons and Dragons*?' he asked. 'The Treacherous Thieves meet-up?'

Oh… That was that… board game? Hattie was pretty sure some of her American counterparts had played it the last time she did a US tour. Rolling dice and pretending to be elves, was it?

'Are you… are you the ones who were here this time last week?' she asked.

'That's right,' smiled the bald man. 'Every Sunday. Well, almost.'

'And is it always the same group of people?'

'Oh, we're very welcoming to newcomers, if that's what you mean. But yes, most of us are regulars. That way we can sometimes do long-running campaigns. Would you like to come in? I'm sure we can find room for you at a table.'

Hattie was half curious to go in and see what all the fuss was about. She knew this was a popular hobby among a certain sort of theatre type. But at this point, explaining to Miguel why she'd followed him here would all get a bit awkward. And she didn't want to embarrass Miguel. After all, he had been very keen *not* to tell her what it was that he got up to on Sunday nights.

'Oh, no… no thanks. I was just… checking. Thank you, you've been very helpful.'

Hattie turned to go, having one last look around the room as she did so. There was Miguel, just sitting down at the far table. For the first time she could clearly see his face. But her reassurance that it was indeed him was swiftly replaced by a new sense of puzzlement. Because, quite uncharacteristically, calm, mild, *Dungeons & Dragons*-playing Miguel was nursing a large and sore-looking black eye.

Act Four

15

Davina was back in the office on Monday morning, to Hattie's relief, and for once seemed relatively attentive to the job at hand. Hattie talked her through the progress she'd made on props in her absence, and handed back to her the tasks that were still outstanding. Davina got stuck into them with vigour, and within minutes had a first achievement, arranging delivery of a set of golf clubs that Hattie had convinced a sporting goods store to lend them the previous week. She gave a delighted chuckle as she crossed it off the to-do list, and for a brief moment Hattie wondered if maybe the props situation was finally under control.

But then, over the course of the morning, a series of messages came through from Kiki in the rehearsal room with requests for *new* props. Hashi was apparently finally turning his attention to such trivialities as where the actors were supposed to be standing at any given moment, and what they were supposed to be doing when they were there. As a result, and as he had threatened in the previous production meeting, new ideas were evidently flooding in. Suddenly they were being asked to provide two 'timeless' chairs, no make that four, plus two umbrellas, and could those chairs be replaced by shooting sticks, and by the way the whole of act one is now being set outdoors in the rain, and Hashi wants to know whether it would be possible to get our hands on some real or realistic shotguns, and actually it's only three shooting sticks and one stool, oh, and as a general note can all the props hint at the 1920s without being too explicit about it… ?

Davina responded to the constant stream of new requirements with at first mild alarm and then rising panic, until Hattie persuaded her that the safest thing would be to ignore absolutely everything until the end of the day, and then take stock, rather than waste time following orders that would probably be countermanded within the hour anyway. There was plenty to be getting on with from the previous week's requests, and if those were then cancelled… well, that would be something to worry about tomorrow.

Hattie, though, had another problem: she couldn't get hold of Steve. She'd wanted to check in with him about something small, and he hadn't answered his phone. Which, in itself, would be nothing. Except that he didn't call her back, and soon after she got a call from Laura the head of lighting, asking if Steve was with her.

'I've been trying all weekend to chase him up, ever since the production meeting on Friday, about what rigging hardware they have at the Tavistock. I don't suppose you know what he's up to today?'

Hattie didn't, and couldn't help but remember how out of sorts he'd seemed on Friday, after Keith went public about the mask being taken. Of course, there were all sorts of reasons why, from Friday lunchtime to the middle of Monday, he might not be answering his phone. And he was a friend, of a sort, and she trusted him. But an awful lot of people were acting a bit strangely when it came to the mask, and in that light, his disappearing act did raise a couple of questions. Hattie resolved to keep trying him when she could.

Mid-morning, Hattie made a cup of tea for herself and brought Davina one too, and encouraged her to take a quick break.

'Did you have a nice weekend?' she asked.

'Um… yes. Yes I suppose I did, in the end,' replied Davina. 'I'm feeling much better now, at any rate.'

'Oh good. I have to say, you're looking much better.'

'Well I think I finally got some closure on… you know.'

'Did you speak to him in the end, then?' asked Hattie hopefully, remembering her conversation with Shane the previous week.

'No, I didn't,' said Davina, calmly. 'Sort of the opposite really. I discovered that the reason he hasn't been responding is because he's actually blocked my number. I even reached out to his new… to my *replacement*, who confirmed it. And once I learned he'd done that, I finally understood just how much, and for how long a time, I've misunderstood what sort of person he really is. And now I know that, I don't miss him any more. I'm still angry with him, but I can cope with that. I know how to be angry. I had a couple of conversations with some friends, who helped me put things into perspective. And I think I'm fine now.'

Hattie frowned. Either she too had badly misjudged Shane's character, or Davina's side of the story was missing some key elements, or… Hmm. She resolved to get to the bottom of this. Still, if for the time being Davina was back, functioning and focused, then perhaps she shouldn't do too much to rock the boat.

Davina's problem, Hattie decided, was that, having fallen for the world of theatre, she couldn't stop herself also falling for theatre *people*. It wasn't that Hattie was opposed to the romantic side of things; she had to concede that, married as she was to a lampie, she was in no position to condemn fraternising with colleagues. No, it wasn't about romance so much as *romanticism*. Davina hero-worshipped, she idolised. She did what she was told by directors not because that was a stage manager's job, but because she believed directors to be infallible. She complimented actors not just because it was a professional courtesy that helped smooth the lines of communication, but because she honestly believed that what they did was something magical. But that was the thing. Yes, theatre was magical. If you were going to stick around in the industry, you had to believe that. A spoonful of starry-eyed naïveté was the sugar that helped the medicine of long hours, late nights and low pay go down. But when it came to the theatre *people*, a healthy dose of cynicism was much more important. You couldn't let yourself be bowled over by an insightful director, a good-looking actor, or a charismatic carpentry tutor, otherwise they'd walk all over you, personally and professionally. At least, that's what Hattie thought, but she didn't have a clue how to convey any of it to Davina.

Their break was interrupted early by the arrival of a van dropping off a large metal dustbin at the main reception. They took delivery, wrote out a receipt and then carried the thing back to the office.

'Looks good,' said Davina. 'Big, sturdy. Does it have a "twenties" feel, though?'

Hattie sighed. 'That's a point. You'd better take a look at what dustbins looked like in the 1920s.'

'In which country?'

'Any country. Ideally one where dustbins just happened to look a little bit like this one. If we can convince Hashi that this bin is at least *compatible* with a 1920s setting, that'll make our lives a lot easier.'

Davina set to work, and soon found a vintage photography website with a black and white picture of a girl sitting in a high chair outside, with a big metal dustbin that wasn't a million miles off what was now sitting in the office.

'There we go,' she said, pointing at her screen. '1929. I'm not sure where this was taken, but in the description they call it a "trash can" so my guess is it's American. Good enough?'

'Good enough,' confirmed Hattie. She took a picture and messaged it to Kiki, with accompanying text:

We've got a big 1920s metal bin for you. Do you still want it?

Kiki replied instantly:

Let me check with Hashi.

A few minutes later she sent another message:

Yes! (Thank God.) Can you bring it over in time for this arvo's session? Sorry.

'Oh for goodness' sake,' muttered Hattie.

'Hmm?' asked Davina.

'The good news is they like the bin. The bad news is they like it so much they want it in the rehearsal room *today*.'

'Can we just stick it in a van?'

'Could do. But a short notice van hire is an expense we really don't want to be footing right now.'

She folded her arms and took a long look at the bin.

'Not sure it would fit in an Uber, be a pain to get it up and down escalators on the tube… Shall we take it on the bus?'

'Would they let us?' asked Davina dubiously.

'We can try. If we sweet talk the driver they might let us, especially if it's not too full. It'll be slow, but the 360 will take us almost door to door.'

'I just… don't want to get yelled at…' said Davina awkwardly.

'I'm sure no one will yell,' Hattie reassured her. There probably were some rules against taking outsize items on public transport, but you had to be prepared to bend the rules sometimes. Davina needed to learn to get comfortable doing that. But, seeing the reluctance in her eyes, Hattie yielded, adding, 'Equally, we need someone to stay here to take delivery of those golf clubs if they turn up. So how about you help me lug this thing to the bus stop, and I'll take it from there?'

'Good idea,' replied Davina, obviously relieved.

So, half an hour later Hattie found herself standing beside a large metal bin, resting a hand atop it to stop the lid sliding off at every turn, on board a red single-decker bus as it wove its way south and east through busy, noisy London streets. Not for the first time, she had a moment to reflect on the ridiculousness of the job. On the one hand, it was the most sensible thing in the world: the director wanted this item in the rehearsal room, it was on the wrong side of town, and they didn't have the budget to hire a van, so why *wouldn't* she haul the thing along via bus? On the other hand, it was easily a couple of hours out of her day, and her hourly rate was high enough that, if you included that in the cost, wouldn't it have been cheaper to just get a van? But then again, the cost of paying Hattie's wages was the same no matter how the bin got moved; the only difference was in how much unpaid overtime she put in to catch up later. So, buses it was.

Lugging the thing the hundred yards from the bus stop to St Eustace's was tough, and nearly got the better of her; by the time she pushed the bin through the rehearsal room door she was red and puffing, and couldn't help making an unprofessionally loud clatter as she entered.

'Ah! Yes. Perfect,' exclaimed Hashi. 'Well, almost perfect. Can we paint it gold?'

'Gold?' repeated Hattie, trying to catch her breath.

'Yes, gold. As a stylistic thing. I'll double-check with Raven, but I think gold would be ideal.'

'Sorry, it's a borrow. Has to be returned as-is.'

'Oh,' said Hashi, crestfallen. 'Well… it'll have to do I suppose. For now. Keep an eye out for one we can paint, eh?'

'I'll see what I can do,' said Hattie, making a mental promise to do no such thing.

Hashi had already turned back to the scene being rehearsed, so Hattie stowed the bin in a corner as quietly as she could, and then took a moment to survey the room. Once again, the whole company was there. They'd all been called in pretty much every day, and clearly for a lot of them, especially those with small parts, the novelty had largely worn off. Several were engrossed in phones or books, and Emile was lying, supine, on what appeared to be a small inflatable mattress, once again dead to the world. Bums was sitting in front of the makeshift shrine to Atlanta she had collaged together of photos and Post-its, and her hand idly stroked the wall as she watched the rehearsal. Kiki was at her desk, scribbling furiously, trying to keep up with the fiendishly complex and constantly revised blocking that Hashi was working out with his actors. Hattie was pleased to see that they were finally working within the confines of the Tavistock stage, as marked out in chalk on the floor, and for the first time appeared to be giving some consideration to what the scene might look like to an audience. Things still seemed fairly stylised, but no longer totally unintelligible.

Perhaps the biggest change was the sound, or rather the absence of it. For once there were no harsh, grating noises blaring from Miguel's speakers. No weather effects, no industrial machinery, nothing. In the absence of sound cues Miguel was sitting quietly at his desk, fiddling with what appeared to be a Rubik's cube on steroids: instead of having six sides, this one appeared to have about twenty, its faces delineated not just by colour but by symbol as well.

Hattie sidled up to him.

'No soundscape for this scene, then?' she whispered.

Miguel looked round at her. His hand self-consciously went up to try to mask his shiner, which had now bruised into an ugly purple with greeny-yellow edges.

'The soundscapes have been cut,' he whispered back.

'What, all of them?'

Miguel shrugged.

'He doesn't want them any more. Says they're too obvious.'

'I see. Er, Miguel, are you… all right?' asked Hattie, pointing at his eye.

Miguel's expression immediately went determinedly neutral.

'I'm fine.'

'Are you sure? Because that looks…'

'Yes I'm fine,' he cut in quickly, loudly enough that a couple of people turned their heads.

'Fair enough,' whispered Hattie. This wasn't like Miguel at all, normally so polite and eager to please.

'If you ever want to talk about anything…' she tried, but Miguel made no response, simply turning back to watch the actors rehearse.

When she got back to ACDA Hattie took a detour on her way to the SM office, and stopped by the workshop. There were now several things she needed to talk to Shane about.

Once again, it was hellishly loud: the second years had made plenty of progress since last week, judging by the pile of amorphous wooden structures laid out in the centre of the space, and they were still beavering away, bashing and cutting and heaving at huge sheets of plywood and enormous lengths of lumber. Shane was doing the rounds, inspecting a join here, offering advice on a tricky bevel cut there, picking flecks of sawdust out of his tea along the way and at all times looking characteristically sage-like.

Hattie started to pick her way over to him, but was nearly flattened by a strip of two by four, which came whistling round at her head out of nowhere. She flinched away, and it missed her by millimetres.

'Oh God, sorry!' came an alarmed cry from near the wall, where a student was holding on to the far end of said two by four, looking mortified. 'I didn't see you! I was so focused on not slicing my fingers off with the bandsaw of doom.'

'Now, Lauren, we've talked about this, haven't we?' admonished Shane. 'Don't focus. Focus is narrowing, it's restrictive, and in a workshop environment it can get you in trouble. Instead of cultivating focus, cultivate *awareness*.'

Lauren nodded, like an eager acolyte receiving wisdom from a revered guru.

'Yes, Shane. Thank you. Sorry. Thank you.'

Shane nodded at her, and she, thus dismissed, turned back to her work. He caught Hattie's eye, giving her a tiny smirk, which Hattie reciprocated. She had started to like him a lot more when she realised that his philosopher persona was at least in part an act.

'Office?' he asked, gesturing.

Hattie nodded, and they made their way to the relative quiet of his lean-to.

'So what can I do for you today?' he asked, pleasantly.

'Oh, it's related to my project at the Tavistock. I was hoping I could talk to you about aluminium,' Hattie replied, thinking she might as well start with the easiest conversation on her mental to-do list.

'Oh yeah? What about it?'

'Hypothetically speaking, if I had a small padlock, about yea big' – she held up a finger and thumb – 'and the body was made of aluminium, and it was attached to one of those yellow hazardous material cupboards, and I wanted to melt the padlock off, in situ, what kind of equipment would I need?'

Shane's eyes widened in bemusement.

'I'm sorry, you say this is a hypothetical?'

Hattie nodded, and Shane took a breath, seemingly considering his words carefully.

'Look... I know that Keith's a bit of a bastard, and I'm sorry if he's screwed you over. Being frank, he did the same to me once. He didn't pay me for some work I did, and I'm still out of pocket. But I think I might know the cupboard you're talking about, and I *really* don't think you want to go down the road of breaking and entering.'

Hattie couldn't help but smile.

'I promise you, I've got no intention of doing any lock-melting myself, and I'm not helping anyone else either. It's just a rather, erm, delicate matter I've been asked to make some discreet enquiries about. Is that OK?'

Shane frowned, then shook his head. 'I mean... sure. Crikey, you move in mysterious ways, don't you? OK, well, for starters you don't want to melt the lock. Get a pair of bolt-cutters, that'll get you in much faster.'

'OK, but let's say I was dead set on melting it, for whatever reason. What would I need?'

Shane paused and considered again.

'Well, aluminium has a fairly low melting temperature, so that's in your favour. Even one of those hand-held little kitchen blowtorches would get it hot enough in theory, but in practice, the flame of those is so small that it'd take absolutely ages. So you're probably looking at some slightly more serious kit that's harder to lug around. Either way though, there's going to be a hell of a lot of mess. COSHH cupboards are generally made of steel, so they won't melt, but you'd be hard pressed not to wreck the paint job, leaving scorch marks everywhere, and kicking up a bunch of smoke and fumes. Good luck if there's a smoke alarm about.'

Hattie thought for a second. This was sounding less and less plausible.

'And would there be anything you could think of that would give the *appearance* of melting the lock, but that didn't use heat? Like, say, dissolving it in acid?'

Shane chuckled. 'Well, I have to say I'm not too familiar with acids. It's all sounding a bit Hollywood to me. You might be better off asking a chemist whether that would work. All I would say is, my guess is that corroding a lump of aluminium with acid would also be noisy, smoky and smelly. I can't imagine it would be a subtle thing.'

'Fair enough,' said Hattie, disappointed. Well, on to the next item on her agenda. 'While I'm here, I wonder if I could ask your opinion on something. There's a young man among the first years, Felix he's called. Have you come across him?'

'Felix? Yeah, I know him. He won't last long, will he?' replied Shane, shaking his head.

'No?'

'No. I mean, he's completely disengaged. Won't get anything done unless you're actually standing over him, barking orders. Mark'll kick him out by the end of term, and no bad thing if I'm honest. People like him just sap energy from a group.'

'I know what you mean,' said Hattie. 'I was hoping it was just that he didn't like stage management. I thought maybe you'd tell me he was a bit more keen in the workshop.'

'I can honestly say I've never seen anyone so disinterested,' Shane said solemnly. 'It'd be comical if it wasn't so frustrating. It's like he hates it here.'

'Ah well,' replied Hattie. 'I'm going to try to have a chat with him. Maybe he'll explain what's up. Well, thanks for your time, as always. I'll let you get back to it.'

She started to leave, and then forced herself to stop. Just because she didn't *want* to talk about the last item on her list didn't mean she could let herself not talk about it.

'The only other thing I wanted to mention was... Davina.'

'Oh yeah,' replied Shane, smiling. 'Yeah, thanks for prodding me about that. I gave her a ring over the weekend, just to touch base. We had a lovely chat, and I think she really needed it. You know, she got dumped recently. And look, she wouldn't tell me who by, but to be honest it kind of sounded like it was someone she shouldn't have been seeing in the first place. I really hope it doesn't turn out to have been a staff member here. Either way, I think she needed to hear a friendly voice. I hope I was able to help her.'

Hattie forced a smile, but underneath she was feeling deeply frustrated. What an idiot. She'd blindly assumed that Shane was Davina's illicit former paramour, and hadn't even bothered to check, and now here was yet one more puzzle for which she had no answer: who on earth was it who Davina had been seeing? Just once, it would be nice to reach the end of the day with fewer mysteries than there had been at the beginning.

She thanked Shane again for his time, and made her way back to the SM office. But here she was to discover that the day had not yet finished dispensing mysteries to her. Because, waiting for her in the office, was the mask.

16

It came in a fairly inconspicuous brown cardboard box. Davina handed it to her as she walked through the door.

'I think it's a prop? I wasn't sure if I should open it or not.'

Hattie took a look at the handwritten delivery label, which began: '*FAO Keith Macaulay, C/O Love's Labour's Lost SM Dept, ACDA...*'

The only other feature of the box was a small label on the reverse, also handwritten, which said: '*If undelivered, please return to Cheap Props Ltd, SW1A 1AA.*'

'That's odd,' said Hattie. 'I don't think I'd ordered anything for the show. Did you?'

'Nothing small enough to fit in a box like that,' replied Davina.

Hattie gave the box a thoughtful look.

'You remember that time last term you thought you'd found some cheap maracas on eBay for the Havana scene of *Guys & Dolls*, and when they turned up they were only two inches long?'

Davina squirmed and nodded.

'I'm very much hoping that this box doesn't contain the world's smallest set of miniature golf clubs, that's all,' said Hattie, with a wink. 'They looked full-size in the photo, but you never know...'

Taking a pair of scissors she carefully cut through the packing tape, and opened the lid of the box. Inside was a selection of cheap plastic carnival masks in assorted colours, the sort you could pick up by the dozen at any fancy dress shop. Hattie, bewildered, held one up to Davina.

'You didn't order any masks for the Russian disguise scene, did you?'

Davina shook her head.

Rooting through the box, Hattie also found a scrap of paper with a note on it, also handwritten, seemingly by the same person who wrote the label on the box. The note said, simply:

Is Frank coming on opening night? Would love a chat.

Hattie frowned.

'Bizarre,' she murmured. 'Well, maybe this is something Keith ordered, although why he got it delivered here...'

She tailed off, as her eyes drifted back to the masks. One of them, she realised, wasn't like the others. One of them...

Her breath caught in her throat. One of the masks, nestled at the bottom of the box wasn't made of plastic. It was covered in black velvet, with gold thread criss-crossing over its face, and small clear gemstones set at every intersection. It *almost* looked at home among all its cheap companions: if Hattie hadn't recognised what it was she might not have spotted that the jewels on it sparkled just a *little* bit more than you'd expect from plastic or glass...

'Oh bloody hell.'

'What is it?' asked Davina.

'Er... never mind,' replied Hattie. 'I know what this is. It's Keith's. I think he'll be pleased to see it. In fact, I may as well go and deliver it to him now. Are you all right to hold the fort here?'

Davina, looking confused, nodded. Hattie closed the box of masks again, tried to fit the whole thing into her handbag, and, unable to, found a shopping bag instead. She was at first slightly concerned that the bag was thin enough to be slightly transparent, so that the box was visible inside. Then she reminded herself that the only person who could possibly know the significance of the box was highly unlikely to want to steal it again, given that they'd only just returned the damn thing. Still, the thought of the value of the item that she was carrying made Hattie nervous, and she clutched the carrier bag extra tightly as she stepped out of ACDA.

So discombobulated was she by the worth of the mask that, upon arriving at the Tavistock, Hattie was perhaps a little over-eager to return it to its rightful owner, dispensing with her normal manners and walking straight into the office without knocking. It was thanks to this eagerness, therefore, that she found Keith and Robin, pressed close up against one another, in the far corner of the room. Keith, whose back was to her when she walked in, spun around and ran his hand with exaggerated casualness through his hair, the gesture not doing much to disguise the stark fact that, seconds earlier, that same hand had been down Robin's trousers. Robin, for his part, turned an immediate beetroot red and swung his hips around to try, unsuccessfully, to get his tent-poled trouser crotch out of Hattie's eyeline.

Hattie and Keith made awkward eye contact for a second, until Keith gave a little shrug, as if simultaneously to acknowledge that he'd been busted and to play down the significance of what (and who) he'd been busted doing.

'Well this is an unexpected—' he began.

'I'm so sorry, I should have knocked—' blurted Hattie.

'—pleasure, but do come in. What can I do for you?' Keith continued firmly, evidently keen not to have to actually *talk* about what Hattie had just seen. For his part, Robin cowered in the corner, eyes fixed firmly on the floor.

'Well… er, I've got…' mumbled Hattie, uncertainly. On the trip over on the Underground she had indulged herself by fantasising about saying something flippant like 'Is this yours?' while showily twirling the mask around one finger. Wrong-footed at the outset, however, it was all she could do to produce the box from her shopping bag, dig the mask out and hand it straight to Keith.

'Oh you bloody darling,' breathed Keith, snatching it from her. 'Oh you absolute showstopper. Where on earth did you get it?'

He closed his eyes and kissed the mask, and looked like a man who has just had the weight of the world lifted from his shoulders. Even Robin forgot his embarrassment and came forward to peer at it.

'It came in the post,' explained Hattie, handing Keith the box. He took it greedily and examined it all over. He frowned when he saw the returns label on the back, and looked perplexed when he discovered the other masks within. But when he discovered the note inside, his good mood evaporated as quickly as it had appeared.

'Oh bloody hell. Oh Helen Mirren's knickers. Oh… *follow-spots!*'

'What's the problem?' asked Hattie.

'The problem? The problem, my darling, is that this is a threat. A pretty bloody diabolical one.'

'I don't understand. Who's this Frank? And what's the threat?'

'That's above your pay grade, my love. But unfortunately, it means that this just swung from a minor drama to a full-scale crisis. I need to know where this parcel came from.'

'It got delivered to ACDA. Davina picked it up. But look, on the back it says—'

'Yes, yes, it's got a fake company name, and the postcode is for Buckingham Palace. Ignore that. But you say Davina gave it to you. Is this her handwriting?'

'Honestly, I'm not sure,' replied Hattie.

'Christ, if it was Davina all along…'

'I'm sure it wasn't,' said Hattie firmly. 'I've got photo evidence that she was at the Menier the evening the mask was taken.'

'You're *sure* about that?' asked Keith, suspiciously.

'Positive,' said Hattie. 'But I've been meaning to talk to you about that too. The staff downstairs say they didn't see anyone go through from the pub on Sunday early evening. Are you absolutely sure that was when it was taken?'

'Positive,' replied Keith, mimicking Hattie's previous response. 'Any earlier and I'd have seen the broken lock, any later and I was either in the theatre or the office door was locked.'

'And you didn't nip out at any point after you came back that evening? There was no point when someone could have snuck in?'

Keith frowned.

'There were maybe three minutes right at the end of the night when I was in the bar having my nightcap. Someone could have conceivably got in the side door then. If they could have been in and out in three minutes I suppose it's possible it could have been then.'

'That sounds unlikely,' mused Hattie. 'I spoke to Sha— to *someone* about what it would take to melt the lock with a blowtorch, and he suggested either it would take an awfully long time, or, if you managed to haul some industrial strength kit up here, you could do it faster but you'd still make a hell of a mess in the process... You do have a smoke alarm up here, right?'

'Oh Lord yes,' replied Keith, gesturing towards a white box on the ceiling. 'Tinderbox, this place is. The insurers would never cover us if we didn't have detectors up the wazoo. Otherwise I'd have burned this place down for a pay-out long ago.'

Hattie had a feeling he wasn't joking.

'Then whoever came in must have done it while you were out for supper, although how they got into the theatre I don't know. But that rules out Davina, and I cannot for the life of me believe it would be any of the rest of the crew. Of course, if you'd tell me what th—'

'Not even Stephen? He's technically skilled, he's got a chip on his shoulder, and he's got the morals of a mediaeval grave robber.'

'That's not true, Keith. Steve's got probably the most straightforward moral compass of anyone. Besides he's so down-to-earth, and all this business with masks and notes is a bit *Phantom of the Opera*, you know? But what does the—'

'The cast then!' insisted Keith, with a glint in his eye that wasn't a million miles off manic. 'Actors are all drama queens, this would be right in character. You'll have to start questioning them.'

'But I don't know what I'm asking about,' Hattie persisted. 'If you'd only tell me what this note is all about then maybe I could help more.'

'You don't need to know about the note. You wouldn't understand the note. All you have to do is what I tell you to do, and I'm telling you to go talk to the cast.'

'Oh for goodness' sake!' cried Hattie, reaching the end of her patience. 'You have the mask. You wanted it back, I got you it back. I've done everything you asked of me, I've gone far above and beyond my responsibilities as your stage manager, and frankly I'm getting sick of all these endless demands that I solve your problems when you won't even tell me what they are!'

They stared at each other in silence for a second.

Then Keith said, coldly, 'Well, thank you for all your input, Hattie. I'm sure you have plenty of things to be getting on with. I'm sorry that you weren't prepared to be more helpful, but I understand that there are limits to your abilities. It's been a not-unalloyed pleasure working together, so I take some comfort in knowing that, when the house goes dark for the last time, at least we won't cross paths again.'

And with that he turned his back to her. It was a ridiculous gesture, Hattie thought, because he was now more or less facing the wall, and there was nothing he could usefully do there without turning back around. So she stood in silence for a second, and then, with a little malicious thrill of defiance, turned to Robin.

'Robin, my love,' she said cheerily. 'While I'm here, I just wanted to finish the conversation we started last week. Have you ever considered working backstage? I thought you might be the sort of person who enjoys being in the thick of it all, instead of cooped up away from the action in an office. It's really not a bad life, after all.'

'Oh, I… I hadn't really thought…' stuttered Robin. Keith, now trapped facing the wrong way by his dramatic gesture, huffed noisily.

'Well, I'd love to chat about it some time. If, you know, you want to find a career path in the theatre beyond… this.'

'Uh… OK. Sure,' said Robin, glancing awkwardly over at Keith's back for support.

'Well, I must be getting along. Bye for now.' Hattie smiled as warmly as she could.

'Bye,' replied Robin shyly.

'And see you soon, Keith,' she called out, aggressively merrily.

Keith, resentfully, shuffled back around.

'Bye,' he muttered.

Well, thought Hattie to herself, that was it then. No more furtive investigations, no more asking difficult questions on false pretences. Whatever he said, she'd done everything he'd asked of her. If the theatre was still in jeopardy, in ways that Keith couldn't or wouldn't explain to her, he'd just have to sort it out himself. And if it all turned out to be related to Miguel's black eye, or Steve's slightly off behaviour, or the whole Atlanta palaver, she was sure someone cleverer than her would work out how. For her, it was over. And just in time too. With the show opening in little over a week, she needed to give it her full attention.

It's just…

No. Don't waste any more brain power on it.

Hattie set off back towards ACDA.

17

She made it back to the SM office just before six: going-home time, really. She'd spent almost the entire day hopping around on public transport, and her hip was beginning to air its grievances. What's more, she had barely touched any of the items on her to-do list. Just once, she thought, it'd be nice to end the day having done the things you said you'd do at the start of it.

'Was Keith happy to see the masks?' asked Davina.

'Yes. Well. Not really. I'm not quite sure what's going on there,' replied Hattie. 'But it's off our plates, that's the main thing. Whatever it is, let him worry about it.'

'Good,' smiled Davina.

'How's it all been here?'

'Well, the good news is that those golf clubs have turned up. The *bad* news...'

She gestured over into the corner, where sat a complete set of golf clubs, in a bag, with a shoulder strap, on loan from a sporting goods store, technically fulfilling all of the requirements given by Hashi the previous week. The problem, however, was immediately apparent. The bag, along with the handles of all the clubs, was a fluorescent yellow-green colour. Everything was emblazoned with space-age logos. Even if the theme hadn't been leaning towards the 1920s, no designer would let a prop like that anywhere near a stage. It was lurid and ghastly.

'I thought maybe they'd made a mistake,' explained Davina, hurriedly. 'I rang them and they said they decided to use the one you spoke to them about last week in a window display, and this is the only one they could spare.'

'I can see why,' tutted Hattie. 'All right. This can be tomorrow's problem. You never know, maybe Hashi will have cut the golf clubs before we have to solve this. Either way, let's go home.'

They gathered up their things, and headed out of the SM office, only to bump into Felix, who was skulking in the corridor. He looked up at Hattie as she came out, with baleful eyes.

'Oh… hello, love,' said Hattie, momentarily confused.

Then she remembered.

'You've finished your sound and lighting classes for the day, so you've come to see me, haven't you? Like I asked?'

Felix just nodded.

'Right! Well, come in. Davina, I'll see you tomorrow. OK?'

She waved Davina off, and ushered Felix back into the office, and bade him find a chair. They sat in silence for a few moments.

'Er…' began Hattie, eventually. 'Thanks for coming by. The reason I wanted to talk to you is that… well, not to put too fine a point on it, I don't think you've been completely *engaged* in my classes so far. Do you think that's fair?'

Felix grunted, not making eye contact.

'Do you mind me asking why you think that is?'

'I dunno.'

As the first words out of his mouth since he'd arrived, they perhaps weren't the most illuminating.

'Well… a lot of the people who do this course are more interested in certain parts of it than others. So some people, for example, really like lighting and stage electrics, but don't really like stage management. Do you think it might be something like that?'

He grunted again.

Hattie had to fight quite hard to conceal her frustration.

'Look,' she said. 'You're not in trouble. I'm not a schoolteacher, I'm not going to put you in detention, or complain to your parents. I just want to help you get the most you can out of this course that you've paid to be on. Does that make sense?'

'Yeah,' he mumbled hesitantly.

'So… if stage management isn't something you enjoy… can I ask what it is you're interested in?'

He didn't answer. He just sat there, staring at the floor. Hattie waited for as long as she could, but when it became clear he wasn't about to offer a response she drew in a breath to tell him he might as well go. But then suddenly he muttered something she didn't catch.

'I'm so sorry, I didn't hear that. Could you say it again?'

Felix slowly looked up and made eye contact with her for the first time.

'I want to be an actor,' he said. His voice was small and strangled, but he spoke with an unexpected intensity.

That was not the answer Hattie had been expecting to hear. Flummoxed for a second, all she could think of to say at first was: 'Oh.'

They sat in silence for a few moments longer, and when he didn't offer anything further, she followed up with, 'Then, if I may, why did you join the technical course, if acting's what you want to do?'

'Can't act,' he said, so simply and straightforwardly that Hattie had to resist the urge to laugh out loud.

For once, he had more to say:

'I'm too shy. Got a shit voice. Got a shit face. Everyone said I should be a techie. Let them talk me into it. Hate it. I just want to act.'

He looked on the verge of tears, and Hattie found herself suddenly feeling that she might be too. This poor young man, armed with precisely *none* of the qualities required, nevertheless yearned for a career that seemed pretty obviously closed off to him. And, not surprisingly, when someone like him gravitated towards the world of theatre, everyone assumed that he belonged backstage, and had gently directed him thither, until he ended up here, in some ways within touching distance of everything aspired to, and in other ways completely out of reach of it.

'I see,' said Hattie, gently. 'Then it seems to me you have a choice to make. There's no crossing the divide between actors and techies in this industry, you know. It's daft but that's just how it is. So either you can take your aspirations and… put them to one side. In which case, if you like the theatre, and you like being involved, you could take the course seriously, and make a nice life for yourself as a lampie, or a chippie, or even an SM. Or, if you really can't shake that desire to be an actor… well, if you keep doing this course, and if you stay in this industry, all you'll be doing is torturing yourself day in, day out, watching from the wings as other people get to have what you want, and you never get any closer to it. So you'd probably need to find another path. I think you'll have to think about it, and then you'll have to choose.'

''S not my choice,' Felix responded blankly. 'My parents.'

'Oh. Oh I see. So… in some ways, would it be preferable, from your perspective, if, for some reason, you were no longer *allowed* to be on the course? So that the decision was no longer in their hands… or yours?'

He grunted. Hattie nodded.

'I think I understand. And I'm sorry, I really am. And if there's any way I can help you…'

Felix said nothing, and didn't meet her eye.

'Well… thank you for talking to me. And enjoy the rest of your week.'

Felix stood up wordlessly and shuffled out of the room. After he had left, Hattie sat for a long while wondering, not for the first time, at the sheer variety of the people who found themselves in the theatre world, and the many diverse motivations that brought them there. She wanted to help the poor lad, but it wasn't entirely clear to her what help would look like.

Eventually, unable to think of a better course of action, she made her way across the building and knocked on the door of Mark's office.

Mark was still in. He was surrounded by mountains of paperwork, and looked exhausted, but he still managed a friendly smile.

'Hello, Hattie. Burning the midnight oil?'

'No more than you, I dare say. You know how it is: just trying to stay on top of things.'

'Of course, of course. Show going well?'

Hattie pursed her lips.

'We've got a few issues,' she replied. 'The director's running a bit hot, and the theatre's a bit disarrayed. And… one of our cast died.'

Mark's eyes widened.

'I'm so sorry. What happened?'

'We don't entirely know. We… I… found her last Monday morning, backstage at the Tavistock, just dead on the floor. We don't know why she was there.'

'Bloody hell. Who was she?'

'A woman called Atlanta Greenwell.'

'Atlanta?' said Mark, visibly stiffening. 'Oh my goodness, the poor thing… and, gosh, poor you for finding… I'm so sorry. So sorry.'

'Did you know her?' asked Hattie gently.

'I got my first break thanks to her. I was doing an unpaid internship at the Lion, they didn't have anything for me to do, so they sent me to sit in on rehearsals in the auditorium. A production of *No Exit*: it was a vanity project, funded by the star. God he was awful. Anyway, the DSM fell out with the director the second day

I was there, then started acting up and sulking, refusing to do her job properly. Atlanta, God bless her, gave this girl a rocket, a real dressing down, enough that she burst into tears, locked herself in the bathroom for a few hours, then left and never came back. So they asked me if I knew how to run a bible, and that's how I got my first stage management gig.'

Mark smiled at the memory.

'Atlanta was playing Estelle, and she was absolutely electric, and great fun to work with. But you know we had to keep a bucket backstage for her. She got such bad stage fright she'd throw up every night at beginners. God, I'm not sure I've seen her since. What a character. So what does that mean for the show?'

'Well, they've given her role to the AD. A few people are a bit shaken, but we're more or less carrying on. I'm sure we'll be there by press night.'

'Good, good. I'm sure she'd want you to make a success of it. It's very sad, but we do have to keep going.'

Hattie nodded, and they stood in silence for a second. Then Mark shifted his weight in his chair and said: 'Listen, while I have you, I just wanted to check in about what we spoke about last time.'

Hattie frowned, momentarily at a loss.

'About Rod,' prompted Mark.

'Oh!' replied Hattie. 'I'm so sorry, I forgot. No, I'm afraid I've not seen him since we last spoke. I will make time to talk to him, though.'

'If you could do it sooner rather than later I'd be grateful. One of the students tried to make a formal complaint about him today, I had to talk her out of taking it to the principal.'

'Oh no! What happened?'

'He fell asleep over lunch and didn't wake up in time for his next class. The students turned up to find him snoring. So one of them complained to me.'

'And what did you say?'

'I told her she should have just woken Rod up. Gave her a line about initiative and personal responsibility. Gave a hint that it may have been a deliberate test. But I can't keep covering for him like this.'

'I'll talk to him. I promise.'

'Thank you,' smiled Mark. 'Let me know when you have.'

His eyes started to drift back to his paperwork.

'Just quickly,' Hattie said, 'have any of the other tutors spoken to you about one of the first years? Felix?'

'Oh yes. Odd lad, isn't he? I think it'll take him a while to come out of his shell. He was practically mute at interview, paralysed by shyness, we had to evaluate him almost entirely on the basis of his written submission. Which was excellent, and convinced me he'd thrive here.'

'I don't know that he's thriving,' she replied cautiously.

'Oh come now, Hattie,' said Mark with a dismissive shake of his head. 'We've seen his type before. He'll never make an SM, but stick him up a ladder with some cables to tape and he'll be happy as Larry.'

'I know that he *seems* like the type,' persisted Hattie, 'but I think it might be a little more complicated than that. And I wouldn't be entirely confident that he didn't have a little, er, assistance with his written application from his family. I don't think he really wants to be here… in fact I think he's sort of hoping to get kicked out.'

Mark's face fell.

'God, the last thing I need is drop-outs this early. They'll use it as an excuse to cut my budget, and there's always people questioning whether having a technical course at all sullies the "creative brand" of the school. Bugger. Well, I won't have it. I don't care if he didn't want to come here originally, we need to find a way to make him stay. Can I leave this with you?'

'As you say, I really don't think stage management is his—'

'Hattie, this is the sort of thing I'm talking about. I'm looking for you to prove that you can be a team player, if you want to stay on here. You do want to stay on, don't you?'

Hattie nodded, uncomfortably.

'Then find a way,' said Mark firmly. 'At least make sure he lasts the first year, so we don't have to worry about fee refunds. OK?'

It wasn't really OK, and Hattie not at all eager to have this dumped into her lap, but Mark was clearly signalling that her job prospects were in the balance. There wasn't much else she could say.

'I'll see what I can do,' she said miserably.

18

On the ride home, Kiki's rehearsal notes came through on Hattie's phone. They made for grim reading: as Miguel had warned, *all* sound effects and soundscapes had now been cut, as had the glowing orbs, and several more of the props they had been working on before. The one small mercy was that the wretched golf clubs were on the list of discarded requirements. In their place were a new list of props, a heap of requests for specific lighting effects, and some urgent costume notes. Much of the production team's work over the past fortnight had been entirely invalidated by Hashi's chaotic indecision, and they were now faced with meeting a new series of demands with very little time and almost no budget remaining. It made Hattie long for her touring days. The companies hadn't been perfect by any means, but they were all old hands, and by God they were disciplined.

As she let herself into her flat, she was mentally working her way through the new props list, categorising each new task according to its achievability, when her phone rang, and she answered it distractedly.

'Hello?'

'Hi. This is DI Burakgazi. We spoke last week about Atlanta Greenwell?'

'Oh... yes. Hello.'

'I just had a couple more questions I wanted to ask about, if you don't mind.'

'Certainly. Yep, now's fine.'

'Good. So, first of all… I was talking to some of the bar staff at the Tavistock today, and it sounded like you had been in contact with them recently. Do you want to tell me a little bit about that?'

Hattie began to feel uncomfortable. Of course the same bar staff she'd spoken to about the mask would have been questioned by the police about Atlanta. And, now that she thought about it, of course they'd have mentioned that she'd been asking questions. Did that paint her as suspicious in the police's eyes?

'Oh… yes… I was curious about whether anyone else had gone into the theatre over that weekend.'

'Did you have any reason to believe that someone else would have?'

Burakgazi's tone sounded just a little bit sharp now.

'Um…' Hattie stuttered. This bloody mask. Now that it was off her plate, should she tell Burakgazi about it? Or would that be the final nail in the coffin of any hopes she had of being hired by Keith ever again?

'The reason I'm interested,' Burakgazi continued, 'is that I've been asking the same question. Because there were, as you may remember, two glasses in the dressing room where you found Ms Greenwell, both of which had had alcohol in them on Sunday night. Which would suggest that she was there *with* someone, doesn't it?'

Oh yes. Of course. Hattie had been so shocked on discovering Atlanta's body that she had completely forgotten about, and never registered the significance of, the second glass.

'Yes, I suppose it does.'

'So if you had some suspicions about who that someone might be, you can understand how I'd be curious to hear them, can't you?'

'I'm afraid I don't know of anyone who was there on the Saturday evening,' said Hattie, feeling defensive. 'I actually... I actually only ended up asking about the Sunday evening, and drew a complete blank.'

'I see,' came the disappointed reply. 'Well, I don't blame you for being curious.'

'Do you know any more about how she died yet?' tried Hattie.

There was a pause, and then Burakgazi let out a sigh.

'No. Or rather, yes, in a medical sense: we discovered a bruise on the side of her scalp above her ear, which suggests she hit her head, fell unconscious, and asphyxiated. She was chock full of brandy, and wearing impractical shoes. So if she was by herself, it's a pretty straightforward verdict of misadventure in the form of a trip and fall, and a sobering lesson on the dangers of alcohol abuse. It's just that if that second glass means that someone else was there with her when she received the impact to her head... well, that changes things, doesn't it?'

Hattie stayed silent.

'Which brings me,' Burakgazi continued after a pause, 'on to my second question. I was talking to some of Atlanta's castmates earlier today, and was astonished to learn about a threatening note that appeared in the rehearsal room soon after Atlanta died. Astonished in particular that I only heard about it through a chance mention. It seemed to me quite incredible that no one had thought to pass it on to me before. The actors told me they had been assured that the production team had dealt with it. When I then spoke to Katherine Bennett – sorry, that's Kiki, isn't it? – she confirmed that the note was indeed discussed in a meeting by the production team, wherein someone successfully argued that the note should be actively suppressed. That someone being you. Why was that?'

Because I don't trust you lot not to bugger up my show, thought Hattie, but she simply muttered, 'I didn't think it was important.'

Burakgazi took a breath.

'Hattie, you're an intelligent woman, aren't you? Intelligent enough that you couldn't possibly not realise how important a note like that could be. And you're also intelligent enough to know that I couldn't possibly *believe* you wouldn't realise it. So please don't insult me by suggesting otherwise.'

Hattie once again chose to remain silent.

'What are you up to, Hattie? Questioning the bar staff, hiding things from the police… I'd hate to think that you were deliberately not cooperating with us. Because I'm going to be honest with you, if we don't find out what happened pretty quickly I'm going to have to widen my circle of investigation. I might have to talk to your employer, for example, since it sounds like half of the production has been operating out of the ACDA premises. I'm guessing your bosses don't know everything that I do about you. And if I wasn't finding any answers from elsewhere, I might feel compelled to have an open and honest talk with them, see if that brought forth any more salient information. Do you see what I'm saying?'

Hattie's blood ran cold. With help from Rod she'd managed to avoid being subjected to an enhanced DBS criminal background check earlier in the year. Burakgazi was now out-and-out threatening to reveal what she had so far managed to conceal, rightly guessing it would mean curtains for Hattie's tutoring career. She had found Hattie's weak spot, and she was squeezing.

'I understand,' Hattie mumbled.

'Well,' said Burakgazi. 'With that in mind, if anything comes to light, do please let me know.'

Burakgazi hung up, leaving Hattie deeply shaken. The *audacity* of it, to bring up things that had happened a lifetime ago, and use them now to squeeze Hattie – no, to *blackmail* her – into docile obedience.

Everyone makes mistakes, she thought to herself. *Why should mine have to hang over my head forever?*

It wasn't as though she was actively doing anything to hinder the police. It wasn't her fault that they were so dim they couldn't work out what had happened to Atlanta. What did they want? For her to solve it all for them?

Mind you, she could see why they were having difficulties. That second glass of brandy showed there was someone else in the room with Atlanta that night, which made it harder to rule out foul play. But who on earth would want to murder Atlanta? She'd rubbed a couple of people the wrong way at the start of rehearsals, but no more so than actors always did. She had mentioned that Joan Haygarth had hated her, but Joan was long since dead herself.

Was there any way this could have been to do with the mask? Had the thief arranged to meet Atlanta on the Saturday night, had a drink with her, killed her… and then returned the next night to break into the cupboard? No, surely that was absurd.

It all felt wrong. Theatres were places of drama, both onstage and off, but at the end of the day you could always walk away, and reassure yourself that it wasn't real, it didn't really matter. The performer tantrums, the backstage trysts, the endless near-disasters that threatened each successive performance, they were all contained in their own microcosm, and didn't impinge on the real world. An honest-to-goodness *death* on the other hand…

Eventually, with the aid of a few fortifying glasses of wine, Hattie managed to put most of those thoughts from her head long enough to settle down in bed and crawl towards the reassuring oblivion of sleep. Sod mysteries, sod masks, sod Keith, sod cryptic notes, and sod Burakgazi more than anyone. She would do her job, get the show up and running, and everyone else could go to hell.

Over the next few days Hattie was kept thoroughly occupied by the play as she and Davina laboured to get Hashi the props he now insisted he needed. To his credit (and to the crew's despair), he succeeded in completely reimagining everything physical, visible and practical about the show in the final week of rehearsals, all the while insisting that the 'heart' of the piece was unaltered. Now there were no wooden blocks, there were no soundscapes, there were no glowing orbs, just a table, a couple of chairs, the enormous bin, and a series of small hand props. But, small though the props may have been, the stage managers still had a struggle on their hands to get everything together in time. They scoured charity shops, they borrowed from friends, they *made* with clay and paper and glue, and assembled a huge mass of teapots, blankets, mirrors, briefcases and more, all with the last £100 or so of their budget. Come Friday lunchtime, at the third and final production meeting, Hattie was quietly pleased that Davina was able to announce that everything was in hand, and that all the required props had been sourced and received at least grudging approval from Hashi and Raven.

Unfortunately, no one else was even remotely pleased with how things were going.

'I don't know, do I?' replied Laura truculently, in response to a request for an update on her preparations. 'I don't have a lighting design to work with, so I don't know if we've got the right lanterns, gels, cabling...'

'Now that's not entirely true,' Carrie complained. 'I've told you several times that we'll work with the kit specified in the design I gave you last week, we just might need to be flexible on the placement of the lanterns and the specific gels.'

'But we don't *have* a bunch of spare gels kicking around. I've got the colours you asked for before, we've got a small number of spare sheets, *not* cut to size, but if you don't tell me what you want I can't just have every possible colour ready to go in case you change your mind at the focus session.'

'It's not the focus session that's the problem, it's going to be in the tech rehearsal, because that's when Hashi is going to see it and hopefully start making some actual, you know, creative decisions.'

'That's even worse!' cried Laura. 'How are we supposed to do a focus session if we don't even know what lights we're supposed to be focusing?'

'But we *do* know—' Carrie started to insist, before Hashi cut her off.

'Ladies, ladies, can I say something? Can I?' he asked, prissily. 'Given that you're all determined to pin all this on me? Can I just… can I make one of these "creative decisions" you're so determined that I'm incapable of? Look, what I've been trying to say, and I'm sorry that it seems to have got lost in communication, is that I don't *want* any complicated lighting. I don't need fancy follow-spots, or rotating leaf patterns projected onto the stage, I just want some basic lights to give me a little bit of delineation between areas onstage at different points in the show, and a few different options, not of colour, just of, you know, *tone*, for different scenes, so we can be flexible. Is that really so hard to put together on the day?'

'YES,' replied Carrie and Laura in unison, who both then tried simultaneously to impress on Hashi how limited their resources were, and how things like delineation between areas and different colour tones were things that needed to be planned in advance.

'Hold up, my loves,' interjected Hattie. 'Now look, this isn't getting us anywhere. We are where we are. How about you rig and focus what you can tomorrow, and then just work with what we've got. I know it's not ideal, but, with no offence intended, this show doesn't stand or fall on the lighting, does it? So let's be pragmatic.'

'Well excuse me for trying to do my job properly,' muttered Laura. 'A professional lighting department shouldn't be—'

'A *professional* lighting team should know when complaining is counter-productive, and work together to deal with whatever situation arises,' Hattie said firmly. She was doing her best to sound confident and calm, but internally she was deeply alarmed. Yes, tempers often got frayed among production teams in the run-up to opening, but that tended to happen a little bit later, during the fit-up and tech, when everyone was treading on everyone else's toes in the auditorium. If people were barely being civil before that even started… well, it didn't bode well for the weekend.

And what the hell was Steve up to? His job was to herd all the techies and keep these meetings in order, and yet he seemed barely to be paying attention. Why was Hattie having to step in? Steve was simply staring at his phone, frowning, ignoring the squabbling around him. That wasn't like him at all.

Still, they got to the end of the meeting without anyone actually coming to blows. Moira assured everyone that the costumes were all under control, but refused to be drawn on which, if any, of Hashi's last-minute requests she'd actually fulfilled.

'You'll see where we are on Sunday,' was all she'd say.

And Kiki was at least polite about how things had been going in the rehearsal room.

'We were hoping to do a full run this afternoon, as it's our last official day of rehearsals, but we're not quite ready for that yet,' she said. 'We're still trying to nail down the last of the blocking.'

'How much do you have left to do?'

'Oh, you know. Act five. And most of act four,' she replied mildly. 'But we'll do what we can this afternoon. And the cast have said they're happy to meet up tomorrow to keep working on it, while the crew do the fit-up in the theatre. We won't have this room any more, but the weather's set to be good, so maybe they can meet up in a park?'

Carrie covered her face with her hand, and Laura gave a bitter laugh, whispering, 'So *professional*…'

At the end of the meeting Hattie checked in with Kiki.

'You're seeming, er, pretty relaxed about the whole thing,' she said.

'I just… stopped caring,' explained Kiki, wrinkling her nose. 'It feels much better, really. All I have to do is get through the next few days, then I can cue the show for a few weeks in the evenings, then I can never think about it again. And… that's that.'

'Fair enough, I suppose,' agreed Hattie. 'I suppose it's just one of those shows. Is there anything you need from me?'

'Can you get the bin over to the Tavistock? We've got to clear out everything from here tonight, and I can pop everything else into a suitcase and take it home with me, but that thing's more than I can manage.'

'No problem,' replied Hattie. 'Me and this bin are old friends. I'll get Davina to help me take it over right now.'

'Also… just be aware, some of the cast are still quite jittery about Atlanta. There's a bit of superstition kicking in. And Sherlock Bums isn't helping matters. She's spending more time playing detective than she is learning her lines. Her latest theory is that Regine killed Atlanta in order to get her part. And she *will* insist on laying out her suspicions while poor Regine is in the room.'

Hattie rolled her eyes.

'Thanks for the warning. I'll be on the lookout for any of it bubbling over.'

On her way out she saw some of the cast milling around, waiting for the afternoon's rehearsal session to begin. As she'd soon be in close quarters with them, she thought it would be helpful to try to get on to friendly terms, so she offered a few greetings, and asked how everything was going. The response was distinctly mixed. The younger, more inexperienced actors seemed energised and enthused, the older ones… less so. Emile in particular just scowled and shook his head. It seemed that those who were more familiar with how a professional rehearsal process was supposed to run were less convinced by Hashi's process. Regine, Atlanta's replacement, was keeping to herself, a little way apart from the others, and wasn't keen to chat to Hattie. She seemed like she'd rather not be there. Which, if Kiki was right about her castmates accusing her of murder, was understandable.

Hattie and Davina lugged the big bin from St Eustace's to the Tavistock. It was a more complicated journey on the bus than the one from ACDA to the rehearsal room, and they had to make two changes, with one of them involving quite a long walk. So Hattie was glad of Davina's assistance in moving it. Thankfully Davina seemed to have got over her fear of getting in trouble with bus drivers over the size of the bin.

In between hauling and puffing and sweating, Hattie took a few moments to watch her young assistant. She had done really well over the past few days. She'd put her all into the work, and proved that she could be creative, diligent and practical. She also seemed much more emotionally stable recently, now that she'd achieved whatever closure she could with her mystery man. Good. Hopefully this meant she'd keep moving in the right direction. In which case she might make a solid stage manager yet.

They got the bin to the theatre and stashed it in the storage space for spare seating.

'What next?' asked Davina brightly.

'Well, that's it, really,' replied Hattie. 'We're more or less as ready for the get-in as we can be. Tomorrow you can bring over the props from ACDA, and Kiki will deal with the last ones in the rehearsal room. Then we'll just see what's needed. In the meantime, why not go home and get a bit of rest? You'll need it for the tech.'

She led Davina out of the auditorium through the pub and towards the exit.

'Oh hello!' called out a voice from behind the bar. Hattie turned and saw the shaven-headed girl she had spoken to a fortnight earlier. Rosie, that was her name.

'Hiya,' she smiled, and then realised that Rosie had been looking at Davina, not her.

'How was *Titus*?'

'Amazing!' replied Davina. 'You *have* to see it.'

She turned to Hattie.

'Rosie's a theatre nerd like me. She's actually thinking of becoming one of us. I'm trying to talk her into applying for the ACDA course. Ro, Hattie's actually the stage management tutor.'

Rosie's eyes widened.

'Cool! Oh, um, did Pavel call you in the end?'

'Yes, he did thanks,' Hattie replied. 'That was very helpful.'

'Good. But yeah, I think I'm going to go for it next year. At ACDA, I mean.'

Hattie smiled at her.

'You should,' she said encouragingly. 'It's a great course. And it's a great life. It's hard work, but it's a great life.'

It was what she always said about the industry. Hard work, but a great life. And it was at least half true: the work was always hard. But on days like this, when the crew were at each other's throats, and half the cast looked like they'd given up on the production, it did make Hattie at least question whether this was *definitely* the greatest of all possible lives.

19

As a stage manager you're always working against the clock, because time is money, and money is in short supply in the theatre. This is never more true than during the fit-up. The fit-up is what happens once all the props, scenery and equipment have been brought into the theatre (the 'get-in'), and is the point where a show 'sets up shop' in the performance venue: scenery is erected, lights and speakers are rigged, props and costumes are put in the appropriate places, and so on. While this is happening, obviously no performances can be happening at the venue, meaning the theatre is 'dark', and no revenue is being generated. As such, producers are always determined to keep the fit-up as short as humanly possible, and sometimes shorter still!

– *From* The Art and Craft of Stage Management
by Donna Fletcher, Chapter 7: The Fit-Up

On the Saturday morning Hattie made sure she was at the Tavistock early. Fit-ups were always chaotic, and the stage managers were at the bottom of the priority list. The day belonged to the lampies, chippies and soundies, with the SMs relegated to doing what they needed to do in gaps and behind backs. So the trick was to turn up early and be prepared for lots of waiting.

Carrie and Laura were already in the auditorium, arguing about lantern placement. Hattie ignored them: the two of them bickered almost constantly when they were working together, had done for years. If it wasn't for the fact that Carrie *insisted* on hiring Laura for every job she did, and that Laura accepted every invitation, you'd think they really didn't like each other.

Hattie made her way backstage. Her first job was to tidy up the dressing rooms. The *Dealer's Choice* cast had trashed the men's dressing room over the course of their run, and their production team had made no effort to tidy up after them. She could complain to Keith, but the other company were long gone, and no amount of whining would change the fact that it would be up to Hattie and her subordinates to deal with the mess and get everything presentable. At least the ladies' dressing room was in a decent state. Hattie inspected the room carefully. There were no lingering signs of what had happened in there: no marks on the floor, no left-behind medical paraphernalia. Hopefully there was nothing that could exacerbate the cast's jitters. She turned her attention to the make-up smears and drink spills in the men's room.

Davina came by a little later, two big bags of props in tow. Hattie helped her set up a props table on either side of the stage, with each item assigned a labelled place. She then helped Kiki set up her position at the prompt desk at the back of the auditorium, and confirmed that the backstage and front-of-house comms systems were working.

And then... she realised she was out of things to do. Somehow this show, this amorphous mess of a show, had ended up being surprisingly simple from a technical perspective. With no scenery to speak of, very little in the way of sound, fairly minimal costumes, a tame set of props, and lighting that was… well, as yet undefined, and therefore not something Hattie could worry about… she realised she was already kicking her heels, even though it wasn't yet eleven o'clock.

She approached Miguel, who was coiling cables in the wings.

'How are you getting on?' she asked him.

He looked round sharply, obviously not having heard her approach, then, seeing it was her, said simply: 'Fine.'

'Can I do anything to make your life easier?'

'No,' he replied abruptly. 'I'm fine.'

There was an awkward pause. Why was Miguel still so determinedly shutting her out? Still, at least his eye was looking a bit better.

'Well,' she said, 'do let me know if there's any errands you need running, that sort of thing.'

He nodded, without smiling, and looked back down at his cables. Hattie turned her attention to Carrie, standing in the middle of the auditorium.

'Anything you need help with, my love?'

'Nah,' replied Carrie, shaking her head. 'Unless you can work out a way to get Laura to shut up.'

'I heard that!' came a disgruntled voice from the top of a ladder.

'And I heard your whole bloody life story today,' muttered Carrie with a wink to Hattie.

'Have you seen Steve at all?'

Carrie shook her head. 'Barely seen him in a week, to be honest. Did you check up in the office?'

Hattie thanked Carrie for the suggestion, and made her way out into the side corridor, then started to climb the stairs. She heard a creaking of floorboards above her.

'That you, Steve?' she called out.

The creaking stopped, but there was no reply.

'Steve?'

There was a bit more shuffling, but no response. Frowning, Hattie made her way to the top of the stairs, knocked on the door to the office, then opened it… to find the room empty. It wasn't that surprising, really. There were some other upstairs rooms that were part of the pub, and the sounds could have come from someone in one of those. Equally, it could have been squirrels on the roof, or rats under the floorboards: Hattie was under no illusion that the premises were free of pests and vermin, and there was a real chance of a bird or a rodent being present in the room. Hattie had a quick look round, but didn't see anything out of place.

She did, however, notice that laid on top of the mess on Keith's desk was a small black diary, lying open. It was Keith's: she'd seen him refer to it before. A little spark of nosiness overcame her, and she let herself sidle up to it. It was open on the page for the first week of rehearsals, the one which culminated in Atlanta's death on Saturday and the theft of the mask on Sunday. On both of those days, Keith had jotted down '9.30–10.30pm: Audition'. Most of the weekdays were fairly bare, apart from a few items marked 'MEETING', with the names of people Hattie had never heard of… except for one. On the Wednesday, he apparently had a session with a 'Frank G'. Could this be the Frank from the note that came with the mask? Hattie had no way of knowing. She was half tempted to start poking through the rest of the diary to look for any other references to this Frank character, but she checked herself: a little light nosing was one thing, but she didn't believe in invading other people's privacy. She let herself out again, and went back down the stairs.

Unable to find Steve, and without anyone else giving her any more tasks, she told Davina and Kiki to go home and get some rest, but to keep their phones on in case something changed. Then she started planning her own day. Faced with an unexpectedly empty schedule, Hattie felt a bit disoriented at first. In the theatre one came to expect to have free time unexpectedly taken away at short notice, not handed out. She took herself home to her flat, but couldn't settle, so she went to the local greasy spoon and had a cup of tea, feeling uneasy.

In the end she decided to use the time to get ahead on prepping for her teaching at ACDA. After the show opened on Tuesday she'd begin tutoring at the school in earnest, and only be at the Tavistock in the evenings and for weekend matinees. The first thing she'd be teaching was the practical side of propping: allocating a budget, sourcing, knowing when and where to borrow, hire or buy. Donna Fletcher's notes suggested delivering the whole thing as a lecture, but Hattie wasn't much of an orator, and was sure she'd bore her students, and herself, half to death. So she decided to make it more interactive. Hattie decided she'd assign the students a script, a fictitious budget, and some notes from an imaginary designer, and get them to actually go and do the research and sourcing as if it was for real.

So she trotted back to the SM office at ACDA, and started busying herself choosing a section of a play, photocopying the script, writing fake rehearsal notes with requests from the director, and so on. It was rather tiresome work, and after a while she took herself off to the staff common room for a cup of tea. There was a kettle in her office, but she wanted a stretch of legs as much as she wanted a drink.

It being a Saturday, she was surprised not to find herself alone in the common room. Even more surprising was that the other occupant was sprawled, sleeping, on the grotty old sofa that one of the voice coaches had donated second-hand in aeons past.

The sleeper's face was directed away from Hattie, but she recognised the general shape of him. It could only be Rod. Attempting not to disturb him, Hattie backed out of the room, and tried to close the door slowly behind her. Unfortunately, the rusty old fire door mechanism – the common room being in one of the older parts of the building – decided to let out a prolonged squeal as Hattie attempted to inch it closed.

'If you're trying to be quiet, you're better off just letting it slam,' she heard Rod's voice rumble. 'It doesn't creak when it moves at full speed.'

Hattie re-entered the room.

'Sorry, Rod.'

Rod looked round and smiled, albeit somewhat blearily.

'Harriet Cocker, as I live and breathe,' he said.

'So it's true then? You really are living in the car park?' asked Hattie, wryly.

'Hmm? Oh, Lord no. No, just dropped in for a nap.'

Hattie frowned. 'I knew you liked to fall asleep in your classes here, but I didn't know you came in specially to do it at weekends too.'

Rod, sitting up clumsily, waved her words away.

'I was just passing through. I got up dreadfully early this morning so I could spend a few hours mucking round in a ditch in Richmond Park. By the time I was done I was knackered, so I thought I'd have a kip here before making the drive home.'

'Couldn't you have napped in your campervan?'

'Can't. It's too full of kit.'

Hattie shook her head.

'So what was it this time? Deer noises? Jogger footsteps?'

'Ring-necked parakeets. I'm trying to get some calls on a clean background, and the middle of Richmond Park at five in the morning is more or less the only place you can hope for a bit of quiet.'

'Ring-necked parakeets you say?' asked Hattie, feigning interest. She had been dimly aware that Rod liked to go out into the world and make sound recordings of a rather mundane kind, even though she couldn't right now remember exactly why he did it.

'Yes indeed. A vital component for my next narrative sound poem,' explained Rod, his eyes glinting with enthusiasm.

Hattie suppressed a grimace. Now she remembered: Rod had occasionally tried to make her listen to these 'poems' he created: half an hour or so of random-seeming sound effects mixed together, with the overall feel of some filler material on the back end of a commercially unsuccessful prog-rock concept album. Apparently each one told a story, but for the life of her Hattie could never work out what was happening.

'So this one is a story about birds, is it?'

'This one is a story about *loss*,' Rod corrected her. 'The parakeets are a symbol of displacement.'

'Oh right,' said Hattie, hoping her voice and face suggested a sincere interest that she in no way felt. 'And what's this poem for, then?'

Rod frowned.

'For? Hattie, my love, it's not *for* anything. The purpose of making a sound poem featuring ring-necked parakeet screeches is to have brought into existence a sound poem featuring ring-necked parakeet screeches. I'll get Robert to upload it to his... Myspace or whatever it is, and then there it shall remain forever. My gift to humanity.'

'Well, on behalf of humanity, I gratefully accept, but ask that maybe next time you consider just buying some chocolates instead. Cuppa?'

'Ooh yes, that would do very nicely.'

Hattie put the kettle on as Rod slowly shuffled and snorted and generally brought himself back to the land of the living.

'I was sorry to hear about Atlanta Greenwell,' he said. 'I read her obituary in *The Stage*. It was your show she was working on, wasn't it?'

'That's right,' replied Hattie. 'Did you know her?'

'Know her? Oh yes. Not, I must sadly concede, in the biblical sense. But I knew her very well back in the day. You know me, I'm normally immune to the twirlies, but I must admit there was a time when my young, naïve, innocent self held something of a torch for Atlanta.'

'Oh yes? Did you do anything about it?'

'I didn't get the chance. She was constantly surrounded by impenetrable walls of suitors. Not that she ever seemed to give them the time of day. Still, I remember her fondly. Heart attack, was it?'

The kettle boiled, and Hattie started pouring water into some mugs.

'Honestly, I don't know. The police say it was probably an accident, some people reckon it was suicide, and some people are even convinced it was murder.'

Rod's eyebrows raised.

'Oh my word. You don't get many murders in theatre. A few, mind. Suicides, though, you get a lot of them over the years.'

Hattie shrugged, and handed him his mug.

'It sounds like she had her demons, and for all her front she was a pretty private person. Who knows what was going on in her life?' she said.

'Who indeed. Speaking of which, what's going on in your life?'

'Apart from putting on a show with a dead cast member, in the theatre she died in? Oh, you know, same old. I've spent half the rehearsal period charging round on a fool's errand thanks to Keith… By the way, you don't know anything about padlocks, do you?'

'Padlocks? Well, I generally know which end to stick the key into, but apart from that…'

'I've been trying to work out how an aluminium-bodied padlock could have ended up… sort of melted.'

'Well, I suppose you could put it in an oven?'

'That's the thing, it was melted while it was still locking a cupboard shut. But the cupboard didn't have any scorch marks or anything.'

'And it was definitely melted?'

'Well, maybe dissolved. Crumbled. Warped and broken into blobby little pieces.'

Rod closed his eyes for a second.

'Oddly enough, that rings some sort of a bell. Only I can't quite… hmm. No, for now it's eluding me.'

He opened his eyes again.

'Leave it with me,' he said. 'Something's rattling round in the old noggin, but I can't quite get it out just now. That's the problem when you get to my age. Your mind is like a vast old library, but with the index cards missing. Tremendous amounts of information tucked away, but even if you know something is in there, it can take bloody ages to actually retrieve it.'

Hattie winced as, hearing Rod talk about getting old, she remembered the task she'd been putting off.

'So Rod,' she began uncomfortably, 'speaking of that great age of yours, have you given any thought to your retirement?'

Rod clasped his hands to his heart in mock shock, as though nursing a sudden wound.

'*Et tu, Hattus*? Why will no one believe me that I'm only thirty-five?'

'I know, I know, but… you must have thought about it.'

'What? Quit showbiz?' asked Rod in tones of horror, before adopting a much more haughty tone as he continued, 'I will retire at such time in the future as suits my purposes, no sooner and no later.'

'And what would it take for it to suit your purposes, then? I mean, how are things looking financially?'

'Harriet Cocker, you are beginning to pry,' chided Rod. 'Unless you are asking because you earnestly intend to leave Nick and shack up with me, and want reassurance that I can provide for you in your dotage, I must ask you to keep that glorious nose of yours out of my beeswax.'

Hattie gritted her teeth.

'I don't mean to be a busybody. It's just that… well, to be honest, Mark has been asking me to—'

'To spy on me? The very thought of—'

'To persuade you to retire, you daft old git!' retorted Hattie, losing patience. 'Your grumpy bugger act is wearing thin, and he wants you out the door. He thinks you're obstinate, out of touch, and tiptoeing round senility. And on two counts out of three I'm inclined to agree. So I was hoping I could persuade you to retire of your own volition before he finds an excuse to force you out.'

There was a silence.

'Sorry,' said Hattie after a while. 'I've been dreading this conversation. You're a good friend. And I owe you for the whole DBS check business. So I suppose I got a bit wound up.'

There was another silence.

Eventually Rod wrinkled his nose, took a slurp of tea.

'Well, at least I know now, I suppose. And I can see why he's keen to get rid of me. I'd be more than happy to oblige, you know, except that this is as much my home as anywhere else. There's more of *me* in my office downstairs than there is in my flat. He's not just asking me to stop working, he's asking me to give up my home.'

'Well,' replied Hattie with a slight smile, 'maybe he'd let you keep the basement. The new sound tutor would move into the new building, anyway. You could be ACDA's resident monster in the cellar.'

'Ooh yes,' said Rod, his eyes lighting up again. 'I could lurk in the stairwell and snatch all the pretty actresses who strayed too close.'

Hattie gave him a stern look.

'No Rod, you couldn't. And frankly, it's that kind of—'

'I know, I know,' he replied dismissively. 'You're no fun when you're serious. Can we please talk about something else now?'

Hattie didn't feel that everything had been said that needed to be, but nodded. Maybe she could bring the subject up again another time.

'How's Davina getting on?' asked Rod.

'She's doing a lot better. Did I tell you she'd been dumped a couple of weeks ago? I think it was something that started while she was at ACDA. I'm slightly worried it was with a staff member, but I'm not sure—'

'No, not ACDA,' cut in Rod.

'Eh?'

'Davina wasn't seeing anyone when she graduated. Certainly not a member of staff. She had that crush on Shane, but thankfully she never did anything about it. I have to say, I rather resent Shane for the number of students who can barely restrain from throwing themselves at him. No one throws themselves at me. Well, almost no one.'

'How do you know all this stuff?' asked Hattie, bewildered.

'Because I *listen*,' replied Rod. 'The students are talking about the tattered state of their love lives the entire time. All you have to do is settle back quietly and pay attention. It helps if they think you're asleep, mind,' he added with a wink.

'Well, aren't you full of surprises, you old devil. I never had you for a gossipy snoop.'

'What's the point of being around people at all if you can't do any gossipy snooping?' asked Rod, innocently.

'I don't know about Davina, then. Because she said working in this building made her uncomfortably close to her ex. So maybe she started seeing someone from here after graduation. Unless...' Hattie frowned. 'I suppose she could have been talking about how working on the *show* was putting her uncomfortably close to her ex. Hey, you don't suppose she got together with Miguel over the summer…?'

'Miguel? No, she'd already had her drama with him,' Rod snorted. 'They were both sound assistants on the same show in their first year. *Elements*, it was called, a daft piece about mad scientists. So they spent a lot of time together, within earshot of me. Miguel was constantly chatting to Davina, telling her about whatever his latest hobby was, completely oblivious that it didn't interest her in the slightest. Bless him, he was just excited to share the things that interested him, but Davina seemed to think that he was trying to *impress* her, and convinced herself that he had feelings for her. Then, and here she really came into her own, she convinced herself that he was worth a go, so to speak, so she made an advance, only to be shot down, because it turned out he wasn't interested in her in that way at all.'

'Ouch,' winced Hattie. 'Even by Davina's standards that sounds… painful.'

'Indeed. Miguel hasn't got the nous to let someone down particularly considerately. And Davina's not the sort of person who responds well to being rejected. She had a huge hissy fit, even dinged up one of my preamps, and then went on a half-hour rant at Miguel about how pathetic he was, how stupid his hobbies were, and how she had only ever felt pity for him. They patched things up a bit eventually, but I don't think he ever quite got over that. At any rate, he stopped being so quick to share things about his personal life from that day on.'

'I did notice he can be pretty cagey about his private life,' said Hattie. 'But anyway, sounds like it's very unlikely anything romantic blossomed between the two of them more recently. So I guess I'm at a loss about Davina's mysterious beau, then. Still, it's not my problem any more. I suppose I'm just being nosy.'

'A gossipy snoop, maybe?'

Hattie smiled. 'Maybe so. Well, I'd better be getting back to it.'

'Very well, my love. I should probably drive back to Epping. Oh, before you go… have you had much contact with the new intake yet?'

'Not much,' replied Hattie. 'I've taught a couple of sessions, though. Why?'

'There's one of them, Felix, who's a bit of a mystery.'

'Ah,' said Hattie. 'I think I'm ahead of you there, for once. It's a bit complicated, but I believe he's doing a little bit in the way of self-sabotage, looking for a way out.'

'I see,' said Rod. 'That would explain it.'

'Mark wants me to find a way of convincing him not to drop out.'

'Does he now? Well, you know I hold Mark in the *highest* esteem…'

'Don't worry, I'm not going to try to rope you into one of Mark's schemes.'

Rod rolled his eyes. 'Mind how you go, Hat.'

'You too, Rod.'

20

She was nearly done with her propping exercise prep when she got a text from Keith:

Emergency. Back to Tavistock NOW. Acknowledge receipt.

Ah, *there* it was. The weirdness of not having anything to do on fit-up day had been bound to last only so long. Hattie sent Keith back an immediate '*On my way: 30 mins*', packed up her bag and got moving. She wanted to ring and find out what was going on, but that would mean dawdling above ground where there was phone reception instead of getting straight onto the tube, so she decided to stifle her curiosity for the sake of an expedient arrival.

She found Keith on the pavement outside the Tavistock, in conversation with a grey-haired man in a smart suit. Keith looked uneasy, constantly shifting his weight and looking around. When he saw Hattie he immediately waved her over, cutting off his interlocutor mid-sentence.

'Hattie my darling! Good to see you, as always,' he beamed, although Hattie thought she could detect a slightly frantic edge to his wide smile. He was certainly behaving oddly: last time she'd seen him Keith had been so cross he'd literally turned his back on her. The warmth of his welcome could hardly be genuine.

'Hello, Keith. How's it going?'

'Great! It's going great! The fit-up's on track, I think. Er, Hattie, this is my very good friend Frank. Frank, this is Hattie.'

'Pleasure to meet you,' said the man, extending a hand, and Hattie recognised his voice at once.

'I think we've spoken before,' she said, carefully. 'Are you… Atlanta's brother?'

'Yes,' replied Frank, looking a little lost. Then recognition dawned. 'You… you rang me. After Atlanta…?'

'Yes, that's right,' said Hattie. 'Sorry, when Keith talked about a Frank I didn't make the connection: Atlanta had you down as Francis on the emergency contact form. I'm so sorry for your loss.'

'Thank you,' he said, with a small, sad, smile. 'She… always struggled with alcohol. I knew it would kill her in the end, I just didn't think it would do it so abruptly.'

Keith looked a little wrong-footed to discover that Hattie and Frank already had a connection, but he soon recovered himself, remarking solemnly: 'What a terrible business. Um, listen, Hattie, I do hate to impose, but Frank wanted to drop in and see how the fit-up was going. Is there any chance you could show him round? I'd do it myself but I must, must, *must* get to the bank in the next half hour. I wouldn't want Frank wandering round the theatre on his own. You never know what, or who, he might bump into!'

Keith let out a forced laugh, which Hattie reflexively mirrored, although she couldn't for the life of her think what the joke was. She studied Keith's face for a second. Was that a pleading look he was giving her? Was *this* the emergency? What an irritating and ridiculous man he was. But still, he was her boss.

'Of course, Keith,' she replied cheerily, 'I'd be more than happy to. Was there anything in particular you wanted to see, Frank?'

'No, no,' he replied. 'I just love the atmosphere in theatres when a new play is, you know, coming in. If you don't mind, what I really want to do is just sit in the auditorium somewhere out of the way. I'm very connected to this show, of course, not just financially but… well, emotionally.'

It was an odd request, but not an absurd one. There was something rather wonderful about a theatre fit-up, although Hattie seldom had the time to appreciate it.

'Of course. Come with me, I'll find a spot somewhere for us.'

'Marvellous,' replied Keith, checking the time on his phone. 'In which case, I'll leave you to it!'

And with that he half strode, half jogged away down the street, leaving a somewhat bemused Hattie to usher Frank inside.

They made their way through the pub into the auditorium. It was dark, apart from a single rectangle of light on the stage, in the middle of which stood Carrie, one foot extended. The rectangle wobbled gently.

'Hold on… there,' came Laura's voice from the top of a ladder halfway up the aisle in the audience. 'That right?'

'No, it's slipped again. My foot, I want the downstage edge right by my foot. See?'

'Oh bugger it, this barn door is knackered. Give me a sec and I'll see if I can find one that stays in place.'

Laura descended the ladder and scurried off into a corner, as Carrie made impatient faces on the stage. Hattie led Frank off to one side, where they'd be out of the way, and ushered him towards a row of chairs. He sat down one seat in from the end, evidently expecting Hattie to sit next to him, so she did. Her phone buzzed gently, and she saw she had another message from Keith:

Do NOT let anyone talk to him. Especially Steve.

Mystified, Hattie put her phone away before Frank could see it. What on *earth* was Keith playing at?

'We'll have to be quiet,' she whispered, 'so we don't disturb the focus.'

'Of course,' he whispered back. 'You know, I sometimes wish I'd been a lighting designer.'

'Oh yes? What line of work are you in?'

'Oh, private equity, M and A, it's all very dull. But I don't do much of it any more.'

They sat in silence for a while. Not very much was happening with the lighting, and Hattie began to feel awkward, so she asked quietly, 'So did you know Keith through Atlanta, then?'

'In a roundabout way, yes. Dame Joan was a good pal of mine. I got to know her through Lala... Atlanta, that is... originally, before they had their falling out. And you couldn't spend much time with Joan without getting a healthy dose of Keith too. I became a supporter of the theatre over the years, so we've kept in touch since Joan died.'

'I see. I'd... I'd heard that Joan and Atlanta didn't get on. I hope that wasn't too awkward for you.'

Frank laughed out loud, and then quickly put a hand to his mouth to stifle the sound.

'Sorry. It's just that... well, I'm afraid it really was rather awkward, you see, because what they fell out over was actually... me. Lala was always very protective of me,' he explained softly, 'especially after I followed her to London. She had it in her head that Joan was leading me on and trying to take advantage of me, financially that is. Nonsense, of course, we were just good friends, even after her divorce. But with drink taken Lala couldn't help but make accusations, and Joan wasn't exactly the sort to back down. One night it got completely out of hand, Joan walked away with a slapped cheek, my sister got a pint of beer poured all over her dress, and they never spoke again. I suppose they were both such big personalities, they were either going to be the best of friends or the worst of enemies. I tried to patch things up between them, but I never could.'

'I'm surprised Atlanta agreed to do a show at the Tavistock, then,' said Hattie.

'Ah. Well, yes, that was actually my idea. I thought it would be a good chance for her to finally bury the hatchet. A bit late, given Joan had already died, but better than never. She grumbled, but I won her over eventually.'

He sighed sadly.

'I was so looking forward to seeing her in *Love's Labour's Lost*. It's probably my favourite play in the canon.'

'Excuse me!' came a petulant voice from the stage. 'Could we have quiet in the auditorium please?'

Hattie looked up. Carrie was directing a very pointed glare at the corner they were sitting in. Frank held up a guilty hand.

'Sorry!' he hissed in an exaggerated stage whisper.

They sat in silence, watching as, one by one, Carrie dictated the exact positioning of every light in the auditorium, often extracting curses and complaints from Laura as she tried to make finicky adjustments at the top of her rather wobbly ladder. It was repetitive to the point of tedium, but Frank seemed enthralled. What a strange man, she thought. Charming, but strange.

Eventually Keith reappeared.

'There you are, my lovelies,' he said in a hushed voice. 'Any excitements while I was gone?'

'No, we've just been sitting here, enjoying the show,' replied Frank.

'Good. Excellent. Hattie, I'll let you get on, but could I borrow you for just a second before you go?'

She nodded, waved a friendly goodbye to Frank, and followed Keith over to the hallway leading to the side exit. She noticed that he kept the door ajar and positioned himself so as to have a clear line of sight on Frank.

'Thank you,' he said quietly, and somewhat uncomfortably. Keith wasn't the sort of man to whom gratitude came naturally.

'For what? I don't really understand what the emergency was.'

Keith sighed. 'It's him. He's the emergency. He turned up out

239

of the blue wanting to see the theatre, and I had an appointment I couldn't skip. But if I let him wander round here by himself he might start talking to people, right?'

'Is that so bad?'

'It is if one of the people he talks is the… the person who sent that note.'

He huffed and scowled for a second, then, seeming to reach a decision, carried on: 'Look, you have to keep this completely secret. You know I said that the note was a threat? That they're trying to hurt me? Well, what I didn't tell you is that the way they want to hurt *me* is by hurting *him*. Frank has been a patron of the house for a long time, and he's got a whole history with Joan, and there are some things that would break his heart to find out. Don't ask me what they are because I promised never to tell *anyone*.'

'But how would that hurt you?'

'Because not only does Frank give a lot of money direct to us as a patron, he's also about to give us a rather large loan, on very favourable terms. The sort of terms that a house like this would never be offered by a bank. That's why the mask matters: it's the collateral we're using to secure the loan. I thought that our anonymous friend took it just because it was worth a lot. But what that note tells me is that they wanted to take it to scupper the loan. After I told everyone I was considering getting the police involved they must have decided it was too risky to hold on to it. But they could still threaten the deal by spilling the secrets about Joan's past to Frank. The only thing I don't know yet is whether they intend to follow through no matter what, out of spite, or whether this is blackmail and they're going to come up with a set of demands soon.'

Hattie took a moment to consider. There was a lot to take in, and she wasn't entirely sure it all made sense. Meanwhile, Laura and Carrie were continuing to fuss over lighting angles, Miguel was pottering round taping down cables, and Frank was sitting in the middle of it all, looking on.

'Hang on,' she said, after a second. 'So you're saying the thief is someone *in the company* who not only knew about Frank's intended loan, but also knew... this terrible secret about Joan that would drive Frank away from the whole thing?'

Keith nodded solemnly.

'It would have to be someone who... look, you're *sure* it wasn't Davina?' he asked, with a sudden intensity.

'I've got photo proof she was on the wrong side of town when the mask was taken. Why?'

'Fine. And her little school friend? Miguel?'

'Was playing *Dungeons and Dragons* that whole evening in a pub.'

'Of course he was, the little weirdo. Then, look, I'm as confused as you are. It must have been someone who knows a lot about the theatre, had plenty of time to do some digging, and doesn't have a clear story for the Sunday night. It could be one of the cast, maybe someone who got pally with Atlanta. *She'd* have known all about it. On the other hand, if it was one of the crew, I'm beginning to think it has to be—'

There was a metal clunk sound just outside in the yard. Keith froze, and then slowly pushed open the side door, which, as usual, was on the latch. He poked his head out, and then said, with an icy politeness: 'What on earth are you doing skulking round the bins, my love?'

He then leaned back and out of the way, as Steve appeared through the doorway.

'Well?' asked Keith.

'Sandwich wrapper,' was all Steve said. He glared at Keith, then, seeing Hattie, gave her a suspicious look, and stomped into the auditorium.

Hattie went home. What a week, she thought to herself. What a month. And in the safety of her flat she took stock. Her hip was fairly constantly giving her grief after all the comings and goings of the past few days. She was feeling grotty, in part because she'd barely been eating. There was never time for a proper meal: at best you snaffled a chilled, overpriced sandwich from a packet, at worst you made do with a cup of tea and some sweets. Plus now apparently someone was having a go at blackmail and attempting to sabotage the show for entirely incomprehensible reasons.

And even before she'd started to make progress on the first mission Mark had given her at ACDA, to get Rod to leave, he'd gone and given her a harder one, to get Felix to stay. Then on top of it all, that wretched policewoman seemed determined to ruin her ACDA prospects anyway, by dragging up a bunch of muck from thirty years ago.

All in all, from a holistic perspective, it was fair to say that Hattie felt she very much deserved and would like a nice relaxing spliff now please. But tomorrow was the tech rehearsal, and while today's get-in and fit-up had been oddly easy, it was safe to assume that the tech wouldn't be. She needed to be sharp, and the rule was no smoking unless you had the next day free.

But God, she needed *something* to take the edge off.

So she poured a large glass of wine, filled a big bowl with some ice cream she found at the back of the freezer, put on Rick Astley's *Love Songs*, and ran a bath. She hoped that in aggregate these would have enough of an impact to approximate the relaxing effect of a joint or two.

It almost worked.

By the time she had drunk, eaten, listened, bathed, and emerged, towelling robe-clad, from the bathroom, she felt much less sick of the world than she had before. But there was still something missing. She sighed, then pulled out her phone and called Nick, planning on leaving him a voicemail.

To her surprise, he actually picked up the phone.

''Allo, cockatoo.'

'Don't you have a show on?'

'Min-Su's on the board tonight. I promised to let him have a go. So I've got the evening off.'

'Oh yeah? What are you up to?'

'I'm in the pub.'

'Who with?'

'Well, there's a bartender, a couple in the corner, a—'

'Oh you sad old man, sitting in a pub all by yourself.'

'I'm having the time of my life! They've got proper pickled eggs and all. I've got a paper, my phone, and a pint of a charming little local ale called Copper Needle.'

'You're a simple man, you are,' said Hattie, then realised she was sounding unnecessarily unpleasant, so added, 'and all the better for it.'

'Don't you get soppy on me, my love. I'm not nearly drunk enough for that. Hey! I've got some gossip for you. About your director. Hashi Whatshisface.'

'Oh really?'

'Mm-hmm. Our new SM just finished a show at the National, got me all the juicy stuff. Did you ever wonder why an up-and-coming director, who's just had a hit show transfer and got rave reviews, ends up doing a show at a crappy little fringe venue as his next gig?'

'It's not a crappy... but yes, I did wonder.'

'Well. Got blackballed, didn't he?'

'Blackballed?'

'Do I mean blackballed? You know, rejected. Shunned by the community.'

'You mean blacklisted.'

'That's the one! Black lists, blue balls, I can't keep up with this stuff. Simple man, remember?'

'What do you mean he got blacklisted?' Hattie pressed, her curiosity piqued.

'Just what I said. He pissed off the wrong people. Well, specifically, he was badmouthing Kathy Meacham, and the stupid bugger did it in front of her.'

'Really? What did he say?'

Hattie was intrigued. Kathy Meacham was a very talented, well-established director, known for a fierce temper and intolerance of fools.

'Apparently he and his pals were getting drunk in the National bar, and he starts giving off about how she's lost her touch and is just regurgitating the same show over and over. Which, well, you can argue the point, but I don't think he said it in a very nice way. At all.'

That sounded believable, thought Hattie. Hashi's tongue tended towards the vituperative at the best of times.

'Anyway, what he *didn't* notice was that she was sitting quietly just behind him with her entourage. He eventually notices her, but doesn't back down, they get into some massive slanging match in front of *everyone*, and don't exactly part ways as friends. And, well, you know how connected she is, especially with the money-men. She lets it be known that he has incurred her displeasure, and suddenly every producer and theatre-owner in London decides it's probably better if Hashi Hassan's name isn't on their next poster. So, there it is.'

'Crikey,' said Hattie.

She took a couple of seconds to digest this information. As she did, she heard a wet munching on the other end of the line.

'You always eat that loud?'

'Only when I want to make you jealous. These really are delicious eggs. They've got bits of dill and all.'

'I wonder why the Tavistock took him on, then?' Hattie mused.

'Well, they were never really part of the London establishment, were they? I can't imagine the sorts of people Kathy hangs round with were ever going to fund Keith's shows anyway. Probably thought Hashi's reputation with the critics was worth it. And poor Hashi, the Tavistock was really the best he could get.'

'It's really not that bad.'

'Really? 'Cos I heard they couldn't even afford to hire decent stage managers any more. Had to rely on grumpy old farts with busted hips.'

'Oh you cheeky bugger!'

They nattered on in their usual way, and when Hattie put the phone down she was in a much better mood. The story about the National gave her pause, though. So, rising star Hashi accidentally torpedoes his career just as it's getting started, because he incurs the wrath of the establishment. It wouldn't be the first time that had happened in the West End. Still, he's desperate to find a next gig, and so has to accept a contract at the Tavistock on Keith's terms, which include picking from a weird list of plays that just happens to include Frank's favourite Shakespeare, and being forced to cast an actress who just happens to be Frank's sister. Keith's no idiot, he'll have known that the choice of show and the forced casting won't help make a success of the show, critically or commercially, but he insists anyway... which means that he's prepared to do absolutely anything to keep Frank sweet. The theatre must be on a complete knife-edge financially. Keith dropping everything to get to the bank earlier had seemed bizarre; maybe it made more sense if the accounts were deeply in the red and he was having to take emergency manoeuvres to avoid bankruptcy...

And this was the theatre that Hattie was hoping to depend on for future income? The outlook's not good, cockatoo, is it? But, as Nick said, who else is going to hire a grumpy old fart with a busted hip who can't pass a background check?

Act Five

21

The technical rehearsal inverts the natural order of things, in that, for once, the actors aren't the focus. During the tech they are simply placeholders whose job it is to stand in the right spots at the right times, holding the right props, so that the techies can weave their own bits of the narrative around them. This is the one time when the stage manager can boss the cast around rather than vice versa. Meanwhile, sitting in the auditorium the director makes decisions in conjunction with the designers, and those get relayed back to the crew who try their best to enact what has been asked for in ways that can be repeated during actual productions. The actors typically get a minimum of three weeks to rehearse. The techies often get less than a day.

– From The Art and Craft of Stage Management
by Donna Fletcher, Chapter 9: The Tech

A decent night's sleep had Hattie feeling in fine form by the time she arrived at the Tavistock the next morning. This was good, because tech rehearsals were stressful at the best of times, and this one promised to be as fraught as any.

The day started with the 'walkaround', when Hattie led the cast through the theatre, pointing out fire escapes, toilets, entrances, exits and so on. It being early on a Sunday morning, it was only to be expected that everyone was fairly quiet and subdued... until Hattie took them backstage.

'Now, here's the men's dressing room. I'm afraid it's fairly tight back here. There's one desk for every three actors, and I've put up names of which trio is assigned to which desk. Be aware that the ladies will need to come through this room to get to the stage, so try to keep yourselves decent.

'Now, ladies, if you follow me through here you'll see you've got a *little* bit more space, but—'

'Wait, what's through there?' asked Bums suspiciously.

'Um, your dressing room,' replied Hattie.

'What, the *actual* one? The one where... you know?'

Hattie had been hoping against hope this wouldn't come up. Idiot, she cursed herself. You don't rely on hope. You make a plan. Now she had to try to make the best of it.

'Yes,' she said solemnly. 'But the place has been thoroughly cleaned, and—'

'But I mean, a woman *died* in there. We can't possibly... *be* in there. I mean... right?'

Bums looked round at her castmates for support. There were, frustratingly, a couple of concerned nods of agreement.

'While I understand it's a very delicate subject, and not wishing to trivialise anyone's feelings, I'm afraid at a certain point we have to be practical,' said Hattie, trying to sound sympathetic but firm. 'There aren't any other changing rooms to be had, and you need somewhere to be when you're backstage. I'm sorry that I didn't bring this up sooner.'

Bums frowned for a moment, but then, to her credit and Hattie's surprise, she nodded.

'OK,' she said. 'OK. Practical. Professional. We can do this.'

The other ladies took their cue from Bums and they all took a few minutes to settle into the dressing room, giving Hattie a chance to give a big sigh of relief. When they re-emerged, it was time to give The Speech.

The goal of The Speech, as given by SMs at the start of technical rehearsals since time immemorial, was to point out that, just for today, everyone needed to stop thinking of the show as an artistic, creative entity, and rather think of it as an intricate clockwork machine. It was to demand, gently but firmly, that the actors see themselves not as artistes, not as performers, but merely as good little cogs, who only spin when they're told to, and are prepared to rotate in whatever direction is required by the spindles and gimbals around them. Hattie had delivered it a hundred times before, and could more or less do it on autopilot these days.

But her autopilot faltered and stalled once Keith's interruptions began.

'Please remember,' Hattie was saying, 'that for the crew, today is our only chance to rehearse. So be patient, because we will have to do things a few times over, and from where you're standing it may not be clear exactly why something needs repeating. So if you're asked to stop, please just wait quietly, and you'll be told where we'll be starting from again. And—'

'And no wandering off, please,' cut in Keith, who had materialised at the side of the auditorium. 'If you're supposed to be onstage, stay onstage. If you're supposed to be backstage, stay backstage.'

'Er... yes, that's right. If you're not due onstage, please remain in the dressing room. We may skip ahead suddenly, and it'll hold up the whole process if we have to go looking for you.'

'So that means, stay out of the pub, stay out of the office upstairs, don't go walking about on the street. Stay where we can see you. I mean it,' growled Keith, eyeing the assembled actors suspiciously.

'I…' faltered Hattie. 'Well, anyway, I know it can be boring and frustrating, but I promise, the best thing you can do to support the show is to just be patient—'

'And supporting the show means supporting the theatre. If the theatre isn't open, the show can't be performed, and it's your career that impacts. So think very carefully about whether you want to cause problems.'

'Keith, could I have a word?' asked Hattie, no longer able to contain her impatience at his relentless interjections.

'Sorry, can't stop,' he replied dismissively. 'That was all I needed to say. I'll be upstairs for a bit, then I'll come back down. To keep an eye on things,' he ended, ominously, before slipping out of the side door in the direction of his office.

'Well, that wasn't suspicious at all,' muttered Steve from his seat, quietly enough that the cast onstage wouldn't hear.

With no more interruptions from Keith, Hattie stumbled through the tail end of her speech, and the technical rehearsal got under way.

'All right,' said Hashi. 'Now, for the opening, I'm thinking we need a big, bold moment. Sort of, house lights snap down, then immediately a quick sort of sound and lighting *oomph*, and then lights straight up into Emile's "*Let fame*", blah blah blah… OK? Ready? Let's go!'

This prompted a chorus of complaints from more or less the entire technical crew. Raven said she thought Hashi's idea was too abrupt, aesthetically speaking; Carrie asked drily for clarification on what counted as a 'lighting oomph'; Kiki pointed out that whatever happened, time needed to be provided for the cast to actually get on to the stage before the lights came up; and Miguel, who only two days before had been told that the only sound cue would be a little light music as the audience first walked in, started flapping about a lack of subwoofer speakers to deliver the bass frequencies required for true 'oomph'.

The commotion continued for several seconds, until Steve, losing patience, roared out, 'Oi! Quiet everyone!'

As they all grumbled into silence, Hashi could be heard whinging plaintively '... the point in a tech rehearsal if I can't voice some opinions about the technical elements of the show?'

'Well, in more *traditional* production processes,' said Steve, completely unemotionally, 'it's customary for the director to discuss these things in advance with the technical team, so they have a chance to prepare accordingly.'

'Interestingly, that's why it's called the tech *rehearsal*, not the tech *make-it-all-up-from-scratch*,' put in Laura quietly from behind the lighting desk.

'I'm sure,' cut in Hattie, before anyone had a chance to respond to Laura's snark, 'that we can find a way of giving Hashi what he wants that works within the restraints we're working under...'

With considerable grousing and grumbling on all sides, a compromise was eventually reached. Hattie didn't let herself get too worked up about any of this: whether or not Hashi was being particularly difficult, it was nonetheless *always* the case that in the technical rehearsal the director, faced with the first sight of what the show might actually look like onstage, would start asking for things to be different, in ways that the technical teams would, as a knee-jerk response, want to dismiss as ridiculous and/or impossible. In many ways the technical rehearsal was just one long series of conflict resolutions. The stage manager became a sort of mediator-cum-group therapist, gently encouraging the rest along the path to reconciliation. It was all part of the job.

The rest of Act one was fairly painless. There was a little bit of faff over entrances and exits, but other than that, once the lights were up, not much of interest happened from a technical perspective. The transition from scene one to scene two went ahead without issue, and even the transition into Act two was relatively straightforward, with just a little bit of time devoted to tweaking the lighting state. Hattie was beginning to think that maybe it was all beginning to come together, when:

'Hang on... Where's my Rosaline?'

'Bums?'

'Miss Morley-Smith to the stage please!'

After an awkward silence, Davina appeared from the wings.

'Um... she says she can't. She's in the dressing room. I think we might need some... help...'

Hashi groaned, and there was a fair amount of eye-rolling from the cast.

'Oh, for God's sake,' came a mutter from one of the men, perhaps Adam, but Hattie wasn't sure.

Hattie cursed herself for jinxing it with her optimism, and called out: 'Ladies and gentlemen, let's take a fifteen-minute break there, then. Please could the cast stay *in* costume, and for now please don't go into the dressing rooms. You're welcome to grab something to eat or drink, but do please cover your costumes to avoid spills and stains.'

Then she hauled herself up onto the front of the stage, and allowed Davina to lead her back to the dressing room. She found Bums crouching in a corner of the room, hugging her knees, looking teary.

'So what's going on, then?' she asked quietly.

'... hnf-cuhhh...' gasped Bums raggedly.

'I'm sorry, what was that?'

'I'm...s-scared...' she eventually replied.

'Of what?'

There was a pause, then Bums said, in a small voice, 'Atlanta.'

She then started sobbing afresh.

'It's all right, my love, it's all right. Take a sip of water. There. And here's a tissue. Now, when you're ready, can you tell me what you mean?'

Bums took some steadying breaths.

'I can feel her presence. I mean, I can really *feel* it. I can feel the pain, I can feel her… un-completeness. She was murdered before her time, she's still here, and she's watching us. She's watching me. I'm scared of what she's going to do to me.'

Hattie considered her options. If she didn't find a way of calming her down, Bums was on track to run out screaming soon and never return, which would completely torpedo the whole show. They were supposed to be holding their press night in a little over 48 hours, after all. Hattie didn't think she'd be amenable to rational argument. There was only one thing for it, and that was to lie completely:

'I spoke to the coroner yesterday,' she said. 'He assured me that they've found a blood clot in her brain. It wasn't murder, it was a stroke. That's all. Of course it's sad that she went before her time, but remember: Atlanta lived for the theatre. The place where she died is the place she loved more than anywhere else in the world.'

Her words didn't seem to be having much of an effect, so Hattie, with a deep breath, took things up a notch.

'And by the way, you're not the only one who can feel her presence. I can sense her too. And I agree, I think she's got unfinished business. But you know what? I think that business is this show. She's hanging around, just until we open, watching to make sure that we do it justice. I've seen it happen before. She's watching over us, and she's rooting for us.'

Bums looked up.

'Really?' she asked, hopefully.

'I'm sure of it. I'm a very spiritual person, and I'm used to reading the signs,' said Hattie, firmly and completely untruthfully. *Acting's not so hard after all, is it?* she thought to herself.

Bums sniffed, frowned, nodded, and picked herself up.

'Well then,' she said, a new note of resolve entering her voice. 'Let's do it for Atlanta.'

*

That nearly did it. That was nearly enough to keep a lid on the whole Atlanta issue. The problem, in the end, was Steve.

Or rather, the problem was how Steve reacted to Keith. Keith, who over the course of the Sunday afternoon, kept sidling up to members of the cast and needling them. He would ask them about how well they knew the theatre, how often they'd been, and inevitably would then demand to know where they had been two weekends previously, surrounding all of his questions with vague threats about how he could use his 'influence' and 'connections' to damage anyone who crossed him.

For Hattie, who understood broadly what Keith was trying to do, it was just rather annoying to have Keith disrupting the rehearsal. For the actors, it was a deeply unsettling experience. Some of those who remembered his cryptic announcement at the production meeting the previous week put two and two together and realised he was all but accusing them of thievery of some sort. The rest invariably inferred, from the fact that he was asking them for their whereabouts on the weekend Atlanta died, that he was all but accusing them of *murder*, which, as well as putting several noses out of joint, re-confirmed all the cast theories that Atlanta had indeed been killed by someone. Hattie could see Bums looking more and more uncomfortable as the day wore on.

Eventually, when Keith started trying to quiz the actors *as* they were standing onstage waiting to deliver their lines, Hattie paused the tech and called him over.

'I need you to stop disrupting my rehearsal,' she told him. 'That's an order.'

She knew he was her superior, but the technical rehearsal had placed her in a temporary position of power, which gave her the courage to stand up to him.

'Of course, ducky, of course,' he replied. 'Just a few more to speak to. I'll be ever so discreet.'

'No Keith, leave my cast alone,' said Hattie awkwardly but forcefully, loud enough for the people around her to hear.

Keith just rolled his eyes and walked back in the direction of the stage.

Hattie was about to go after him when, from the seating bank behind her, Steve called out, 'How did the auditions go, Keith?'

Keith turned round, confused.

'Which auditions?'

'Two weeks ago. You were doing auditions right here, weren't you? Remind me what show that was for?'

Now everyone had stopped what they were doing and were listening to this bizarre exchange.

'Just something we're putting together,' Keith replied stiffly.

'Really? Because I've spoken to every show that's on this season, and none of them were doing auditions that night.'

'Steve, the amount that goes on here that you don't know about is considerably—'

'I'm just saying,' bulldozed on Steve, 'that it's a bit strange that two weeks ago you were apparently here doing something with other people, but there were no other people around, and now you're intent of grilling all my cast members to confirm that *they* weren't around to see what happened here either. Worried that someone saw that you weren't auditioning anyone at all? That you were actually doing something else entirely?'

Keith stared at him in open-mouthed fury, but couldn't seem to come up with a response. Eventually he raised his hand and pointed viciously at Steve.

'*Not helpful!*' he barked, then, vibrating with anger, stalked out.

In the silence that followed you could practically hear every mind in the room whirring to process Steve's speech. All was still for a second, as no one knew how to respond. Then Hashi broke the spell with a hushed, delighted 'Oh my God!', and suddenly everyone was talking at once. Steve had discovered that Keith had murdered Atlanta. Steve was working with the police. Scratch that, Steve *was* an undercover police officer. Keith was running an illegal drug ring from the theatre. Or maybe he was a serial killer. Keith was about to be arrested. Keith mustn't be allowed to escape.

The men in the cast suddenly looked on the verge of forming an impromptu posse to round up Keith and detain him until the authorities arrived. Bums was back in tears, Hashi was wringing his hands in glee, and Steve was sitting, silently, his face turning progressively angrier shades of purple, until finally he stood up and stalked out.

Hattie was left with no choice.

'LADIES AND GENTLEMEN,' she bellowed, as loud as she possibly could. By some miracle, her voice managed to carry over the hubbub, and everyone quietened down and looked round.

'May I remind you that in this room we are all professionals, and it is our duty to behave as such! We are here to do the technical rehearsal, and we don't take a break until I say so. Did I say we were taking a break? No! So let's carry on.'

'But Keith—' began Emile.

'Keith is heading upstairs to carry on doing his job, and it's our duty to carry on doing ours,' Hattie declared.

She looked at their faces. She didn't have them. Not quite. She could see that if she tried to simply ignore what had just happened they would rebel. A compromise was necessary.

'Now,' she continued grudgingly. 'Clearly some questions have been raised here that need answering. So I'm going to go upstairs and have a calm conversation with Keith. In the meantime, Kiki is going to continue running the tech, *and God help any one of you who doesn't do exactly what she says!*'

Hattie surprised herself with the aggressiveness of her tone, but it seemed to do the trick at least. Satisfied that something was being done, everyone more or less calmed down enough to at least go through the motions of readying themselves to carry on. And once they were up and running again they'd get caught up in the process, Hattie was sure. Anxious not to upset the apple cart any more, she quickly slipped out to the hallway by the side entrance and closed the door behind her. Then, with a deep breath, she made her way up the stairs.

22

Hattie knocked on the office door, and received only silence in response. She knocked a second time, and then, still receiving no reply, turned the handle and entered.

Keith was sitting hunched over his desk, a furious frown on his face, pounding away at his laptop. Robin was hovering by the kettle, looking alarmed.

Keith glanced up as Hattie walked in.

'Sod off,' he snarled. She didn't oblige. Robin looked pleadingly across at Hattie, but she ignored him.

'Well now,' she said, after a while. 'I've got a rather agitated company downstairs. And it's messing with my tech rehearsal. With you going round one by one and riling everyone up, and then Steve making his speech like he did, everyone's a bit aerated.'

'That is not my problem,' replied Keith coldly.

'I'm not so sure about that. For one thing, if we can't get through the tech we won't open the show on time, and that's lost revenue for you. For another, with everyone on edge about Atlanta, there's a group of strapping young men down there who are on the verge of coming up here and lynching you, to be honest.'

'Oh for goodness's sake, are you actually accusing me of killing her now?'

Keith's hands, Hattie realised, were shaking. And he was looking very pale.

'No I'm not,' she replied. 'But some of them are thinking it. So I think it's time for us all to have an open discussion about that weekend, so that I can tell everyone what's what, calm them down, and get on with my show. Does that sound fair?'

Keith made no reply, which Hattie decided to interpret as tacit acquiescence.

'So... these auditions, the ones happening between half past nine and half past ten over that weekend. Were they taking place in the auditorium?'

Keith remained silent.

'Because if so, then on the Saturday night you'd have been *right next to* the room where—'

'We were upstairs. In here,' said Keith abruptly.

'All right,' said Hattie slowly. 'It's just that you told me that, on the Sunday night at least, you *weren't* up here after nine o'clock, which is why you didn't notice that the lock had been broken.'

Keith was silent for a good few seconds. Then he turned to Robin.

'Rob my love, be a good boy and bugger off for the day, would you? I'll call you later.'

'Oh, um...' said Robin, looking confused.

'*Now* please,' Keith commanded, and Robin, gathering up his jacket and satchel, did as he was asked.

Keith waited until his footsteps on the stairs had receded before continuing.

'He's a lovely boy,' he said with an air of forced casualness. 'Lovely but a bit naïve. Doesn't understand that we grown-ups don't always follow the same rules as the young ones.'

He made no further comment, so Hattie prompted him again.

'So what was happening on those evenings?'

'You know, there was a time when stage managers like you were very literally the servants of people like me. You'd have called me "sir" if you knew what was good for you, and I wouldn't have to put up with any lip. A better time, if you ask me. Actually—'

'Keith…'

'Oh come *on*, Hattie, what do you expect late-night one-on-one "auditions" with a man like me to be?' Keith snapped. 'If you must know, on the Saturday night a charming young man called Cosimo was playing the role of a well-endowed rent-boy providing much-needed relief for an overworked artistic director. And on the Sunday night, a slightly less charming and less young woman called Zelda, whose hourly rates were therefore somewhat lower, was attempting to impress me with her ability to play an instrument colloquially known as a "rusty trombone", and if you don't know what that means then trust me, you don't want me to tell you.'

He closed his eyes and sat back in his chair.

'We were up here, nowhere near Atlanta. I always bring them up here. The point is that on the Sunday I was *far* too distracted by Zelda's spirited performance to pay a blind bit of notice to the padlock in the corner. We'd barely made it through the door when she got started.'

There was an awkward silence, and rather too much colour returned to Keith's cheeks.

'I… see,' said Hattie eventually. 'I hadn't realised your tastes were so… diverse.'

Keith couldn't help himself: he burst out laughing.

'That's one way of putting it. My appetites are wide-ranging, and rather hard to sate.'

'And your… date… on the Saturday night. Would he be able to confirm that that's what happened?'

'Oh, he already has,' said Keith. 'I had to give over his number to the police. That woman Burakgazi insisted on getting contact details for everyone who was in the theatre. Digging up his number from my little black book while PC Plodette peered over my shoulder was a uniquely humiliating experience, I can tell you.'

'Well then,' said Hattie. 'I can see why you were a little bit coy about what you were up to. Thank you for clearing that up.'

'You're very welcome. And now that you've had your fun humiliating me, it's time to start asking the real questions, isn't it?'

'Such as?'

'Such as how on earth did Steve know about my "auditions", and what the bloody hell was he playing at, mouthing off like that?'

'I think I might know the answer to the first part,' said Hattie, and she told him about the previous day, when Steve had been nowhere to be found, and she had heard noises up in the office and found Keith's diary open on his desk.

'Ha!' snorted Keith. 'The idea of big Steve being disturbed by you and, what, hiding under my desk while you hunt around for rats in here? It's just too precious. Still, it's certain now: he's trying to collect as much dirt on me as possible. So it is him, and it is blackmail.'

'You think this proves he took the mask?'

'Yes,' said Keith, exasperatedly. 'I just said that.'

'But it doesn't make sense. He was having a go at you just now because you were buggering up the tech rehearsal. If he was really trying to engineer the downfall of the whole theatre, why would he care about the tech? I just don't believe it.'

'Then we'll just have to agree to disagree,' replied Keith coolly. 'Now, will you please bugger off out of my office so I can get some actual work done? And, Hattie, I'm going to trust that you're going to find a way of getting your rabble back in order without being *indiscreet*, understand?'

'I'll see what I can do, Keith.'

*

She made it out of the office, down the stairs, and halfway along the corridor, before the absurdity of this whole encounter caught up with her and Hattie found herself having to suppress guffaws of laughter. Unfortunately, as soon as she walked back into the auditorium, all eyes turned to her, and whatever had been happening in the tech rehearsal ground to a halt.

'What's so funny then?' asked Hashi.

'Oh lordy,' said Hattie, desperately trying to keep a straight face. 'Nothing. Let's just say that I've established very reliably that Keith was otherwise engaged when Atlanta... you know. I'm afraid I can't say anything more without betraying his confidence. He apologises for acting a bit strangely today, and assures me it won't happen again.'

As an explanation it combined fudge, hedge, and, with respect to the apology bit, outright mistruth, but it seemed easier than to try to get into the details. Of course, the whispers and theories and gossip started among the crew and cast immediately, but that was fine: chatter and scandal were part and parcel of theatre. So long as no one was actually accusing anyone else of murder, Hattie was confident they could press on with the rehearsal. At the end of the day, that was all she wanted, all she *ever* wanted: to get the job done.

So they carried on, and over the course of a gruelling afternoon they made it all the way through to Act five, scene two, the final scene in the play, more or less on schedule. Steve never returned, Carrie and Laura bickered, Hashi made snarky remarks about some of the props, Miguel curled up on the back row of seats and fell asleep, Kiki got impatient with the actors continually getting confused over their lines and needing prompting, but they got there.

Unfortunately, *when* they got there, they hit a bit of a snag.

'Ladies and gentlemen, we're going to go from Holofernes's

last line in act five scene one, "*Most dull, honest Dull.*" Stand by please... and when you're ready, thank you.'

'*Most dull, honest Dull! To our sport, away,*' said one actor, and he and five other men capered off stage left.

'And lights down...' called out Hashi from the auditorium, as Laura pressed the appropriate button on the lighting desk, 'then the ladies come on, and take a beat... And lights up there.'

The lights came up slowly onstage.

'Does that timing work for you?' asked Carrie.

'Yes, glorious, marvellous,' nodded Hashi distractedly. 'Um... where are my ladies?'

The stage was, indeed, completely bare.

A head poked out from the wings.

'Sorry,' she called, awkwardly. 'We just... didn't know where to come on.'

'Right there is fine. That's the side you left on, so that's the side you can come back on from,' said Hashi, encouragingly.

'No, I mean... we don't know where to come on *to*. We haven't blocked this scene.'

Hattie shot an alarmed look over to Kiki, who shrugged resignedly.

'I suppose they didn't get to it yesterday,' she said quietly.

There were various groans and mutters from the assembled crew.

'Not to worry,' said Hashi. 'We've got plenty of time to work out the details tomorrow before the dress rehearsal.'

'With all due respect,' said Laura, 'how are we supposed to tech a scene if we don't know what the scene is going to be?'

'Does it matter where they'll be standing?' asked Hashi. 'We just need lights onstage from the beginning to the end of the scene. There's nothing to tech, really.'

'Apart from the Russian disguise sequence,' pointed out Carrie. 'Lots of lighting cues for that.'

'Well, yes, but apart from—'

'And the whole "Nine worthies" bit,' she added.

'Sure, but—'

'And the Winter and Spring bits at the end,' she finished, with just a hint of venom in her voice.

'Oh. Christ. Fine. All right, well, we'll just have to work it out as we go. OK?'

There were more groans. Working out the positioning of the actors alongside everything else would take an age. It was going to be a late one. But, to be fair, Hattie couldn't remember a tech that wasn't.

Three agonising hours later, they crawled over the finish line, as Hashi signed off on the timing of the blackout at the end of the final scene. They were all tired, hungry and irritable, but there was a grim satisfaction in getting to the end. There was still the curtain call to work out, of course, but tradition dictated they worry about that only at the end of the dress rehearsal.

Hattie called the full cast to the stage, thanked them all for their hard work (even the ones who'd been distractedly half-arsing it), and sent them home.

'Don't forget, line run at lunchtime in the park, then meet here at five to start getting ready for the dress!' called out Hashi.

Next came what Hattie called the Just Hour, because it was a period when all of the crew were supposed to go home, and when prompted they all said that they would, but then they would invariably follow up with 'I *just* need to…' or 'Let me *just*…'

Finally, with several lights refocused, several bible notes rewritten, and several props repaired, Hattie managed to shepherd everyone out of the auditorium. By tacit agreement, with the exception of Moira, who had made herself scarce as soon as the last costume change was done, the crew and designers all went straight into the pub, where Hattie bought the first round:

tradition dictated the production manager should do this, but Steve had not returned. It was crowded, but Laura had that magical ability to sniff out a table that was about to be freed up, and pester those sitting around it until they vacated their seats. Most of them managed to squeeze around the one she magicked up, borrowing chairs and stools from the other tables. They sat in silence until Hattie and Kiki brought all the drinks over.

'Well, cheers, everyone,' Hattie said, and was met with a chorus of 'cheers' in return, followed by a few solid seconds of the sound of gulping.

'… aaaaand breathe,' said Laura with a satisfied sigh, setting down her empty pint glass, and Hattie watched as around the table shoulders sank gently, chins raised, and eyes began to regain their twinkle.

'Bloody hell,' murmured Davina, in summary of the day that had just been.

'Next time round, and I know this is controversial, but could we maybe not have someone *die*? I think it would simplify a lot,' complained Carrie. 'I mean, it's hard enough to deal with a director who's having a mid-life crisis at the best of times, but having everyone stop the tech to go on a manhunt for a murderer really takes it to another level.'

'Mid-life crisis? He can't be more than thirty,' countered Laura.

'If he makes it to sixty without someone dropping a speaker on him from a great height he'll be doing well,' Carrie muttered.

'Still, he's not having a mid-life crisis, he's just a crap director,' argued Laura.

'I dunno. His show at the National got good reviews,' said Miguel.

'I saw it,' Davina piped up. 'It was really good. Really powerful.'

'But it was a very different sort of piece,' said Carrie. 'He can pull off a kitchen sink drama, but his range is pretty limited beyond that.'

'Exactly,' Laura put in. 'No range: crap director.'

They went back and forth over Hashi's qualities and deficiencies for a while, before the conversation inevitably turned to the Keith incident.

'So what on earth happened there?' asked Kiki. 'One second Steve's making it sound like Keith was the one who murdered Atlanta, the next we're all told to drop it and Steve is AWOL. Again.'

Hattie sighed.

'Well, first of all, and I can't believe this still needs saying, Atlanta wasn't murdered,' insisted Hattie. 'She drank too much, fell and hit her head. The police say it was an accident.'

Almost certainly, she added mentally. Almost certainly an accident.

'So then why the hell was Keith acting so weirdly today?' Carrie asked.

'I'm telling you, it was the mask,' said Laura. 'Someone's nicked it. That's what his whole speech was about last week, that's why he was interrogating everyone today. What's that thing worth? Ten grand? Twenty?'

Raven had been, up to this point, sitting quietly in the corner. She had never really got to know the rest of the team, and was obviously a friend of Hashi's, which made it hard for her to get pally with a group who were united primarily in the intensity of their complaints *against* him. But now she snorted.

'I doubt it,' she said.

'What? Like... more?' asked Miguel.

Raven shook her head.

'I did some jewellery design before I moved into theatre. Worked with diamonds quite a lot. I don't think that mask is worth as much as Keith thinks it is.'

'Excuse me,' cut in Carrie, 'but can we *please* talk about the big secret thing he was doing in the evenings over that weekend? Come on, Hattie, spill the beans.'

'Let's just say... let's just say he has a very active and varied social life,' said Hattie carefully.

'Oh, for God's sake,' snorted Davina. 'He was shagging someone, wasn't he?'

'Oh my God, it was Robin, wasn't it?' asked Carrie. 'He and Robin are definitely, definitely bumping uglies, aren't they? I swear to God, half the time that office reeks of sex when I go in.'

'I couldn't possibly comment,' replied Hattie, solemnly, and she refused to be drawn further.

They stayed on in the pub, bitching about Hashi and Keith, gossiping about the cast, and generally setting the theatre world to rights, until at the end of the night the bar staff unceremoniously kicked them out. When they all went their separate ways, a great deal of the tension that had built up over the course of the previous days and weeks had been dissipated. There was, Hattie thought, a lot to be said for pubs.

She also felt as though some of the weight had been lifted from her shoulders. Yes, there was still a lot to do, but it would all get easier from here. Now that the tech was done, the show would increasingly start running itself, and Hattie could get progressively less and less involved, until she was nothing more than a spare pair of hands in an emergency. And then in the blink of an eye the show would be over entirely, and all those annoying niggling questions, that kept popping up like... badgers? No, moles. It was whack-a-mole, not whack-a-badger. Although badgers lived underground too, didn't they, so presumably they also had to pop up sometimes ... Hattie realised that, with the warmth of three large glasses of wine inside her, she was thinking a little more groggily than normal. Anyway, the point was, all those unanswered questions would cease to matter. Because she'd have done her job, and her work for the Tavistock would be over, and the only thing she needed to care about was how *on earth* she was going to pay the heating bills over the winter.

Well. That was something to look forward to, wasn't it?

23

The next day was rather quiet, at least for the first few hours. Every crew member had, over the course of the previous day's rehearsals, put together a list of things to fix, as they discovered that, say, when one particular actor stood in one particular place they were *slightly* too tall for any of the frontal lighting to reach their face, or that a certain prop wasn't strong enough to withstand a rather more frenetic-than-expected onstage wielding, or, purely for sake of argument, that despite having been assured that absolutely no sound effects were needed, the director did in fact want several sounds to play at various points, and therefore the speakers that had previously been thought unnecessary were now actually needed to be rigged in certain specific places.

For the most part, everyone had their own list and worked through it independently. Miguel and Carrie clashed over whether certain lighting stands could be moved just slightly to accommodate an unexpected subwoofer, and Carrie got her way by sending Laura up to the roof on a ladder while keeping Miguel stuck in conversation on the ground, so that Laura could use her unchallenged aerial dominance to achieve control over the front-of-house rigging bars. Moira had more costume alterations than she could handle, so occasionally requested assistance from Kiki, who was reasonably adept with a needle and thread. But other than that, each department did their own thing.

Hattie assumed a rather more pastoral role, providing a steady supply of tea and biscuits to anyone who seemed to be flagging, and helping out with all those little 'Could you hand me that…?' requests that risked otherwise slowing down the momentum. Spirits were reasonably high, in that, more so than yesterday, it was generally believed that by hook or by crook they would actually get through the dress and be ready for the first preview the following night.

Not preview, Hattie reminded herself. Press night. It was fairly standard for shows to do a couple of preview performances to real audiences before letting the critics in. This gave them a chance to work out the last technical gremlins and let everyone settle into their roles without the added pressure of press in the crowd. Keith, however, was a firm believer that reviews were the main driver behind ticket sales, and that, therefore, reviewers should be invited in at the earliest possible opportunity, to maximise bums on seats over the course of the run.

'If a show's any good, it'll be good enough for a review on its first performance. If it's not, an extra couple of days won't save it,' he'd explain, to the horror of actors already prone to first-night jitters. Hattie thought it was slightly daft, but then again, box office receipts were neither her job nor her problem, so she chose not to pick a fight about it.

Steve was nowhere to be found. He hadn't been seen since storming out in the tech, and wasn't answering his phone. It was unheard of for a production manager to go missing at this stage in the proceedings, but they muddled through without him, and apart from his absence it was a relatively straightforward day at the Tavistock for everyone, free from crises and disasters. Free, that is, until the actors arrived at five o'clock, bringing with them, as is so often the case, a full complement of drama.

They all appeared in a group, having got an early meal together following a line run in the park in the afternoon. The first excitement was that Regine had been neither seen nor heard from all day. She'd missed the line run, and wasn't picking up her phone. This, of course, was problematic in and of itself, because her part, while considerably reduced since she'd taken on the role, was nonetheless crucial to the show, and, short of getting Davina into costume, they had no backup plan if a cast member didn't turn up. Regine had been the backup plan.

But the practical inconvenience of a missing cast member paled in comparison to Bums's new take on the situation.

'It's cursed,' she announced. 'It's a cursed role. First Atlanta, now Regine. I mean, maybe the whole play is cursed. It has had a certain… odd feel to it, hasn't it?'

'Do you really think Regine might be dead?' asked one of the other actresses, breathlessly.

'Christ on a bike, will any of you ever just *shut up*?' muttered Adam.

'Oh God, please let her not be in the dressing room again, not in the dressing room, I can't cope if I see that,' wailed Bums theatrically.

With all the authority she could muster, Hattie assured the company that everything was in hand, that people had been going in and out of the dressing rooms all day and there were definitely no (more) bodies in them, and that there were a thousand reasons Regine might have missed the line run, none of which was cause for alarm. Having, at least temporarily, calmed the actors enough to shepherd them backstage, she immediately sought out Davina.

'Right, I've got a mission for you. I need you to find Regine *right away*.'

'OK,' said Davina. 'Um… how, though? I mean I can try calling her, but…'

'Start with that. If you can't get through, try emailing her. If she doesn't immediately reply, we've got her home address, so if it's anywhere nearby I want you to nip out and see if she's home, or if she's got housemates who know where she is. If all else fails we've got contact details for her next of kin.'

'Should we really be calling them for something like this?' asked Davina, sounding dubious.

'Ordinarily no, but the cast are so on edge that if Regine doesn't make an appearance they'll have a collective fit,' Hattie replied. 'They're already wittering on about curses. We can't let this get out of hand.'

'All right. If she's findable I'll find her,' Davina assured her resolutely, and hot-footed it away. Hattie was pleased. *That* was what made a stage manager: when a crisis loomed, you didn't flap, you just got on and fixed it.

With Regine's absence in hand, the next thing was to start trying to wrangle the crew away from the stage. Through the fit-up and the tech, they had owned the space, and actors were permitted to occupy it only to the extent that it served the interests of the crew. Now the dynamic was shifting, as the cast needed to start preparing to give actual performances, which meant feeling comfortable in the performance space. They needed to start taking ownership of the stage from the crew, and sometimes the crew needed a little chivvying to cede power. Hattie started gently, and then less gently, reminding Miguel, Laura and the others that their window for putting ladders onstage and dumping cables everywhere was drawing to a close, and they needed to start taking themselves off to the darker corners of the theatre as the actors stepped into the light.

With the stage finally clear, Kiki was free to call the performers out of the dressing rooms for a vocal warm-up. The weird mishmash of yoga, singing, tongue-twisters and aerobics that ensued always struck Hattie as faintly comical. It had none of the grace of, say, an orchestra tuning itself in the pit of an opera house, and felt more like what you might expect to see from the inmates of a Victorian lunatic asylum. But it was as integral a part of the process as any other, and respect for the process was key.

A minute or so into the warm-up, Bums nipped backstage to collect her water bottle… and moments later started screaming.

'Oh lordy,' Hattie murmured, as she sprang into action. Ignoring her complaining hip, she vaulted up onto the stage, pushed her way through the milling actors and hurried as fast as she could back through to the dressing rooms.

Bums was collapsed in a heap, a rictus of horror frozen on her purple-red face, tears streaming from her eyes, hyperventilating, her hands pressed into her cheeks. In front of her, on the floor, was a piece of paper.

It was a single A4 sheet on which someone had written, in biro:

2 DOWN.
1 TO GO.
B. U. M. S.
YOU'RE NEXT.

'It's all right, my love, it's all right,' she cooed gently to Bums. 'You're safe, I promise you're safe. It's only a piece of paper.'

Her words, though she kept repeating them, had no kind of effect on Bums, who remained a bundle of tears and gasps and misery on the floor. Hattie rubbed her back awkwardly, but it seemed that nothing would comfort the poor young actress. Hattie was getting sick of mysterious handwritten notes.

Within a few seconds, cast members started to try to shuffle into the room, all peering to get a look at what had caused the commotion. Hattie snatched up the piece of paper so no one would see it, and shooed them all out. Eventually Kiki appeared at the doorway, and Hattie gave her strict instructions to get the cast back onto the stage to finish their warm-up. Once the last rubber-necker had been chased off, there was a moment's silence in the dressing room. Then Bums said quietly: 'It's the same handwriting.'

'As what, my love?'

'As the other note. The one in the St Eustace's. No one took it seriously. No one believed me. And now there's another one. Regine is dead. And I'm going to be next. They're going to kill me and I'm going to die and I'm going to be gone and no one believed me and now I'm going to die and all this time we could have been trying to find the killer and all we've been doing is *rehearsing* and you said Atlanta was an accident and…'

She kept talking faster and faster, but so heavy and frequent were her sobs and gasps that Hattie couldn't make out any of the words. So, rather than try to reply, she wrapped Bums up in a big hug, and simply waited.

Through the backstage relay she heard the cast awkwardly resume their vocal exercises onstage. Was one of them really a serial killer? Absurd and overblown though it seemed, Atlanta was dead, and now Regine was missing, and this new note seemed pretty unambiguously a taunt, and a threat. But who had written it? And what on earth were they trying to achieve? Did this mean Regine really was dead? Hattie now found herself worrying about Davina, whom she'd just sent after her. But no, whoever was behind the note must have only just put it there. They weren't with Regine's corpse somewhere out in London. They were in here.

She looked again at the note. It was pretty stark. It felt different, somehow, from all the others. She couldn't say for certain it was in the same handwriting as the ones pertaining to the mask, but the tone was the darkest of any of them.

On the stage, the actors had clearly judged themselves to be sufficiently warm, because they had quietened down, and Hashi had evidently decided to use the opportunity to give some notes.

They were fairly brief, mostly comprising some new thoughts he'd had about the blocking of the final scene since they'd muddled through it the previous day.

'Remember,' he was saying to them encouragingly. 'Intention is everything. We've put a tremendous amount of work into discovering the intention of every single character, in every single line. We've stripped everything else away, and that can leave you feeling awfully exposed. But trust in the work that we've done, deliver that intention, and the show will really fly. And enjoy it. It's a great piece, it's witty, it's funny, it's got emotional depth, it's got tremendous dynamic energy. If you enjoy it, they'll enjoy it. OK? OK. Now I'm not sure if we can go backstage yet, or…'

Hattie realised she was deliberately putting off the inevitable. Someone was endangering members of her cast. Possibly someone who was part of the production. There was no way they could carry on. She had to admit defeat. It was time to gather everyone together in the auditorium, and keep them there until the police came. Opening night was cancelled, of course, and…

There was a knock on the door, and the young actor Adam sheepishly poked his head into the dressing room.

'I just wanted to say—'

'Not right now, please, Adam,' said Hattie, perhaps a little sharply.

'No, sorry, I really… I do need to say something.'

He stepped into the room, closed the door, and cleared his throat.

'It was me, Bums. I wrote that note. And the other one.'

Bums looked up, horrified.

'Why…?' she whispered.

'It was… it was a joke,' Adam said, screwing up his face.

There was a pause.

Then Bums launched herself to her feet.

'What do you mean a joke! You threatened to murder me!'

'No, I just wanted—'

'What the hell is wrong with you! I thought someone was going to kill me!'

'I'm sorry, I really—'

'That is sick, it's disgusting, it's… Why would you do that?'

'BECAUSE YOU DESERVE IT!' Adam suddenly yelled back, stunning Bums into silence again.

'You're so self-centred, Bums,' he carried on, quivering with emotion. 'A woman died, she actually *died*, and you still found a way to make it all about you. First you're trying to turn the whole thing into a murder-mystery so that you can play amateur sleuth, then you're saying that Atlanta's ghost is talking to you, then you're saying you've discovered that the show is cursed… you're just using her as a prop for your one-woman show. You're the sick one. You're taking something serious, something real, and twisting it into your own perverted fantasy. Show some… some goddamned respect for the dead!'

'How *dare* you!' snarled Bums back, and the two of them launched into a shrieking match of accusations and insults that Hattie was quite unable to tear either of them away from. Hattie began to get concerned they would actually come to blows, when Kiki and Laura appeared, and each of them wordlessly and bodily hauled one of the squabbling pair out of the room in different directions. It wasn't the most elegant solution, but it was, Hattie had to concede, broadly effective. Once separated, both parties started to calm down, or at least to quieten.

Hattie allowed herself a moment to slump into a chair. She sat for a little while, vacantly, imagining to herself how nice it would be to be back in her flat, with a chair up against the window, smoking a nice big spliff with Nick. No, with Nick on the phone, that was probably better. Present but not imposing. Maybe she could eat a plate of chips with a fried egg on top. Some Michael Bublé playing. Oh, and…

'Hattie?' asked a timid voice.

Returning, reluctantly, to the here and now, Hattie looked round to see Davina. And behind Davina, she was delighted to see a puffy-faced Regine.

'Oh, thank God,' she said, not entirely meaning to.

'I'm sorry,' began Regine, hesitantly. 'I…'

She faltered, so Davina took over.

'She had a bit of a wobble, but I think we're all OK now.'

Regine nodded. Hattie had never seen her so cowed.

'I'm really not an actor,' Regine explained, apologetically. 'I said I'd step in because I wanted to show initiative, and I didn't think there was any other way, but then yesterday, in costume, onstage, under lights… It all got a bit real. And so I freaked out a bit. But I'm much better now. I can get through it. Sorry for… causing a fuss.'

'Well I'm *very* glad to see that you're OK,' said Hattie fervently. 'And I'm sure you'll be absolutely fine. You're very brave for stepping in like you did, but Hashi wouldn't have asked if he didn't think you could pull it off. Can I get you a cuppa?'

'No thanks. I should probably go and say hi to Hashi and the cast.'

Hattie nodded, and Regine slipped away. When she was gone, Hattie looked at Davina.

'Well done. Where was she?'

'Just round the corner, it turns out. She was really trying to psych herself up for coming. I think she just needed a little extra push.'

'Excellent work, Davina. You handled that perfectly.'

Davina smiled.

'I'm just so used to emotional crises of my own that I'm quite good at recognising them in other people, and I sometimes can help offer useful advice.'

Hattie sucked in a breath.

'Well, if you're up for solving some emotional crises, I could use your help with Bums and Adam...'

It took a lot of time, plus plenty of gentle words, and a fair few sharp ones, to get Adam and Bums to agree to share the stage with one another. Few had realised quite how deeply Adam had come to resent the actress who played his love interest over the course of the past few weeks. The Atlanta thing was central to it, but beyond that, he just seemed really to not *like* her. Bums, for her part, didn't seem to have had any particular opinions about Adam prior to his prank, but was now adamant that he was the worst of the worst, and consented to work with him only on condition that he never speak to her except to deliver his lines, a condition that he was only too happy to accept.

Eventually, with all the actors in costume and marshalled to their starting places, with the director and designers watching from the front row and the crew in their required places, Hashi gave Hattie the all clear to give Kiki the all clear, and she started to cue the show. The house lights went down, the actors assembled onstage, then with a fanfare of pre-recorded noise the stage lights came up...

... and the next two hours were utterly dire.

It wasn't just the sound and lighting issues (which abounded) and the forgotten lines (which were manifold). It wasn't the costume that ripped, the props that got lost, the actors who left on the wrong side of the stage and found themselves stranded, unable to get round to where they needed to make their next entrance. It wasn't even the drunk punter from the pub who wandered in looking for the toilet and had to be shepherded out by Hattie.

What it was, what the real core problem was, was that the performance was unutterably *dull*. The humour was flat, the emotions muted, the actions stilted. It wasn't entertaining. Everyone in the audience could see it, everyone onstage could feel it, everyone behind the scenes could hear it. This was supposed to be the moment that everything came together into a glorious edifice of art that revealed itself to be far more than the sum of its parts. Instead, what was finally assembled for all to see was, fairly unmistakably, a turkey.

They shuffled their way through the piece at an excruciatingly slow speed. It took them far longer than the ninety minutes Hashi had envisioned, that number being the justification he had used to avoid having an interval – an interval that was sorely missed now. The cast got more and more dejected as the piece went on, which only contributed to the maudlin pace.

After an absolute aeon, the final lines were spoken in barely more than a whisper, and the lights went down, leaving the building in dismal silence for a second. Then of course, as is required in these situations, the company members front of house started up some defiantly enthusiastic applause, with Hashi, Raven, Carrie, Hattie, Kiki, Laura and Miguel all doing their best to mimic the enraptured response of a packed house.

'Marvellous,' declared Hashi, smiling as though his life depended on it. 'Great work everyone. Great job. Great, great job. Now, if I could have you all to the stage, please, I do have *some* notes…'

'Some notes' turned out to be an hour's unstructured lecture about the nature of theatre, the eternal relevance of Shakespeare, and, rather bluntly, the many, many ways in which the show currently missed the point of both. The cast and crew listened in meek silence, occasionally jotting things down on the few occasions Hashi veered towards specificity. The gist was that subsequent performances needed to differ from the dress primarily in that they were uniformly, radically and quantitatively better. Hattie found it hard to disagree, but dearly wished Hashi would offer some advice on how they were to achieve this miraculous transformation. He was clearly waffling, panicked and embarrassed.

Then, when he finally shut up, they had to endure the technical notes shared by the crew. Everyone kept their words polite and their tone positive, but from the slumped postures and the weariness in the eyes, Hattie could see that spirits were low. Once everything was said that needed to be said, she dismissed the company, and no one seemed keen to stick around for a drink.

Hattie shuffled and tidied and fussed and fixed and, as always, was more or less the last to leave. She took herself out from the side door, and made her way round to the front of the building. It was dark outside, and she was distracted by her thoughts, so she didn't notice the figure hovering at the corner of the building until she'd bumped into it.

'Whoops!' she exclaimed. 'Sorry!'

'That's all right,' said a voice she recognised, and, peering through the gloaming, she realised it was Rosie, the shaven-headed girl from behind the bar, who was having a huddled cigarette break.

'Oh hello, my love. How are you?'

'I'm all right,' said Rosie. 'How's the show going?'

'It's… getting there,' Hattie replied cagily.

Rosie laughed. 'I'm sorry. That's what Davina said on the last show she did here, some god-awful devised piece about mental illness. I think I know what "getting there" means. That's a real shame, though. Davina told me the read-through was absolutely brilliant.'

'Well,' said Hattie awkwardly. 'We've still got a bit of time. You never know.'

'Well, fingers crossed,' said Rosie. 'Have a good evening!'

'You too,' said Hattie, and made her way home.

24

This is what it all comes down to. Yes, once a show opens it can run for weeks, months, or even years, and yes, your job as a stage manager extends far beyond the first performance. But all the grit, all the stress, all the heart that goes into the rehearsal period: the fulfilment of all those emotions happens on opening night. You can spend your entire life in the industry and never lose that feeling that comes around thirty minutes before the first curtain up. Conversely, if you ever do lose that feeling, that's a sure sign it's time to quit.

– From The Art and Craft of Stage Management *by Donna Fletcher, Chapter 11: Opening Night*

Tuesday, the day of the show's official opening, was expectedly manic. Overnight Hashi had started thinking in more concrete terms, and first thing in the morning he unleashed a torrent of changes and reworkings prompted by the disastrous dress rehearsal. Davina was rushing around all day, trying to accommodate often conflicting notes on what needed doing to the props from not only Hashi but also Raven, who had her own ideas, as well as fielding requests from the cast members themselves. Kiki was frantically bouncing between the actors and the lighting team, trying to keep everyone abreast of changes to who would be positioned where and when onstage, and how they needed to be lit at the time. Then there were the adjustments to entrances and exits that needed to be worked through: 'Mr Williams will come off stage *right* in act three now, so his props for act four need to be pre-set on the other side of the stage', and so on, not to mention, of course, the last-minute cuts Kiki had to add to the bible, which affected the timings of everything. Hattie did her best to support both of her subordinates, whilst also helping out Moira and Raven where needed. It didn't help that Steve was *still* absent.

In the midst of all this it was hard not to call to mind certain sayings involving lipsticks and pigs, polishes and turds, or deckchairs and iceberg-afflicted seagoing vessels, but, despite suspecting that some of her colleagues were entertaining similar mental comparisons, Hattie kept those thoughts to herself. Saying what everyone was thinking wouldn't help anything. Like a rowing eight trailing in distant last place in a race, the job of the crew was to focus on nothing more than getting to the finish line, regardless of the likely final result.

At lunchtime she took a brief break and checked her phone. She was surprised to see she had an email from Rod, of all people. Never the most comfortable with technology, he had sent a message with no content beyond the automatically inserted ACDA signature, while in the subject line was a YouTube link. After a couple of false starts Hattie worked out how to copy the link into her phone browser. She was surprised to find herself watching a video entitled *Exhibition Fight 27: Gallium vs Aluminium* on a channel called Chemistry Deathmatch. Despite the aggressive title and fancy graphics at the beginning, the video itself was very simplistic. It showed, on a black workbench, a strip of silver metal, onto which the hands of an off-screen presenter scraped from a little beaker a blob of a viscous silvery paste that looked a bit like mercury, only sludgier. The paste sat on the metal strip... and nothing happened. The hands retracted, and in the lower corner of the screen a 'fast forward' icon appeared, suggesting the footage was now being played at faster-than-normal speed. It was hard to tell, though, because still, nothing happened. Then the paste suddenly slithered off the strip, leaving behind some lumpy silvery residue. The corner icon disappeared, and the hands returned, moving at a normal pace. They picked up the strip, which they then pulled, with apparent ease, into little crumbly pieces. Then another fancy graphic flashed up, with the text 'Victory, by dismemberment: Gallium!!!' and the video ended.

Hattie watched the video again, perplexed. Why on earth had Rod sent her... hang on. Those little chunks of metal at the end of the video: they looked sort of melted, or crumbled, in a way that was oddly familiar. Of course! The remains that Keith had shown her bore a striking resemblance. Did that mean... was the metal strip made of aluminium, the same material as the padlock? If so, the metallic paste was presumably gallium, whatever that was. It seemed to have the ability to melt metal, quietly and without mess. But goodness, it was very slow. It seemed to take several hours to eat through the thin strip of aluminium. Surely the thief hadn't had time to pour gallium on the padlock and hang around waiting for it to take effect? Still, it was at least as plausible as the blowtorch theory.

She rang Rod to thank him.

'Told you there was something in the noggin,' he said, smugly.

'When on earth did you start watching chemistry videos?' asked Hattie. 'And weird ones about "deathmatches" at that?'

'Students,' he replied. 'It was that show last year, *Elements*. The director wanted all the sound effects to be based on chemical reactions, so my students spent a full week trawling through the internet looking for fun things and buying samples. That reaction didn't have any sound, of course, so they couldn't use it, but they ended up chatting about it anyway and, well, I listened. Anyway, does it look like the right sort of thing?'

'Very much so. Possibly raises more questions than it answers, but still, I think you might have solved at least part of a bit of a mystery that's been bothering me for a while now.'

'Delighted to help, oh heart of my heart. I shall claim a kiss on the cheek as my reward next time I see you.'

'You bloody well won't,' Hattie warned him.

'No… no I suppose I won't,' said Rod ruefully.

'But I'll buy you a box of doughnuts if you like.'

'Oh, well, yes, that'll do nicely. Pleasure doing business with you.'

'I'll see you later, Rod.'

'Yes you will, Harriet. Yes you will.'

She hung up, and then Kiki came out to find her about a problem to do with space in the wings and it was back into the fray, and before she knew it, it was five o'clock and she was shooing everyone out of the auditorium so that Keith and Hashi could host a pre-show drinks reception for VIP audience members. Keith was looking extremely flustered, and grabbed Hattie by the elbow as she tried to leave.

'I need you,' he hissed. 'Frank's coming, and I can't watch him the whole time. I need you to keep an eye on him. Don't let him speak to *anyone* from the company.'

'But I have to…' Hattie started to protest.

'I *need* you. Frank needs you.'

Before she could point out all the many other things she was supposed to be doing in the run-up to curtain up, Keith had swerved away.

'Oh… bugger,' she muttered to herself, then went to find Davina to try to offload the bulk of her to-do list onto her.

*

In the end, Hattie parked herself in the tech booth at the back of the auditorium. Here she was out of the way enough that she could get on with a few bits and pieces of preparation without disrupting the ambience of the drinks reception, but she could still keep an eye out for Frank and pop out if needed. She watched the great and the good file in. In this instance, the great were a slew of second-tier critics, and the good were a small crowd of what were presumably benefactors of the theatre. Keith devoted the bulk of his attention to the latter, while Hashi was rather more keen to sweet-talk the former. Keith appeared to be in his element, loud and boisterous, cracking jokes and telling stories. Hashi was also working hard, but was much more obviously nervous. So much so, in fact, that as Hattie watched, he lifted a wine glass to his lips with a shaky enough arm that he splashed cheap Cabernet Sauvignon onto his jacket.

Hattie instinctively raced out of the booth, handbag at the ready, already digging out the Kleenex. She whisked the glass out of Hashi's hands and dried it off while handing him a tissue to dab his sleeve with.

'Thanks, Hattie,' he said, shaking his head. 'I'm all over the place at the moment. I've got a horrible feeling this is going to be my last ever press night.'

Hattie found it harder to dislike him when his vulnerable side was showing.

'It's no problem,' she assured him. 'And I'm sure it won't be. Feeling prepared?'

'Not even remotely,' he replied. Then he gestured over to a pale, rather overweight man in the corner, whom Hattie vaguely recognised. 'Oh God, and there's Marcus, the critic from hell. I was really hoping he wouldn't review us. He's rubbished everything I've ever done. He'll have an absolute field day with this one.'

'I'm sure he'll judge it on its merits,' said Hattie diplomatically.

'That's what I'm afraid of.'

Poor Hashi. He had tried, she'd give him that. He'd put the effort in. Not always in the most constructive way, but directors had to be allowed some leeway with that. He'd found himself in a situation where the only opportunity he had was to direct a piece he had no idea how to approach, and he'd given it his all. The fact that he knew just how much he wasn't succeeding did a lot to excuse some of his behaviour over the past few weeks. Hattie felt genuinely sorry for him. Was there something she could do to help him? She looked again at Marcus, and cast her memory back...

'If you want to butter him up, ask him about his garden,' she said. 'He's *obsessed* with dahlias, and loves to show off about them.'

Hashi gave her an odd look.

'Really? How do you know that?'

Hattie smiled and tapped the side of her nose.

'It's a small industry, and I've been in it a while,' she said.

'You techies really are full of surprises,' Hashi said, with a small smile. 'Very well. Gardening it is. Wish me luck!'

'Break a leg.'

He plunged away into the crowd, leaving Hattie alone for a moment and able to take in the room. To her dismay, she saw that Frank had arrived, and Keith was, for the time being, nowhere to be seen. Time for her to assume chaperone duty, then. She started to make her way towards him, but as she did so she noticed that she wasn't the only person in the room moving in his direction: Steve had reappeared, and was also making a beeline for Frank through the clumps of VIPs with an air of determination and purpose.

Hattie was momentarily unsure. Was it really Steve all along, then? Who'd somehow discovered some dark secret about Joan, and was hoping to reveal it to Frank, so he'd... renege on his loan agreement with Keith...? It didn't make much sense to Hattie, but then again, Steve had been acting so strangely. And now here he was, doing exactly what Keith had predicted.

Whatever was going on, she wasn't supposed to let Steve talk to Frank. That was the only certainty Hattie could cling to. She started moving, trying to get to him first, but found her way blocked by a group of old biddies who were wittering on about Gilbert and Sullivan. Meanwhile Steve had just rounded an outcrop of trendy young theatre bloggers, and was almost within touching distance of the oblivious Frank, who was standing by himself, gazing up at the stage with a look of profound sadness on his face. There was no way Hattie could get to him before Steve. She had to find another way.

In her hand, she realised, was Hashi's wine glass. He hadn't taken it back from her before setting off for his encounter with the dread critic Marcus. Now it offered her a hope of salvation. She raised the glass above her head with one hand, and tapped it hard with the fingernails of the other, at the same time bawling, 'LADIES AND GENTLEMEN!'

The room fell silent, and everyone turned to face her. Hattie felt her face going bright red, but more importantly, noted that Frank had turned to face her, putting his back to Steve, who for the moment had no way of initiating a conversation with him.

'Er,' said Hattie, as she realised just how temporary her reprieve was likely to be. Well, at least the biddies had drawn slightly out of the way as they looked to see what the fuss was about. Now she just needed a few more seconds…

'Can I… can I take this moment to welcome you to the Tavistock, and… and also to draw your attention to the fire exits, which are located through the doors you came in by,' said Hattie, pointing and shuffling forward awkwardly, 'and also over there on the right. Er… We will ask you to vacate the auditorium at seven o'clock for our final preparations, and then you will be readmitted to take your seats from around seven fifteen. Thank you and enjoy your evening!'

There was a short silence, in which she saw Steve draw in a

breath and start lifting an arm to tap Frank on the shoulder. So Hattie lunged forward with her hand extended, heartily shoving an old lady out of the way as she did so, and exclaimed, 'Frank! How nice to see you.'

'Oh hello,' said Frank, shaking her hand. Hattie tightened her grasp, and smiling inanely, hauled Frank a couple of steps towards her, at the same time directing what she hoped was a warning look at Steve, who glared back at her.

'Er… Have you seen Keith yet?' she asked Frank. 'I know he wants to chat to you.'

'He wants to chat to my wallet,' replied Frank, a touch distractedly. 'He knows he hasn't squeezed every last penny out of it yet. But no, I haven't come across him so far. As I walked in I thought I saw him disappearing backstage, though.'

Behind him Steve gave up and stalked away, and Hattie allowed herself to breathe a sigh of relief. The relief was short-lived, however, as she realised Frank was already making to turn away from her. She'd never been one for small talk, but if she couldn't hold him in conversation she'd have no way of stopping Steve, or anyone else for that matter, from getting to him. She didn't think she could use her trick of making announcements to the whole room more than once.

'Um, you must feel very sad,' she said. 'About Atlanta.'

It was a crude way of keeping his attention, and probably a cruel one, but it was all she could think of. Frank looked at her curiously, then nodded.

'Of course,' he replied. 'I was hoping that spending more time in this building would help. I thought it would make me feel a little bit more connected to her. But if anything, it just makes me feel more guilty.'

'Guilty?' asked Hattie, genuinely surprised.

'Well yes. She wouldn't have been here, that night, if it wasn't for me.'

'Oh? Did you... did you arrange to meet her here? Was that second glass for you?'

'Second glass?' he echoed, frowning. 'Oh... no. No, she wasn't here to meet *me*. The second glass will have been for Joan.'

'*Dame* Joan?' asked Hattie, bewildered. 'But she's... I mean...'

Frank smiled sadly.

'You didn't know our Lala very well, did you?'

'No,' confessed Hattie.

'That's all right,' he said. 'Very few people did. She was a rare soul, and like all rare souls she had her quirks. One of them was a very active and visceral, although perhaps somewhat confused, belief in the afterlife. She'd have long conversations with people she'd lost, and swore blind that they sometimes talked back. She hadn't been on speaking terms with Joan since the big falling out, years prior, and she didn't feel remotely comfortable being on Joan's turf, given how they'd left things. But I'd pressured everyone into it. So she popped by to have a drink and bury the hatchet. She was hoping to get Joan's blessing to perform on her stage. But she and Joan could never just have *one* drink. So, presumably to honour old times' sake, she made her way through most of the bottle. And then, blotto, she slipped, hit her head, passed out, and choked. On her tongue, I suppose, or maybe on vomit. They've spared me the details, at least. Marvellous work they do, the police, but they do get rather over-excited. It took me weeks to convince them that she went backstage by herself. In the end I had to get quite cross with them, tell them that I needed some *closure*, although it's a ghastly word, of course, and that I couldn't get it with them hopping around like a bunch of Clouseaus.'

'Don't you feel it at all?' asked Hattie. 'A sense of closure, I mean.'

Frank shook his head, and Hattie could see his eyes beginning to tear up.

'I think a part of her hated it, you know: *performing*,' he said, after a pause. 'She lived for it in one sense, but it also made her desperately unhappy, and it ruined her health. In another life she might have stayed away from acting entirely, and been better off for it. But it wasn't to be. Her friend… Well, when she was fourteen her best friend in the world died, very suddenly. He had always been the passionate actor, school plays and drama clubs and so on; she followed him into it because she adored him. And afterwards she carried on because of him. Partly to honour his memory, as it were, but partly… well, I think after she lost him she found it very difficult to get close to people and share her real feelings, her… authentic self. She felt safer making everything a performance. And if you're doing an act all day anyway, why not be an actor? Maybe it's fitting that it should have ended in a theatre, but I can't help but feel…'

His eyes, which had drifted off into the distance, focused on Hattie.

'Sorry,' he said, 'ramblings of a sad old man.'

'Not at all,' replied Hattie softly. 'I completely understand how you feel. Um, listen… about that loan that Keith is asking for. I don't think—'

She was cut off by a scruffily dressed man, of a similar age to Frank, who appeared beside them.

'Francis! Francis my God, my condolences, my condolences!'

The newcomer pulled Frank into a bear hug.

'I hadn't heard, I hadn't heard until tonight. You poor man, such a great loss. Great!'

Over the man's shoulder Frank gave an apologetic smile at Hattie. The scruffy man didn't appear to notice her, and even if he did, he clearly had no intention of sharing Frank, whom he steered off in the direction of the drinks table.

Hattie was left alone for a few moments, and in those few moments she did some thinking. She thought about Raven's experience as a jewellery designer, and about gallium, and about Rosie the bartender. Then she went backstage.

She found Davina setting up costumes ready for quick changes in the men's dressing room.

'Hello, my love!' said Hattie. 'I need you to help me find Keith. I think he's backstage somewhere.'

'Sure. Can I just finish hanging the fur coats?'

'I'm afraid that will have to wait. There's something rather serious I need to talk to Keith about.'

They made their way through the women's dressing room, round to the stage left wings. Keith was nowhere to be found. Hattie was nonplussed for a second, then, spotting a slight movement behind one of the thick black masking curtains, strode across the stage to the wings on the far side, Davina in tow. She pulled the curtain aside... and discovered Adam and Bums, tightly intertwined, embracing passionately.

Bums, noticing them, giggled.

'We made up,' she said, cheerfully.

'Oh God,' said Adam, looking horror-stricken. 'Sorry. I'm sorry, this is completely unprofessional, I really...'

Hattie rolled her eyes, and wordlessly put the curtain back in place. Now was not the time to worry about cast entanglements, no matter how unexpected. She made a mental note to have a jolly good chuckle about it later, then turned to Davina.

'He must have gone back upstairs to his office. Would you mind coming with me? I don't want him to have the chance to sneak away.'

Davina nodded, uncertainly, and followed Hattie back across the stage, through the dressing rooms, into the side hallway and up the stairs. The office door was closed. Hattie knocked, waited for a couple of seconds, then entered.

Keith was pacing around, his phone clasped to his ear.

'... No I understand...' he said impatiently, 'darling, of course I understand, but I had very much hoped to see you here because I wanted to talk to you about… I… OK, go on.'

He caught sight of Hattie, and his eyes widened.

'Get downstairs!' he hissed, covering his phone with his palm. 'If Frank turns up…'

'Frank arrived some time ago,' Hattie replied.

'Oh Jesus,' muttered Keith, then turned back to his phone. 'Eddie, Eddie darling, can I call you back? Show emergency. Thanks!'

He put his phone down, then immediately snapped at Hattie, 'Then get the hell down and protect him!'

'He doesn't need any protecting,' replied Hattie.

'But the mask thief—'

'The mask thief is right here,' said Hattie, cutting him off and gesturing at Davina.

25

Hattie gently closed the door of the office behind her, then looked pointedly at Davina.

'I think you'd better sit down, my love,' she said firmly, and Davina quietly complied.

Hattie then turned her attention to Keith.

'I'm sorry it took me quite this long to put it all together. You know me, Keith. I'm not the quickest, but I am thorough, and I do get there in the end. Still, I'd have got there a lot faster if you'd been more honest with me from the get-go. But that was the problem, wasn't it? You couldn't be honest. That's why you were so desperate to keep the police out of it.'

'Oh, for God's sake, Hattie, leave the speeches to the actors,' huffed Keith. 'Just tell me what's going on. You said it couldn't possibly be Davina before.'

'Yes, and I was wrong about that. I was wrong about a lot of things. But I think there's still time to make amends. You really are the most breathtakingly self-centred man, you know that? It blinds you, and it makes you greedy, Keith. You'd have the shirt off poor Frank's back if you thought you could get away with it.'

Keith snorted.

'"Poor" Frank is a multi-millionaire banker who wants to pretend he's a producer.'

'*Poor Frank is mourning his sister,*' Hattie shot back. 'And all you can think of is whether you can con him into giving you more money.'

'It's not a con, it's a loan,' Keith snapped. 'I'll pay it back.'

'Will you? How many of the loans from Joan's friends have you actually managed to repay over the years? Oh, you want to, I'm sure. You'd very much *like* to repay the loan, because otherwise there's always the danger that Frank will actually take a closer look at the mask that you offered him as collateral, and if he looks at it a little too closely he may come to realise what someone like Raven saw immediately, that this supposedly priceless piece of theatre history is really just a cheap prop.'

'Hattie, I don't have time for this nonsense,' said Keith.

'And you roped me into all your lies,' Hattie continued. 'Telling me there was some terrible secret about Joan that would hurt Frank so much to find out. But there was no secret about Joan. The only terrible secret was just how much you were trying to rip him off with a worthless fake. How much did you tell Frank it was worth?'

'Hattie,' said Keith firmly, 'you are poking your nose into things you don't understand. Frank and I have a long-term working relationship, and the financial arrangements we make are no concern of yours. Without Frank, this show would never have even happened.'

'Yes, yes, I know he's paying for the damn thing, as it's his favourite play, and his sister got a guaranteed part in it. Was getting Atlanta to make peace with Joan like that really his idea? Or did you plant that seed as a way of convincing him to fund it?'

'I'm not prepared to talk about—'

'But this is all a tangent. The thing that you *really* should have told me about from the start,' Hattie ploughed on, 'was your tryst with Davina. Do you sleep with all your interns, then? Regardless of gender?'

'Oh, for goodness' sake, must you worm your way into *every* aspect of my private life?' Keith snapped.

'How did you know?' asked Davina, quietly, from her chair in the corner.

'I pieced it together. After graduating in the summer you do a spot of work here helping out with a one-off cabaret show, right? But then, according to Mark, you keep coming back, again and again over the course of a summer, although he can't understand what you're doing here – it's definitely not stage management. You're here enough that you strike up a friendship with Rosie who works behind the bar. Enough that she assumed you were working on the next show that happened here... What did she say it was? Some devised piece about mental illness? But you weren't technically working on that show, were you? So what were you doing here, night after night? Well, eventually even I worked it out.'

'I know it was stupid,' said Davina.

'Don't upset yourself, my love. The heart wants what the heart wants, and all that. But it turned sour, didn't it? He got himself a new intern, and abruptly lost interest in you, just stopped answering your calls... that hurt a lot didn't it? And at first all you wanted to do was to hurt him back. You knew all about Frank by then, and the mask, knew how much Keith was dependent on it – Keith's such a blabbermouth, isn't he? So you thought you could get back at him by taking it. Right?'

'I... I wanted to provoke a reaction,' said Davina. 'I just couldn't bear being ignored. I assumed, with the note, he'd immediately know it was me, and at the very least he'd call, or come see me, or *something*. I was always going to give it back.'

'Oh, for God's...' huffed Keith. '"Love's Labours Repaid"? That's your idea of an explanation? Well I'm sorry, *darling*, that I didn't originally take you for the burglarising type, but the number of people who want to hurt me is pretty long and you don't even make the first page. By the time I got round to suspecting you, this bloody bag lady was assuring me that you couldn't possibly have taken the thing because you were at the theatre all night.'

'Well, not all night,' said Hattie. 'Just between six-thirty and nine, right? Which is when *you* told me that the mask was taken, Keith. Unfortunately, you were off by a couple of hours. See—'

Hattie was interrupted by the door slamming open to reveal a red-faced Steve, who stormed in angrily, jabbing a finger in Keith's direction.

'I've got you now, you bastard. I've been through your entire history. Every dodgy deal, everyone you've ever screwed, every penny you've squandered, I know everything,' he growled. 'I know about Frank, I know about the mask, and I know about Atlanta. They'll throw away the key, they will.'

'Steve…' said Hattie, calmly.

Steve, spun round to Hattie.

'And I don't know why you're protecting him. He's a fraudster and a murderer. That mask is worthless, Atlanta found out and he killed her for it, then he destroyed it and faked the theft to try to cover his tracks. What's he got on you, eh? Why are you helping him?'

'I'm not helping him, Steve,' said Hattie, patiently. 'He didn't steal the mask, and he didn't kill Atlanta.'

'Nah,' Steve shook his head. 'I've just been talking to Frank, I know all about this supposed loan. And I've been doing my research on that mask. That production of *Antony and Cleopatra*: Joan Haygarth never wore a mask as part of her costume. The whole thing is a sham! And Hattie, shame on you. Busy doing his dirty work ever since Atlanta died, trying to find witnesses to silence them. Was it you who gave Miguel his black eye? To warn him off?'

'Oh for goodness' sake,' said Hattie. '*Yes*, I've been asking a lot of questions and poking my nose in odd places, because I've spent the past fortnight trying to work out what the hell is going on. Just like you, it sounds like. The only difference is, and I'm sorry to say it, but I think I've got the *right* end of the stick. Yes, the mask is a fake. But it was actually stolen. By Davina. It hasn't been destroyed, by the way, it's in the cupboard over there. She returned it a week ago. I'm guessing when Keith sounded off in the rehearsal room you realised how much trouble you might get in if you were found with it, my love?'

Davina nodded.

'But by then, having had a chance to get up close and personal to it, you'd realised it was a fake?'

Davina nodded again.

'And you couldn't help yourself, you couldn't just send the thing back, you had to try to get at Keith another way, with that note.'

Davina's eyes started to fill with tears.

'I… I'd just found out from Robin that he'd actually blocked my number. That hurt so much… I wanted to hurt him back, that was all.'

Steve was looking increasingly perplexed.

'Hang on… what?' he said.

'The whole thing was just a lover's tiff,' replied Keith sourly. 'Apparently, after making my life a living hell for the past fortnight, Davina here is the one who deserves all the sympathy. Naughty Keith is the villain of the piece, and she's the *real* victim.'

'Well, not quite,' said Hattie. 'After all, she does have a bit of a runaway temper. When Miguel worked out what you'd done, and confronted you about it, you were… shall we say *emphatic?*… in your insistence that he keep quiet. That was a hell of a thump you gave him, but it worked. He clammed up entirely after that. He won't even give me the time of day.'

'I'm sorry!' cried Davina. 'I was so scared of how much trouble I'd get in if anyone found out, when I realised how seriously everyone was taking it. He kept on telling me he was going to dob me in, and I got flustered.'

'So flustered that you punched him in the face?'

'I… I just get very upset sometimes.'

There was a silence. Everyone had a lot to digest.

Hattie eventually looked at Steve.

'I'm so sorry, Steve. We've spent the past two weeks coming at the same thing from two different angles, and every time we've crossed paths we've got more suspicious of one another. Up until just now I honestly thought you were involved in this whole thing.'

Steve gave her a hard stare, and she returned his gaze, unflinching. Then his mouth slowly formed into a reluctant smile.

'Well, it sounds like that was the only thing you got wrong,' he replied. 'So you're sure Keith didn't kill Atlanta?'

Hattie nodded. 'Pretty positive.'

'Then I've got some egg on my face, eh?'

'I suppose an apology is out of the question?' asked Keith, stiffly.

'I suppose it is, yes,' replied Steve. 'You're still a shifty bastard, and I had every right to suspect you. And your loan scam is shameful.'

'You can judge me however you like,' replied Keith with venom, 'but I do what I need to do to open shows and get everyone paid. You think it's been easy, keeping the lights on these past few years, through everything? You think that a little rebellious fringe house like ours would survive a *month* if we played by the rules? I'm trying to do something with the Tavistock, make something that matters, make something to be proud of. And so yes, I squeeze the money men every which way from Sunday. You think Frank's the only one I've used the mask on to get a loan? Half a dozen of them think they have exclusive rights to it if there's a default. And I found the damn thing behind the dressing room radiator! I lie, I cheat, and I sleep like a baby, because I see what happens down on that stage night after night, thanks to me. And you know what, if it's all too dirty for you, we'll shut up the house right now, and you can all hand back all the tainted money I've paid you. But if not, I suggest you shut up and put up.'

Steve growled quietly, but didn't reply.

'All right,' said Keith, turning to Davina. 'I've got to know. How the hell did you get the mask, then? And when?'

Davina looked over at Hattie, who looked meaningfully back. She eventually mumbled: 'It was on the Sunday night, after I'd gone to see *Titus* at the Menier, just before closing time. You went for your evening drink just before eleven. You always do. I just waited outside till I saw you in the bar, then I went in the side door and grabbed the mask.'

'And the padlock?' asked Keith.

'Gallium,' muttered Davina.

'Come again?'

'Gallium paste. It eats through aluminium. Me and Miguel were playing with it for a show we did at ACDA once, and I'd kept some.'

'Oh bloody hell,' said Keith irritably. 'I knew you were smart, but I didn't know I'd been shagging Marie sodding Curie. How on earth did you think of that?'

'I didn't. It was Miguel. He was just getting into lock-picking at the time,' said Davina mournfully. 'When we were messing round with gallium he had this idea that you could use it to break padlocks. But he said no lock artist would use it seriously, because it didn't take any skill.'

'"Lock artist"? Christ he's a weirdo. So this gallium stuff, it just... poof!... and the padlock fell apart? All while I was having a whisky.'

'Yup,' said Davina with a nod.

Hattie took a deep breath.

'Oh, Davina,' she said, sadly. 'I really wish you hadn't said that.'

'How do you mean?' asked Keith.

'I mean that you're still lying, and that means you're still trying to hide something, and that only serves to confirm... Well. You see, gallium doesn't act quickly. It acts very, very slowly. It needed to be smeared on that padlock hours, maybe a whole day, before it would work its way through it. Davina knew that. Which is why she took *two* trips to the Tavistock over the weekend. Sunday night was the second one. The first was Saturday night.'

'No—' began Davina, but Hattie cut her off.

'Stop. Just stop, Davina. Rosie saw you, didn't she? As you arrived? She was having a cigarette break, and you bumped into her. You couldn't get away without a chat, so you told her that the read-through had gone well, and told her that you were going to see a production of *Titus* the next day. Didn't you?'

'I...' said Davina, and then tailed off.

'But Rosie being in the alley threw a spanner in the works,' Hattie continued. 'You'd wanted to loiter there quietly until you heard Keith come down and go through to the pub, but you can't do that if she's nattering to you. So instead you finish off your conversation, head inside early, and need a place to hide until he goes for his drink. The obvious place is the ladies' dressing room, so you sneak in there. That's the perfect spot... except it's rather unexpectedly occupied. Atlanta's in there, drunk off her head. I'd imagine she yells out "Darling!" or some such greeting, starts making a hell of a racket, and you know that if Keith hears it, it's game over. You needed her to be quiet, and let me guess... you got "flustered"?'

'Bloody hell,' breathed Keith in the silence that followed, looking appalled. 'You *Chicago*'d her.'

Davina was shaking her head.

'No, no, I didn't, I promise I didn't. I just left, I went straight through to the other dressing room and I left her behind, I didn't kill her, I just... pushed past her. That's all. I had no idea she'd died until you told me on the phone. It wasn't anything to do with me. I just pushed past her, that's all. I promise. I promise!'

'I believe you,' said Hattie. 'At least, I believe you didn't mean to kill her. I believe it was an accident, in that sense. But she still died. And at the end of the day it's not up to what I believe.'

Kiki's voice came crackling through the speaker: *Ladies and gentlemen, this is a call for Hattie Cocker. Could Hattie Cocker please make her way to the prompt desk.*

'Oh, bloody hell,' said Keith. 'Look at the time. The house should be opening now, but they've got no SM, PM or producer to give them clearance. They can't even send an ASM round to look for you, because she's here too. Hashi must be having kittens.'

He walked to the office door and opened it.

'Right, well this has all been fascinating, and I'm sure we've all learned something here today, but now that we've had our fun, I believe our jobs are calling. OK? All three of you are different varieties of idiot, and Davina, I hope it goes without saying that as soon as the curtain call finishes tonight you're fired, and also you're an unutterably awful human being, but can we please get this horrible, horrible show open?'

Steve looked at Keith, then looked at Hattie, and shrugged.

'He's right. We've got a show to put on. Come on.'

'All right,' said Hattie. 'I'll do the show. But we need to call the police first.'

'No,' said Keith firmly. 'We shouldn't. If any of this story gets outside this room, then that's going to cause an awful lot of people to ask some very awkward questions about the mask, meaning that a whole bunch of financial agreements I have in place are going to fall through, with Frank and several other creditors too. With the immediate consequence that the building owner evicts us for repeated non-payment of the lease. So your play doesn't get to finish its run, and no one gets paid. No cast, no crew, no one. So we're not going to do that, are we?'

Steve sighed. 'You're a slimy bastard and I hate to say it… but I take your point. We can't do that.'

'Well, there you and I must disagree, Steve,' said Hattie.

Steve turned to look at her.

'Seriously? Come on, Hattie, you know how it works: we get the job done. Hook or crook. It's not the end of the world if the police never know a few details about what happened. Either way, it's a tragic accident.'

'But it's not *right*,' said Hattie.

'My love,' wheedled Keith, 'are you telling me that you'd rather bring this whole playhouse down around you – with the consequence, by the way that I will personally see to it that you never work in the industry again – than get off your moral high horse for just *five sodding minutes*?'

'Maybe,' said Hattie.

Keith threw his hands up in the air.

'Hattie, I *order* you not to tell the police. This is a theatre matter, and you answer to me. And if you don't answer to me, you answer to Steve, don't you? So do what we say, do the right thing, let's get the job done, and we can all get on with our careers. Tell you what, I'll even hire you on for the rest of the season, to show how sweet and nice I am really.'

Hattie looked over at Steve, who gave a resigned shrug. She then looked across at Davina.

'I just pushed her,' the ASM said in a quiet voice. 'She wouldn't be quiet when I asked, and then she wouldn't get out of the way. It was just a little push. Just a push. While I was waiting in the other dressing room I thought I heard her get back up again. I just… I didn't have time to go and check.'

Hattie thought about how nice it would be for this all to be over, and how painful it would be for the theatre to go bust mid-run. She felt the pull of forty years of experience training her to do what she was told, and never to say no to her superiors. Then she thought about Atlanta, and then she thought about Atlanta's brother, downstairs, wretchedly blaming himself.

'Sorry, Davina,' she said eventually. 'I would imagine this won't be easy for you. But DI Burakgazi seems nice, and I'm sure she'll hear you out. If you want to take the evening off that's fine. I'll do the props and quick changes tonight. Now, if you'll all excuse me, I need to make this phone call before the house opens.'

Epilogue

'At the end of the day, we're not superheroes. We can't do everything, and we can't make everyone happy all of the time. We just have to use our judgement, and do what we can. That's what people always misunderstand about "*the show must go on*". It's got two sides. It doesn't just mean you do what you can to try to get the job done. It also means almost the opposite: theatre has an inevitability about it. It always keeps going. Even if you make a mistake. Even if the costumes go missing, or someone forgets a line, or the lights blow. It's very hard to completely derail a production. So do what you can, and forgive yourself for the rest.'

Hattie realised she was rambling, and forced herself to stop and take a breath.

'All of which is a long way of saying, if you can't find every prop on the list, that's not a problem. You're not going to fail the exercise so long as you can show me that you've done your best.'

She handed out the last of the exercise sheets to the students, and realised she had one left over. Was someone missing? With a sinking feeling, she realised that yes, indeed, she was one short: Felix. She'd completely forgotten about him in all the chaos of the last few days. It appeared that he'd given up. What a shame. She hoped Mark wouldn't be too cross with her. She was getting a bit tired of people being cross with her.

Burakgazi had been unexpectedly grouchy, especially given that Hattie had just solved her case for her. She took issue with the fact that Hattie hadn't involved her earlier on, and grumped and sighed every time Hattie couldn't back up an assertion with some form of documentary proof. She did eventually admit to being grateful for the assistance, but when Hattie had gently suggested that, with the culprit now identified, it might no longer be necessary to talk to Mark, or to bring up any unnecessary particulars about Hattie's past, all she received by way of reply was a grudging 'We'll see.' So, *maybe* her secret was safe. For now.

Never trust the police, thought Hattie. Weasels, the lot of them.

Steve had been all right, in the end. He wasn't happy that she'd just risked his team's pay cheques for the show, as they were very much his responsibility to ensure. But it helped his mood that, given the truth about the mask was now bound to come out eventually, he had been able to be the one to tell Frank about it, a task that he had undertaken with gusto, not even trying to hide his glee in causing Keith pain.

'Steve, are we... all right?' Hattie said to him as he was leaving at the end of the night.

He looked at her coolly, for a second.

'I suppose so. You probably did the right thing, in the end.'

He blew out a long, slow breath, then continued: 'I'm wondering if it's time for me to get out of this game. I always thought theatre was a bit more light-hearted than... what I did before. Thought it would be good for me to take it a bit easier. But recently it's just getting me down. People like Keith, self-absorbed, manipulative little sods, they crop up everywhere. I can smell them a mile off, and I can't stomach 'em. At first I tried to just avoid him, then when I got a sniff that he was up to something... well, that took over. All I could think about was bringing him down. I basically dropped the show and spent the whole time digging up everything

I could on him. It's not good for the blood pressure. It's not good for the soul.'

Hattie, who would never in a million years have expected Steve to share with her a meditation on the state of his soul, tried to keep the surprise out of her face as she replied, 'Maybe. But you got the show open on time even so. The industry would be worse without you in it.'

He shrugged, and walked away, leaving Hattie shaking her head. He was a strange one, was Steve Felton. She hoped to have the chance to get the measure of him one day.

Keith, for his part, had uttered the most dramatic series of threats and predictions, most of which involved Hattie ending up destitute and alone either as a direct result of her actions or through his own retributive steps. He'd even tried to call the company together after the show to issue some cryptic warnings about the financial future of the production, and drop heavy hints that Hattie was responsible for any coming difficulties. But thankfully no one had paid him too much attention: they were all buzzing far too much with adrenaline.

Buzzing because, against all odds, the evening had turned out to be one of the most well-received opening nights of any show at the Tavistock in years.

Of course, whoops and cheers were pretty common at any such performance – producers were always careful to pad the audience with enthusiastic well-wishers whenever the press were in – but it was rare, when a show received a partial standing ovation, to see so many of the critics join in.

They were as effusive in their praise in print as they were in their applause in person. The first reviews had been published online late that night, and they didn't hold back. One pronounced that '*Hassan's vital production seethes with a dark and intense energy, transforming one of the more lightweight comedies in the canon into a brooding reflection on the destructive war between the emotional and the intellectual.*' Another insisted that not since Peter Brook's legendary production at the RSC had *Love's Labour's Lost* been made to feel so powerful and relevant. And even the fierce Marcus, although he couldn't bring himself to use any positive adjectives, nevertheless concluded: '*Don't worry if you can't get tickets for this rather short run at this rather small venue; I have a feeling that this production will find itself on a larger stage soon enough.*'

All in all the consensus among the critics was that the production was nothing short of a triumph. And they were right too, Hattie conceded. Somehow, in the presence of an audience, the cast had tapped into an energy that lifted the whole piece, and suddenly brought all the loose elements together into a cogent and compelling whole. When it was funny, it was hilarious. When it was poignant, it was heart-breaking. The rest of the time it was simply spellbinding. Despite, in all specifics, being exactly the same piece as the dismal dress rehearsal the day before, it was nevertheless unrecognisable. And everyone could feel it.

Theatre, Hattie thought, not for the first time, was a funny old thing. Still, if it meant there was a chance that the show could survive the probably imminent closure of the Tavistock then she wasn't complaining. At the very least, if the show was cancelled, it would end on a high. Although Hattie couldn't really believe that the run wouldn't finish. Keith was a bastard, but he had his own brand of genius. She couldn't help but assume that he would somehow find a way to survive for a little longer.

She finished briefing her students on their assignment, and then spent half an hour getting them all started on it, which largely involved explaining and re-explaining the point of it to the gloriously dim Alexander. Once they were all more or less working independently, she realised she was, for the moment at least, not needed. So she excused herself and made her way towards the staffroom. She told herself it was in case someone had left some posh biccies by the kettle, but really she was just hoping for a little peace and quiet. However, just as she turned into the final corridor she bumped into Rod coming the other way, clutching a mug of tea.

'M'lady,' he greeted her, tugging an imaginary forelock.

'All right, Rod?' she replied with a smile.

'Did you get the show open?'

'We did. Went better than I expected. A lot better.'

'Well then, congratulations. And your padlock mystery?'

'All solved. Thanks to your tip about gallium. And, in fact, to your penchant for eavesdropping on student gossip.'

'Oh?' frowned Rod. 'Well, what can I say? I listen. I've put a lot of work into these ears over the years, and it does occasionally pay a dividend.'

'Well, thank you,' said Hattie, sincerely.

'You're most welcome,' he smiled, before making a face. 'Which makes this as good a time as any to apologise: sorry.'

'What for?'

'One of your students. I may have slightly poached him. You may have noticed he wasn't in your class this morning.'

'Felix?' asked Hattie. 'What do you mean?'

'I've been... well, come with me and you'll see,' said Rod, with a mischievous smile, and without another word he led the way down to his basement. He stopped at the door, through whose small window he pointed silently, gesturing for Hattie to look for herself. She stood up on tiptoes and did so, and was surprised to see Felix, sitting hunched over a mixing desk, headphones clamped over his ears, hard at work.

'What's he doing?' breathed Hattie.

'Learning,' replied Rod in a whisper. 'I got chatting to him about this and that, you know, trying to find out what makes him tick. He explained that he really wants to be an actor, but he's very self-conscious about his voice. So I asked him what it was about acting that appealed to him, and he said, and I thought this was rather insightful of him, it was about telling stories and having people listen. And I sort of suggested to him that a voice is just one of many tools you can use to tell a story, and talked to him about some other ways of doing it, and pretty quickly we got on to the topic of my sound poems.'

'Oh lordy. Like the parakeet thing?'

'Exactly. He was a bit wary at first, but I convinced him to have a bit of a play... and now he's got the bug. He's been here all morning. I know he's got other classes he's supposed to be doing but... well, I thought it might be best to let him keep at it, considering, you know.'

Hattie looked at Rod. Then she leaned forward and gave him a peck on the cheek.

'You really are a bit marvellous, you know that?'

Rod looked away, bashfully.

'Oh now, I'm blushing. Anyway, I should get back to him. He keeps asking me to dig out obscure sound effects from long-forgotten corners of my library. Some of this stuff was originally made to be played back on *gramophones*.'

'Righto, Rod. Well, I'll see you later.'

'I very much hope so.'

Hattie made her way back towards the SM office to check on her students, but before entering had a thought, and took a detour, finding herself outside Mark's door. She knocked and entered.

'Hattie!' beamed Mark from his desk. 'What can I do for you?'

'I won't keep you Mark, I just wanted to say: all things considered, I wouldn't be too hasty to push our Rod out the door if I were you. He's a silly old sod, but he does have his uses.'

Mark's smile turned into a wince.

'I do wish you'd try to see it from—'

'I know, I know, there's politics with the administration, and I know Rod's not the easiest to work with. But all in all he does a lot to help steady the ship. Underneath it all he's one of those *team players* you're so keen on. And if you don't believe me, I'd strongly encourage you to pop down to the sound basement right now and see for yourself. You might just change your mind. Anyway, must get back. Catch you later.'

With a grin on her face, and without waiting for Mark to reply, she turned on her heel and went back to the SM office. She had a class – possibly her last – of bright young things who were waiting for her to instil the ethos and discipline of a professional stage manager into them. In her experience it was a blooming long process, so she might as well get stuck into it.

Acknowledgements

I owe an enormous debt of gratitude to James Wills, my agent. Not just for taking a punt on me in the first place, but also for continually pushing me to improve the manuscript, and in particular for responding with patience and compassion when, at a particularly low moment, I tried to self-sabotage my way out of the entire thing. He, along with Helena Maybery and the excellent team at Watson, Little, have been constant in their support throughout the whole process, and I couldn't ask for better representation.

Huge thanks also to Carolyn Mays, my marvellous editor, and her team of renegades taking on the entire publishing industry from their garret in Bedford Square. I'm immensely grateful to Swati Gamble for copy-editing, Kay Gale for proofreading, Heike Shüssler for the beautiful cover design, Polly Halsey for her editorial and production work, Anastasia Boama-Aboagye for marketing, Abi Walton for publicity, Laura Fletcher for sales and more, and to everyone else who had a hand in bringing this book to print. Together, somehow, they have transformed a poorly-punctuated Word document into an actual, physical, complete and beautiful thing, and they've made it look effortless.

Thanks to my mum, my dad, my sister Kate, and Ben Dunn, for early feedback on the first draft and words of encouragement, and to my wife Ellie for putting up with me when I got unhealthily emotionally over-invested in getting published. And lastly thanks to all the wonderful, diverse and gloriously weird people of theatreland, for providing a wealth of inspiration for me to draw from when putting together this story.

About Patrick Gleeson

Photo credit courtesy of Patrick Gleeson

Patrick has a degree in philosophy and classics, another one in technical theatre and stage management, and one more in business administration. He has worked as a theatre sound designer, an 'interpretive naturalist' at an aquarium, a software developer, a business mentor to fledgling entrepreneurs, and a voice actor.

He composed the music for a musical about taxidermy that *The Stage* said 'put to shame the hackneyed standards of the contemporary musical scene', and has been performed in London, Edinburgh, Suffolk and, weirdly, Alaska.

He now lives in Norfolk with his wife and two children, where he brews mediocre cider.

patrickgleeson.com

'A very smart, independent publisher delivering
the finest literary crime fiction' – *Big Issue*

MEET NO EXIT PRESS, the independent publisher bringing you the
best in crime and noir fiction. From classic detective novels to
page-turning spy thrillers and singular writing that just grabs the
attention. Our books are carefully crafted by some of the world's
finest writers and delivered to you by a small, but mighty, team.

In over 30 years of business, we have published award-winning
fiction and non-fiction including the work of a Pulitzer Prize winner,
the British Crime Book of the Year, numerous CWA Dagger
Awards, a British million copy bestselling author, the winner
of the Canadian Governor General's Award for Fiction and the
Scotiabank Giller Prize, to name but a few. We are the home of
many crime and noir legends from the USA whose work includes
iconic film adaptations and TV sensations. We pride ourselves in
uncovering the most exciting new or undiscovered talents. New
and not so new – you know who you are!!

We are a proactive team committed to delivering the very best,
both for our authors and our readers.

Want to join the conversation and find out more about what we do?

Catch us on social media or sign up to our newsletter for all the
latest news from No Exit Press HQ.

fb.me/noexitpress @noexitpress
noexit.co.uk/newsletter